'Where is everyboc

'I'm sure we'll 1

Kingsfield.

'If my time in the N

we see here can only be bad news,' added Miller.

Miller was a relative newcomer to Northamptonshire Police, still fully aware of the dangers of inner-city housing estates that she had left behind in London. She'd already served twenty-two years in the job. A reasonably stout and stern-faced woman, she was nevertheless a good police officer with high standards.

'It's always a worry when things seem this quiet,' continued Miller, putting on a bit of a scary voice, 'you know - like in the films?'

'All right, all right,' Kingsfield put in, as they all started to get out of the car. 'Let's not put the poor girl off before she's even got started.' They both looked at Parker.

'You want to stay here or come with us?' asked Miller.

'No, I'll come with you. It'll be OK. Can't be that bad, can it?'

'Hope not,' replied Kingsfield. 'You stick close to us, Steph, we'll be OK… Promise.'

He gave Parker a wide grin, but both Miller and he could see the uncertainty on Parker's face.

As the sun set on what had been an unusually dry mid-August day and in the twilight of this particularly quiet Monday evening, the three of them looked towards the open front door of the house. All the lights in the house were switched on. Usually domestic incidents on council estates such as this brought other residents out from their houses. This had nothing to do with what was going on, other than that they wanted to be nosey and hassle the police. In this case however, it was eerily quiet, with no signs of other residents being attracted by developing events.

Kingsfield looked around the street, becoming more and more concerned that this might be an ambush. A few nights before, Kingsfield had been sent with his tutor constable to another area of the town, where they were pelted with bricks and bottles. At 6' 5' tall, the sight of a stick-thin, gangly eighteen year old legging it back to the safety of his police car must have been a sight that the perpetrator of the false 999 call had had a good laugh about. Although still in his probation and with another six months to do, Kingsfield resolved, after that incident, to turn his gangly body into something a bit more substantial. The lack of onlookers and the heavy silence pervading the street on this current job was making him more and more aware of that previous incident.

Kingsfield heard Miller speaking into her radio, as she informed the controller of this initial situation.

The three walked up to a small wooden gate. Parker looked at the state of the gate and noted that it was rotten and only just hanging on to the gatepost by the top hinge. Parker watched Miller trying to push the gate open as best she could, but it scraped across the broken footpath, getting stuck against a broken piece of path. She lifted it slightly to overcome the obstruction and, as she did so, it fell off the one rusty hinge that was holding it upright. She let the gate fall and took a step in.

'Shit!' she exclaimed.

'What?' Parker remarked, thinking she was talking about the gate.

'No, shit!' Miller said, indicating the bottom of her boot and looking around the garden, 'There's piles of it. Watch your step.'

'Where's the dog, then?' Parker asked, looking around warily. The day's hot sun had given the garden a sickly, dog-shitty smell as they began to make their way up the path. Parker watched Miller cleaning her boot on the overgrown grass, swearing to herself under her breath, as Kingsfield stood there smiling.

'It's no good smirking, Jimmy boy. Come on,' Miller said, in a tone indicating she was decidedly pissed off with getting dog shit all over her boots.

A slammed-down Ford Escort passed by with the thump, thump of some inane tune playing, causing Kingsfield to look around and give it a good stare - a signal, perhaps, he wondered.

They continued up the footpath towards the front door. Kingsfield led the way and was the first to enter the house.

'Hello! Police! Anyone here?' Kingsfield called loudly, but cautiously.

He called again. There was no response. Parker staying close behind Miller, admitting to herself as they stepped over the threshold, that she felt even more uneasy than she had when they'd arrived. Her operational inexperience and the developing situation made her feel even more frightened.

'Who lives like this?' she mumbled to herself.

She looked around, wary that there was still nobody in the street and still no dog. Moving a bit further into the house, Parker was hit by a smell that made her gag.

'What's that smell?' she asked Miller disgustedly.

'That,' Miller replied, 'is the smell of a dirty, filthy household. You'll get used to it, coming to places like these.'

'They don't all smell like this, surely?' asked Parker, as she managed to identify some smells. Old cooking fat, cigarette smoke, human sweat–and probably a bit of damp thrown in for good measure.

'Well, most of the time, it's a case of wiping your feet when you leave, not the other way around,' remarked Kingsfield.

'Ah, I understand now what my training officer meant by saying that some houses needed to have mud-guards on the Hoover.'

They all chuckled. 'Yeah, as Jim said wiping your feet when you leave,' countered Miller, chuckling.

'You have to take the bad smells as well as the good ones. And this, at the moment, is definitely bad,' said Kingsfield, turning up his nose.

Slowly moving further into the house, Parker saw that there was a living room to the right and stairs going off to the bedrooms on the left. There was no carpet on the stairs or the hallway floor. The kitchen was directly in front of them and the hallway was tiled with small redbrick square tiles. A battered old moped without a number plate leant against the under-stairs cupboard door. Oil had leaked from the moped and congealed in a thick, black, viscous pool underneath the engine.

They went into the living room first, still calling out as they went. The room was unkempt. There was a brown, three seat vinyl-covered sofa and two chairs in the room. The plastic sheeting it was delivered in still covered the suite – 'obviously to try to protect it from all this crap,' Parker thought.

In the middle of the room was a small circular 1970's style glass coffee table, with silver aluminium legs. The three-piece suite surrounded the table, which was piled up with magazines, dirty cups, plates and takeaway cartons. Kingsfield nonchalantly moved some rubbish on the table. A magazine fell to the floor, revealing what appeared to be two lines of cocaine ready to be snorted up someone's nose.

'Looks like they were getting ready for a party,' he said to Miller as he pointed out the lines of coke. A well-used credit card lay beside the lines of drugs. Miller examined the table and peered more closely at the credit card.

'Obviously didn't buy the lines on this credit card,' she said light-heartedly, 'it expired some time ago!'

At the opposite end of the living room from where they'd come in was another door, leading to the kitchen. Parker, in an effort to at least look the part of a police officer even if she didn't feel it, moved toward the kitchen door, taking note of what she was looking at. She watched the other two as they continued to look around the living room and walked into the kitchen. Startled, she shrieked loudly.

Miller and Kingsfield both rushed into the kitchen on hearing Parker's startled cry. Parker was standing staring at a woman lying on the floor. The woman was looking straight at her, unblinking, pupils dilated. Blood had congealed around her open mouth, twisted at an angle that looked as if she'd had a stroke. The white t-shirt the woman was wearing was torn and soaked with a large bloodstain around the area of her abdomen. Blood also stained her blue denim jeans from a stomach wound and her bladder had released its contents, covering her jeans further around her crotch and down her legs. A large bloody kitchen knife lay in a pool of coagulated blood that surrounded the woman's body.

It was all Parker could do not to be sick. 'I think I'm going to heave,' said Parker.

'It's always difficult the first time,' said Miller, 'but you will have to be able to deal with it, believe me.'

'Don't know whether I want to. My first shift and I get this! I'll be traumatised forever,' Parker exclaimed. Miller noted that the colour had drained from Parker's face and she was looking decidedly green. Kingsfield turned to the dead woman. He was somewhat perturbed by the sight too, but nevertheless checked for a pulse. He did not expect to find one - and didn't. Looking at Miller, he shook his head.

'Still warm?' Miller asked Kingsfield.

'Yeah, this didn't happen too long ago.'

Miller radioed her controller, updating him of their find and asking for the appropriate people to attend the scene. Miller continued to get the ball rolling with the major incident team, as Kingsfield began to start to record their movements in his police pocket-book.

Glancing across the kitchen, Miller realised that Parker was still staring, transfixed at the dead woman on the floor. Moving closer to her, she tapped her on the shoulder and said,

'Come on, let's go outside for some air. I think you need it.'

'Yes, we all need to leave until the others get here,' said Kingsfield. 'We don't want to contaminate the scene any further.'

They all agreed and went outside. The hot summer evening did nothing to abate Parker's nausea. Instead, she leaned against the wall just outside the front door and, holding her long blonde hair away from her face, the tea she had just finished before being called out to this job came up in a sticky mess. Miller took a step back out of her way just as it happened.

Miller changed her demeanour towards Parker and became more motherly. She suddenly saw this young girl in a police uniform in front of her and realised she'd just experienced the sight of a dead body for the first time. Miller knew the image of that woman would remain with Parker for the rest of her life and she would have to find somewhere in her head to park it. Despite her professionalism, Miller had to admit that the sight was unexpected, even for her, too. On these occasions it was difficult not to be affected. Miller realised that she had to remain professional for Parker's, and even for Kingsfield's, sake if nothing else.

'Feeling any better now?' asked Miller.

'Mm, a bit,' Parker nodded, still feeling a bit green.

'We need to look upstairs,' said Miller, addressing Kingsfield. He nodded his agreement, as he continued to write in his pocket book.

'Are you up for that?' she asked Parker.

'Mm, I think so,' Parker nodded.

'You can go and sit in the car if you want –you don't have to do this,' said Kingsfield.

'No, I want to,' Parker said, wiping her mouth with a tissue she'd fished out of her trouser pocket. Looking around for somewhere to put it, she ended up chucking it where she had thrown up.

The duty inspector was the first of the back-up team to arrive. Inspector Andrew Prentice—a tall, military-style man with a handlebar moustache—asked his two constables what they'd discovered. Miller explained what she'd found to the Inspector and told him they had yet to check the upstairs. Prentice sent Miller and Kingsfield back into the house to check the upstairs. He instructed Parker to sit in his car and then began to arrange for the arrival of the senior detective on call and the 'scenes of crime' van.

Miller first showed Parker into the passenger seat of the Inspector's car.

'Are you going to be alright?' she asked.

Parker looked at Miller,—her eyes were beginning to water, something the Inspector must have picked up on, Miller thought. Parker had another tissue out and was dabbing her eyes.

'Look, once I've done upstairs, I'll come back and we can go back to the nick, OK?'

Parker nodded. 'I don't know what to think,' she whimpered. 'I've never seen a dead body before, let alone someone who has been murdered.'

Miller dropped down on her haunches, so she was at eye level with Parker, who by now was sitting in the passenger seat of the patrol car.

'There's not a lot I can say. This is part of the job. This is some of what policing is all about. I know that you didn't expect this on your first day out, but try not to think about it, otherwise it will consume you. I know...'

'I'll try,' said Parker. But Miller knew that this event would define whether she stayed with the job. It will either make her or break her, she thought.

'Miller!' shouted Prentice.

'Coming, Sir.'

'Stay here, OK?' she said to Parker and stood up and joined Kingsfield to go back into the house.

The arrival of further police vehicles had finally aroused the attention of other residents, who had begun to stand out in the street or were lazily leaning in the front door- way of their houses, smoking and watching the proceedings.

Miller and Kingsfield went back into the house to search the upstairs rooms, as instructed by the Inspector. The rooms were just as unkempt as the downstairs living room: one had no wallpaper; the other had what used to be floral print wallpaper that had become discoloured and was peeling off the walls. Large patches of mould covered parts of the ceiling, where there had obviously been a water leak in the past. There were no beds, just mattresses on the floor, the linen of which hadn't seen a wash for a good many months. Clothes—what little there were—hung on an old shop rail. The smell of dampness and filth in the room was overpowering.

'How could anyone live in this crap?' asked Kingsfield.

'What? You've been in the job, how long?' questioned Miller.

'Eighteen months, why?'

'You've not seen this before then?'

'Well… not as bad as this, no.'

'I do agree, it's a bit of a shit hole, but this?' said Miller, spreading her arms wide to take in the whole room, 'This is a palace compared to some I have seen.'

'You are jo-'

'Shh,' said Miller, indicating to Kingsfield to be quiet.

Just as they had turned to leave the main bedroom, Miller thought she'd heard a noise. Standing in silence, they both listened. Miller heard the noise again. It was a soft bang from the cupboard in the corner of the room. She pointed to the in-built cupboards in the corner of the main bedroom. They crept slowly towards the cupboards and both stood silent, listening again.

'I think there's someone in there,' Miller whispered.

'Get your peg out... Just in case?' hissed Kingsfield.

Kingsfield carefully lifted the latch on the door and opened it just enough to let light in. Fearful that the killer was going to startle them, heart pounding, he opened the door further. There were no more sounds, but they still could not see in.

'Ready?' whispered Kingsfield, 'I'm going to open the door fully. On three.'

Miller nodded. 'Ready,'

Kingsfield silently mouthed the words, 'One - Two – Three.' He then flung the door open as far as it would go.

'No, no, don't hurt us!' came a girl's cry from the cupboard. When the door was fully open, they both saw three children huddled together in the far corner of the large recessed cupboard. Miller extended her hand to the girl who had shouted and told them to come out.

'It's OK, you're safe now,' Miller said to the young girl. The girl took Miller's outstretched hand and all three children sheepishly climbed out of the cupboard.

'What are you doing in there?' Kingsfield asked.

'We're hiding,' a tiny voice from behind the girl said.

'Who are you hiding from?' asked Kingsfield. He bent down in front of a little boy.

'We always hide in here when they argue,' the youngest boy offered.

'It wasn't our fault,' continued the eldest girl.

'No, it wasn't us,' the eldest boy confirmed.

'What wasn't your fault?' Kingsfield asked.

'Why he run off,' the girl said.

'Who ran off?' Miller asked.

'Mum's boyfriend,' replied the boy.

'Mm, how often does that happen?' asked Miller.

'Almost everyday,' the girl replied, 'doesn't like any of us, I think he wishes we were all dead.'

'Why would you say that? Surely your mum wants you?'

'Not so sure about that,' replied the girl.

'How old are you all?' asked Kingsfield.

'I'm sixteen, he's fourteen and our step-brother, the youngest, is nine,' said the girl. 'He's living with us just for now,' she added in confirmation, giving the youngest boy a contemptuous stare.

Miller noted that it seemed that there was no love lost between them all - or was it perhaps just the state in which they were living?

The youngest boy kicked out at the girl, as she continued to glare at him.

'Hey!' Miller shouted to the boy, 'that's not very nice is it?'

The young boy stuck his tongue out at Miller then emphasised it towards the girl. Throughout this time the boy had been holding onto a battered shoe-box.

'What's in the box?' asked Kingsfield.

'You don't want to know,' the eldest boy responded.

'Oh, why is that?' interjected Miller.

'You just don't,' said the girl.

'Well, we need to have a look - what have you got in the box?' demanded Kingsfield.

'Fug-off, copper!' shouted the boy, tightly holding the box.

In more gentle tones, Miller asked, 'can we have a look in the box?'

'Give them your box,' the eldest boy said.

The youngest boy moved the box from in front of him to behind his back. 'No!' he squealed.

Swiftly the eldest boy grabbed the box - there was a brief tug-o'-war between the two boys, until the box split open. The youngest boy screamed and stamped his feet. The shoe-box, now on the floor, had spread its contents: a dead rat, two dead sparrows and a number of small insects in a jar with a lid on.

'Told you, you didn't want to know,' the girl exclaimed. 'Kills anything he can get his grubby little hands on.'

The youngest boy quickly tried to kneel on the floor to pick the objects up, but was held back by the older boy, who grabbed the back of his dirty blue t-shirt.

Inspector Prentice, on hearing the commotion, made his way upstairs and entered the bedroom.

'What's going on here?' he demanded.

'Found these three hiding in a cupboard and this boy here has this box of corpses!'

Prentice raised his eyebrows and indicated to Miller and Kingsfield to get the children out of the house.

'Come on,' Miller said to the three, 'let's get you out of here.'

'I want my box!'

The young boy screamed and started to stamp his feet again. Prentice went over to the boy and picked him up, tucked him under his arm and took him downstairs, still screaming.

'Come on you two!' said Miller, turning back to the other two children, 'let's get you out of here as well.'

'Where are you taking us?' the girl enquired.

'Somewhere safe,' responded Miller.

The boy and girl nodded to each other and left the house without further argument, not knowing whether they would ever see their mother again.

Chapter 1 - Eighteen Years Later

Arriving at the scene of the county's latest murder, Detective Inspector Jim Kingsfield peered out of the windscreen of his black Audi TT at the small end of terrace cottage he was about to step foot in. The tranquillity of the typically English country cottage built of Northamptonshire sandstone, with its small cottage garden, belied what carnage he knew was going on inside.

Pulling heavily on his Havana cigar, the smoke circled around the car before finding its way out of the partially opened driver's side window. Clouds were gathering and it looked like rain was going to spoil what had been a pleasant summer evening.

Stubbing out the cigar in the car's ashtray, Kingsfield realised how pissed off he was, having to leave the dinner he was attending with his wife. 'Didn't they realise that this was the only night off he'd had in the last month?' he thought as he got out of his car.

As he walked over to the SOCO van parked on the opposite side of the road, he noticed his wife's car had arrived as well. Removing his tuxedo jacket, he was acutely aware he was overdressed, as he helped himself to a SOCO suit from the van and climbed into it. He crossed onto the other side of the road and entered the small garden of the cottage, the PCSO on the gate acknowledged him and 'arrived' him in the scene log.

He stood on the threshold of the little cottage and viewed the scene before him. No longer the six-foot-five-gangly youth of his probationary years, he now had the physique of a rugby player. He was an imposing figure who managed to fill the little doorway into the cottage. His delay at arriving at the scene allowed the

Scenes of Crime Officers—SOCOs, as they were generally referred to—to arrive a few minutes before him. In their white paper SOCO suits, they buzzed around the scene, preparing for the long task ahead.

Kingsfield sniffed the air and became conscious of the recognisable stench that permeated the cottage from weeks of human decomposition. The sweet, sickly smell of decay that overpowered the senses was well known to most coppers, reflected Kingsfield, a smell that invades every pore of the body, lingering forever.

Kingsfield could see, from the vantage point of the doorway, human remains lying at the bottom of the stairs, discarded like a child's rag doll. He could see a large proportion of the cottage – the front entrance opening directly onto its one main room, with no hallway. There was a very old and battered collection of armchairs and a sofa, none of which matched. These were gathered around a fireplace with a wood burner that looked as if it had never been cleaned out. Kingsfield saw that the cottage had been completely trashed. Someone had ripped the stuffing out of every chair back. An untidy and destructive search, he thought.

Although not a stranger to crime scenes like these, it was something Kingsfield never got used to, but was a necessary part of the job he did. It still beggared belief what human beings were capable of doing to each other and their property, thought Kingsfield, and not for the first time.

Kingsfield's Detective Sergeant then came towards him, dressed in his own SOCO suit – clearly too small for him – hat, gloves and mask. A veteran CID man with a few good years experience in major crimes, he had kept himself in shape and had not taken on the beer bellies that a lot of well-trodden CID officers tended to develop. As he walked over to Kingsfield, he pushed a large shock of light brown hair from his forehead back under his cap and removed his mask.

'Bit over-dressed, aren't we, boss?' Detective Sergeant Dave Heart exclaimed, as he walked towards his senior officer from the middle of the cottage, and noticing his bow-tie under the SOCO suit Kingsfield had stretched almost to bursting point.

Kingsfield smiled. 'Thought I would add a bit of culture, Heart,' replied Kingsfield. 'You mark my words, we'll all be wearing these at crime scenes soon,' he smiled again, adding, 'well, you going stand there looking like a spare prick at a wedding or are you going to tell me what's gone on here?'

'Well, seems like the place has been trashed for no reason,' said Heart, as he handed Kingsfield a pair of blue overshoes that he just happened to be holding.

'You don't say–tell me something I can't see for myself!' replied Kingsfield, sarcastically. He hopped about on one foot trying to get the overshoes on over his black patent leather dress shoes, before entering the cottage, but gave up and instead leant against the outside wall. Kingsfield indicated to Heart to carry on.

'It looks like a trashing, boss, but there is some evidence of a meticulous search first.'

'Ah, now you're talking. Go on.'

Heart continued talking as Kingsfield stepped over the threshold and into the cottage. 'The woman has been here for around two weeks, we think. Probably in her mid-seventies, assuming at the moment that she lives on her own and may have fallen down the stairs when she was coming down to see what the commotion was. Doc says that the blackened putrefaction of the body makes it difficult to see any obvious signs of a suspicious death, but we'll have to wait till the post-mortem.'

'Any idea what the intruder was looking for?'

'Nothing we've found so far. The scenes of crimes' manager said it's going to take some time for his other SOCOs to sift though all this mess.'

Kingsfield had a good scan of the cottage as he talked to his DS. 'Do we know who she is?' he asked.

'Yes, a SOCO found this,' said Heart handing Kingsfield an identity card in an evidence bag. Holding the bag up to the light, he examined the card through the bag. Heart, reading from his notebook added, 'she appears to be Eleanor Smyth, retired social worker with the DHSS, as was,' he turned to a passing SOCO and called to her. 'Where was this found?'

'There was a pile of DHSS papers in the kitchen drawer,' the SOCO replied and then confirmed by saying, 'mostly about her pension.'

'Thanks,' he turned back to Kingsfield.

'Any idea about next of kin?' enquired Kingsfield.

'No, not at the moment, there is some reference to her work rehoming children and she appears to have kept in touch with some of them, but we've only got pictures and no names at the moment.'

'OK, let's see if we can get some details of next of kin,' said Kingsfield as he moved towards the body.

He and Heart walked over to the forensic pathologist, who had also arrived a few minutes before him.

'She's dead, Jim,' exclaimed the forensic pathologist, feigning 'Bones McCoy' in *Star Trek*. Kingsfield smiled in acknowledgment of the joke – not heard that before, he thought to himself.

'I bloody well hope she is dead, if she's in that state,' he remarked, pointing to the blackened body in the corner of the stairs. 'How?'

'Not sure at the moment,' the doctor said. 'Have to wait till I do the PM, but her neck is broken, probably when she came down the stairs.'

'I see,' said Kingsfield, 'and how long have you been a doctor, doctor?' he questioned.

'Why?'

'Even I can tell her neck is broken, 'cos it's almost sitting in her bloody lap.'

'Oh, so you're the doctor now, then,' she replied with a hint of sarcasm in her voice.

'Yes, dear,' he replied, adding, 'you've taught me well.'

'We really must stop meeting like this,' Kingsfield continued with a grin. 'We see more of each other at crime scenes than we do at home.'

'Should've stayed on the Northern division then, my love,' she replied. 'I wouldn't see you at all then, would I?'

Dr Kirsty Kingsfield had been married to Jim Kingsfield for two years.

'True,' replied Kingsfield, 'and don't call me 'wood eye' in public please! I've told you before about that,' he grinned at his wife and she winked back.

Kirsty was four years younger than Kingsfield's thirty-seven years. He remembered that they'd met at a national crime conference. It was not a particularly good first meeting. Kingsfield, the big clumsy oaf that he could be sometimes, knocked a plate of vol-au-vonts down the front of her dress on the evening of the first day of the conference. It was a difficult time for Kingsfield and the conference distracted him from the marital traumas that had been preoccupying him then.

Though the mutual attraction between him and this young, redheaded forensic pathologist was the last thing on his mind, both seemed to take an instant liking to each other. Kirsty told him later that she thought Kingsfield manufactured the accident with the plate of vol-au-vonts and that he'd done it deliberately. Kingsfield always denied it and, in truth, it had been an accident.

After the conference the two started seeing each other casually. Kingsfield's divorce was close to being finalised and he felt it was time to move on and put the past behind.

Although, he realised, there were some things that would never go away. He'd found closure over the breakdown of his first marriage, but an open sore was the disappearance of his friend WPC Stephanie Parker, which he'd never resolved. As a detective there were always cases that stuck with you, cases that were permanently open, cases that bugged the hell out of you and Kingsfield knew he was no different.

Kingsfield momentarily allowed his eyes to drift over towards his wife, allowing himself to be distracted by her good looks. Kirsty had deep red hair and green eyes, truly titian in every sense of the word. He'd always had a liking for redheads, never understanding why so many derogatory remarks were made about them. And Kirsty didn't have the quick temper historically associated with redheads, either– or if she did, he hadn't found it yet. At five feet eight inches tall, she had a pair of legs that went on forever, which he loved. She liked to show off her legs whenever she 'had the bottle,' as she'd confided to him a long time ago.

This evening, Kingsfield had been happy to go with his wife to a charity ball she'd been invited to as the new forensic pathologist at the hospital. A chance, he thought, to forget work and enjoy the company of his wife and professionals other than just coppers. The ball had taken place in one of the town's best hotels, 'The Collingtree Hilton.' Kingsfield had thought as the evening progressed, that his luck may be in and hoped that–well – not going to happen now, is it, he thought to himself.

They'd only been there for about two hours when his wife had been contacted to attend the scene of the murder. Although he was number two on the call out list this evening, he knew he would get the call eventually, particularly at a scene like this one. Nevertheless he was intrigued as to how she got there before him.

Now though, Kingsfield noted, his wife had changed from her ball-gown, in which he told her she had looked stunning, to her all-in-one whites.

Turning away from his wife and the victim, Kingsfield went to move back into the main part of the cottage, but as he did so something caught his eye. It appeared that something had been placed under the table lamp, which was sitting on an old telephone table next to the stairs. He pointed this out to Heart and the other SOCO standing nearby. The SOCO photographed it in situ, then carefully removed and unfolded it. She placed it in an evidence bag and handed it to Kingsfield.

'DHSS-1515/495', Kingsfield read aloud through the evidence bag. The letters and numbers had no real meaning to Kingsfield. He could hazard a guess that DHSS was the Department for Health and Social Security, but the rest was meaningless. Heart made no sense of it either.

'Looks like it may be some sort of reference number,' Heart remarked as he handed the packet to the exhibits officer, who duly recorded the find in the evidence log.

'Possibly something we can work on. Anything else we can do here?' Kingsfield enquired of his Detective Sergeant.

'No, not really, boss. I think that SOCO and your missus have it about wrapped up.'

'How did we find out about this? We're not exactly central here are we?'

'Three nines from a concerned villager, works in the post office. I think she hadn't seen the victim for a little while, although she never visited regularly anyway. She came up to see if she was OK and found the back door had been broken down.'

'Did she touch or move anything, do we think?'

'Not had a chance to talk to her yet. I think she just saw the body and ran.'

Kingsfield turned towards the body 'Think I'd run if I saw that, 'nuff to give anyone nightmares!' He indicated the victim with the nod of his head in her direction.

'I'll arrange for some elimination prints to be taken, just in case,' added Heart.

Kingsfield and Heart moved further into the cottage. Kingsfield made a mental note of the layout of the cottage, while Heart was writing everything he could in his notebook.

'OK, let's have a look at this back door,' said Kingsfield.

DS Heart went on, 'It's a bit strange, because apparently the door was unlocked and it seems that somebody broke the window to make it look like a genuine burglary.'

'Why would someone break the window when the door was already unlocked?' Kingsfield said, thinking out loud.

'Well, the only reason I can think of is that they wanted it to look like some sort of bungled job.'

'Surely though, they would have tried the door first?' suggested Kingsfield.

'And if they entered this way they'd have known it was unlocked, so why go to all the trouble?' said Heart. Kingsfield couldn't help smiling at Heart squirming away in his SOCO onesie.

'What is the matter with you, Dave? You got St Vitas' Dance or something?'

'I hate these bloody suits, they're always too small and I sweat like a pig in them,' retorted Heart.

'Perhaps you should make sure you get a big one next time–arrive early.'

'Right, says the man who turned up *after* his wife.'

'Touché–anyway what were you saying?'

'I said, if they knew the door was unlocked, why go to the trouble of staging all of this?' Heart indicated the glass on the floor by the back door.

'So,' replied Kingsfield, 'are we to assume then that the assailant may have been known to the victim?'

'It's a possibility, I think–angry parents perhaps?'

'Mm, let's make sure we get plenty of photos and do a video of the inside of the place as well as the outside. I don't want this to turn into a bloody press fiasco. They'll be all over it like a swarm of locusts in the morning.'

'Right-o.'

'I have a feeling we've missed something here, but I don't know what.'

'Got one of your hunches, then, have you?'

'Yeah,' Kingsfield said looking at his Detective Sergeant, waiting for the next question. He knew he had a reputation for going out and doing his own thing on a hunch and usually without back up. Sometimes it paid off, but in one that hadn't, a witness had ended up as a paraplegic. It was something Kingsfield had to live with. The civil case and compensation hearings went on for years and still weren't finished, but it finished him – nearly – and it certainly finished his marriage. Fortunately having met Kirsty by then, she'd provided him with the support he needed– and occasionally the pills.

Kingsfield knew these things were hit and miss – that's half of what coppering is about, a hunch, a feeling you can't quite put your finger on. Nine times out of ten, however, he tended to be right.

He continued to survey the scene with his Detective Sergeant, as his wife walked over to him.

'OK,' she said, 'I've done as much as I can do here. You can have her taken to the morgue.'

'Will you be doing the PM straight away?' asked Kingsfield.

'That all depends.'

'On what?'

'Whether you want her to wait the night. I'll get onto it first thing in the morning, if you do.'

'Well, she's been waiting for a few weeks. I don't suppose one more night is going to hurt, is it?'

'No, not really,' said Kirsty, adding quickly, 'nice way to end a romantic evening, just as you were getting amorous!'

'Pardon?' Kingsfield exclaimed. Heart stifled a chuckle.

'Don't think I didn't know what you were after tonight,' she said with a beaming smile.

'Well,' he said to his wife, 'you certainly know how to command an audience.'

As he looked around the room, he noticed a couple of SOCOs had stopped what they were doing, more out of disbelief than anything.

'Of course I do, sweetie,' said Kirsty flashing her big green eyes. With another wink, she turned and walked out of the cottage.

'Sounds like you were on a promise tonight, then, boss.'

'Shut it, Heart,' Kingsfield drawled. 'OK, back to work, show's over,' he added, indicating the SOCOs. 'Never going to get any work done now, am I? She can be such a tease sometimes.'

'Whatever you say, boss.'

Kingsfield turned and followed his wife out of the cottage. He found her standing on the small manicured square of lawn and immaculately kept borders. He stopped and stood with her for a moment. Both were silent. She took his hand then said quietly,

'I'll see you at home.'

He turned to her and smiled 'Mm… OK.'

Kingsfield watched his wife enter the SOCO van and come out a few minutes later dressed in blue scrubs with her gown over her arm. She got into her ageing VW Golf and drove away, leaving Kingsfield to his thoughts in the garden. He inhaled deeply taking in the sweet scent of garden roses he was standing next to and thought about the scene. He considered lighting up another cigar, but thought better of it. Kingsfield shivered as the cool of the evening hit him. Or was it that little tug at the back of his neck he got when he felt things were not quite right? This, he thought, was not quite right and he had a foreboding feeling that he was being watched.

Chapter 2

Rosemary Jordan gave a loud sigh. 'And what time do you expect to be home tonight?' she asked her husband, who was sitting at the kitchen table casually eating a piece of toast, while listening to the local radio news. Rosemary Jordan was a petite brunette with bobbed hair. Dressed ready for work in a grey pin-stripe trouser suit, she was becoming increasingly frustrated with her traffic sergeant husband, Jacob- Jake- Jordan.

'Midnight, hopefully,' Jordan said without looking at her.

She slammed her mug of tea down, causing it to spill on the table.

'God, don't they ever give you any time off?'

'Christ, Rosie,' he said, looking up at her for the first time, 'it is my job you know. What the hell has got into you lately? You've been on my back now for weeks– just give it a rest,' irritated, he noisily turned the page of the morning paper he was reading. Rosie got up from the kitchen table and began to bustle about the kitchen. Eventually, she put her coat on ready to go to work. As she opened the kitchen door to leave she stopped and turned, looking contemptuously at her husband.

'It would just be nice if they allowed you to see your wife in the evening occasionally. They just don't give a shit about family life, do they?'

'Well, perhaps you'd like to write to the Chief Constable and ask him to tell all the criminals only to commit crime between nine and five?'

Rosie huffed, walked out of the kitchen and slammed the door. Jake heard the front door slam, the car start up and screech off the drive.

'For Christ's sake, woman, what do you want from me?' Jake mumbled under his breath, as he finished eating his toast.

He couldn't concentrate on the morning paper anymore and, as he closed and folded it hastily, his attention was drawn to the radio that was reporting the murder of a woman in Willoughby. He wondered whether his old mate Jim Kingsfield had been called out to that one. He recalled they'd worked together on the same shift when they first started in the job. Jake always knew he would go into Traffic, whereas Jim went on about becoming a detective. Putting the radio report to the back of his mind, he drained his mug of tea and poured another one. He got to thinking about the fact that he knew the job took its toll on families. Reflectively, he stirred his second mug of tea. All the officers he had known and worked with – a percentage of them, he now realised, were either separated or divorced. In fact, he knew that at least two of his colleagues were having affairs. 'Over the wall' or 'playing away,' as many would describe it.

How did the trainer on his Family liaison officers' course put it? Ah yes, divorce was the policeman's disease. Well, when all was said and done, he was a just a normal traffic sergeant. And, as the sergeant in charge of the Family liaison team, he was used to dealing with road death and the aftermath within families. He knew that it did not make it any easier when he or his colleagues had their own personal troubles. They usually kept silent and didn't come clean about it until it was too late, he thought.

Jake realised to some extent his life was different, too. After all, he didn't have a family. He'd met Rosie nearly fifteen years ago. She was a slim twenty-three-year-old, who he met while he was trying to sort out a loan for one of his classic cars. It was very much the long and the short of it – as he was six foot and Rosie was a petite five foot two inches. They married quickly, but ten years ago he discovered that he was not able to father children. 'Not enough little soldiers' was how it was explained to him at the time. But when they found out that Rosie was also unable to bear children, it was a double blow and had meant that Rosie needed counselling for depression. She had not taken it well and it took her years to recover, whereas Jake had accepted the situation without much further thought. He supposed that deep down he wasn't that bothered about having a family, which was why he was able to accept the situation better than his wife. Perhaps the argument this morning was a deep down brewing resentment against that – and everything else.

He remembered a recent conversation with her that hadn't ended well. Rosie had two brothers and one surviving sister out of three. She was the youngest. They had all produced children and the family naturally assumed that he and Rosie would add to the growing entourage of grandchildren. Apparently, she had told her family that it was all down to Jake. It was something he found upsetting at the time, that his wife had put all the blame on him. The grand argument that followed had sent Rosie off to stay with her sister for weeks to cool off.

Counselling sessions and severe periods of depression were followed by years on anti-depressants that made it difficult for Jake to know what to do for the best, but he thought that over the last few weeks, the growing anger and frustration he had seen in her about his work was different. He could not put his finger on it, but something wasn't right.

The shrill tones of his work mobile phone interrupted his thoughts. Although he was not due to start work until two o'clock, as the sergeant in charge of his team of family liaison officers, he was always called to allocate an appropriate Family Liaison Officer for the job.

After his morning upset with Rosie, Jake was grateful for the interlude. He answered the phone.

He listened. 'OK, give me forty minutes or so, I'll come in.'

Jake cleared the call and got up from the kitchen table, thinking that as his plans for the rest of the morning were now in ruins, he may as well go into the office. He went upstairs to change and, glancing out of the landing window, he noticed it had started to rain.

Several years ago Jacob Thomas Jordan had managed to buy a brilliant white Ford Sierra XR4i in immaculate condition. Being a traffic cop also meant that he had a decent understanding and interest in cars that made his job a whole lot better. In fact, he thought that being a traffic sergeant was probably the best role in the job. It wasn't just the classics, but modern cars as well – although he did want to build up a museum collection of old police cars, ancient and modern. Something he'd thought about doing in his retirement.

Pulling into the police station car park, he parked up against the rear wall of the station yard. The rain had started again, soon filling the ruts and dips in the car park, which sent Jake hopping over the large puddles that were quickly forming, as he walked towards his office.

The traffic sergeant's office was home to four sergeants. The duty sergeant, Robin Tellmann, was sitting at his desk, tapping furiously at his computer and banging the mouse on the desk.

'Why do these bloody things always pack up at the most crucial point?' he said, acknowledging Jake as he entered the office.

'Because,' Jake said, 'it's a secret ploy by software manufacturers to frustrate you into buying their upgrades.'

'Doesn't work though, does it? Because I'm just gonna throw the feckin' thing out of the window.'

'Calm, calm,' Jake said quietly as he walked over to the desk and stood behind Robin. 'What you have to do is use the executive switch,' he said smiling.

'The what?'

'The executive switch.' Jake leaned over the desk, pushing Robin out of the way and switched the computer off.

'There,' he said, 'problem solved.'

'Right... Good job, I'd saved all my work, then, wasn't it, you wassack?'

'Anyway, what's so important that you needed to bring me in early?' Jake asked Robin as he went and sat at his desk.

'Well, we had a fatal, early doors. Single vehicle into the central barrier on the motorway.'

Robin was in his mid-forties with thinning and balding hair. One of the more senior traffic sergeants on the department, the uniform he wore tended to hang on him like a coat hanger. He got up from his desk and handed Jake a brown folder. The file contained a preliminary hand-written press release from the collision investigator and the officer in the case, which he quickly read.

'OK,' Jake said. 'Nothing spectacular here, single vehicle, alcohol suspected. So why do you need me?'

'Bill thinks that you would be better doing the trauma message.'

Jake was about to argue the point, when Bill walked in.

'Ah, Jake,' he said. 'Just the man I need, with your special talents.'

'It's not really a talent, Sir,' he replied. 'Anybody can do this trauma message.'

'Yes, but I don't just want anybody doing it. I want you to do it and I want to come along too.'

'Why?'

'Look at the name of the deceased.'

'And?'

'Don't you know who he is?'

'Should I?'

'Some years ago Detective Chief Superintendent Porter got drummed out of the force - unreasonably in my mind - for being involved in a serious collision in a CID car. He was drunk at the wheel, celebrating some murderer they had just banged away. Well, it's his son, so we need to tread a bit carefully.'

'But why me, Sir?'

Chief Inspector Bill Gorman indicated to Jake to step outside out of his office into the corridor. Lowering his voice, he said, 'Look, Jake, I am asking you to do this as a favour for me. He was a good cop, caught out by one mistake for which he paid the price. Spread all over the newspapers at the time when it happened and he has not worked since. Nobody would employ him and this was his only son, so this news isn't going to be good for him or his wife.'

'OK, OK Bill. But I don't think you should come. What's your relationship with him, as you seem so concerned?'

'He was my tutor constable and the best man at my wedding.'

'Ah, all the more reason then for you to stay here. I'll take Bob with me, and then you can see him later.'

'OK, thanks.'

Jake started to walk away.

'Jake?' Bill called.

'Yes, Sir?' Jake replied, turning towards Bill.

'Thanks, I owe you one.'

Jake grinned. 'Yes, Sir, you do.'

Returning to his office, Jake collected his kit, made a quick phone call to his training officer, Bob Evans, and then met him in the car compound.

'What's this all about then, Jake?' asked Evans, as Jordan got into the driving seat of their five series BMW estate patrol car. Evans lumbered his overweight body into the passenger seat, the mere act of which seemed to make him breathless.

'This 'fay-tacc' this morning, son of an ex-copper, apparently.'

'Why do you need me then, Sarg?' Evans said, with an out of breath wheeze. Anyone would have thought he had just run a marathon, thought Jake to himself.

'Best to be on the safe side, under the circumstances, belt and braces job, so to speak.'

'Right,' Evans just replied, still puffing.

'Anyway, you of all people should know how hard the job of the FLO is, because that's what you taught us. Makes it even more difficult when it's one of our own, even if they have retired. And you really ought to get some more exercise, Bob. Jesus, you're puffin' and blowin' like an old man.'

'Yes, I know, so everyone keeps tellin' me, but it's harder than you think.' Puff.

'Yeah, right, it'll be even harder when you're pushing up the daisies.'

'OK, less about my health! Why didn't the Inspector go with you, instead of me?' Puff.

'They are mates and this guy was Bill's tutor and best man at his wedding, so he tells me.'

'So, how do you want to play this then?'

'No different to what we normally do, but just leave the talking to me, would you?' Jordan said.

'Ah, only a supporting role then?' Evans remarked.

They sat in silence for a moment as Jordan pulled out of the police station yard.

'You know there are a lot of people out there,' Evans said, making a sweeping gesture with his arms as best he could in the confines of the patrol car, 'who think that this isn't our job.'

'What, death messages?' Jordan sometimes slipped into the old, pre-politically correct expressions.

'No, family liaison.'

'Why? Don't they understand that this is some of what coppering is all about, supporting the community and all that?'

Jordan had volunteered for the role of Traffic Family Liaison Officer, as he didn't see his job on traffic as all speeders and traffic tickets. He knew that was part of it, of course, but this role addressed his more compassionate side and was one of the reasons he became a copper.

'A lot would argue against that,' said Evans.

'Yeah, a lot are probably politicians or the Police and Crime Commissioner, looking to reduce the budget.'

'You know, I've always found the intimation of death quite difficult when we first meet the relatives.' Jordan said, changing the subject. He went on, 'We are taught how to communicate with people, but you can't just blurt it out.'

'Yeah, I know what you mean. Remember that example given in the training school, when we were young, green PC's?'

'What, the story on how *not* to deliver the death message, as we called them then.'

'Yes,' said Evans, thinking, 'I remember now. How did the story go, a woman answers the door to a policeman. The policeman asks – 'widow Jones'? 'No', the woman replies. 'Well, you are now', the policeman replies. I seem to recall that it was quite funny at the time.'

'It seemed to get the message across to most of the class,' Jordan responded chuckling.

'Mm, but you can't tell stories like that in training school today,' said Evans, jokingly making sure that the in-car 'ProVida video system' microphone was switched off.

'I know that a lot of officers are unsure about delivering the actual message,' Evans continued, as he settled back into the passenger seat as best he could. 'I see it in the training I deliver all the time. They tend to go around the houses before they get into the main message.'

'I'm not really like that,' remarked Jordan. 'I like to get the message over as quickly as I can, then get on with the job of supporting the family.'

'Ninety per cent of the time if you turn up on someone's doorstep, they know it's trouble anyway.' Evans reminded Jordan.

'Yeah, the old adage that a policemen turning up at your front door means bad news is never far from the truth.'

The discussion continued as they drove towards their destination, arriving at the home of ex-Detective Chief Superintendent Alan Porter.

The 1930s style semi-detached house was in the centre of a well looked after middle-class estate. The lawn at the front of the garden was tightly cut with a square border of shrubs and roses. Evans and Jordan glanced around the well-kept garden.

'I hope I have more to do than just tend the garden when I retire,' commented Evans, quietly, as they rang the front door bell. Mrs Porter opened the door. She was shocked to see two policemen standing in front of her and called to her husband immediately. Alan Porter joined his wife at the front door and invited the two into the house. Jordan could see that Mrs Porter was close to tears already. This was going to be difficult, Jordan thought to himself. Jordan and Evans were ushered into the large lounge that was plainly two rooms knocked into one.

'Please, take a seat,' Alan Porter said, as they entered the room. He indicated the sofa, and they sat on the edge of it, not really feeling comfortable enough to sit back on it. Jordan quietly cleared his throat before he began to speak to the couple who had sat down opposite him.

'What's all this about, Sergeant?' asked the ex-policeman, with some concern in his voice and perhaps, thought Jordan, a little defensively. Despite Jordan knowing the family, after his conversation with his boss, he still needed to go through the motions of making sure that they were who he thought they were. Many a message had been passed on only to find that it was the wrong family, so Jordan confirmed that they had a son and the exact vehicle he owned and drove.

Leaning closer to the couple, he said quietly 'Mr. and Mrs. Porter, I'm sorry to have to tell you that your son, Vincent, died in a road accident this morning on the motorway near to Watford Gap Services. Vincent has been taken to the general hospital and I need one or both of you to come to the hospital to do a formal identification. I'm sure you understand, Sir.' Jordan directed this last comment towards Mr Porter.

Porter nodded his head slowly, as the couple sat in stunned silence for what seemed like ages. Mrs Porter was the first to speak.

'Where are my manners? Thank you, officer. Would you like a cup of tea?'

It was not an uncommon reaction to such news, Jordan thought.

Mr Porter sat back in his chair and Jordan could see that tears were welling up in his eyes, while he was desperately trying to remain composed. Mrs Porter quietly rose from the chair, patted her husband's arm and moved swiftly into the kitchen.

Mr Porter had not spoken.

'Are you OK, Sir?' Jordan asked.

Mr Porter solemnly nodded his head. 'He was on his way home, you know. Although we were not expecting him till tonight,' he added.

'Is there anything I can do for you now?'

'No, Sergeant.'

'My name is Jake, Jake Jordan'

'Thank you, Jake.' He stumbled a bit over using Jordan's first name.

'Unusual name, Jake.' commented Porter.

'Mm, yes. Short for Jacob.'

'I see. I, I, just need to sit for a moment, if you don't mind?'

'No, that's fine, sir– whenever you're ready, we'll continue – no rush.'

As they were speaking, there was a loud crash from the kitchen. All the men got up to follow the noise. They entered the kitchen to see Mrs Porter staring at a broken teapot on the floor and sobbing uncontrollably. Her husband put his arm around her and guided her back to the living room.

Evans, who had said nothing until now, stood up and volunteered to continue making the tea. Mrs Porter explained where everything was, between sobs and nose-blowing.

As they sat drinking their tea, Jordan explained the procedure of identifying their son. Although, Jordan thought, Porter probably knew the procedure better than he did. Mr Porter began asking questions. He asked whether Jordan was aware of who he was. Jordan felt that he was only asking the questions in an effort to be sociable. He could also see the spark of the detective was not quite dead in the man and he wondered whether that might be a problem for the investigation. He must remember to speak to Bill about it when he returned to the station.

Jordan made arrangements with the Porters to attend the hospital and do the identification. Jordan and Evans gave their condolences and then both quietly left the house.

Chapter 3

'Come in Bingham, have a seat,' said Eleanor.
Bingham quickly glanced around the room, as he stepped over the threshold into the cottage. He followed Eleanor as they walked through the lounge into the kitchen. She offered him a seat at the small kitchen table. He went to sit down but Eleanor turned her back to him, as she went to fill the kettle with water.
He moved up behind her and grabbed her with one swift movement. With his right hand, he took hold of her head and swiftly snapped it to the right, instantly breaking her neck. She never felt a thing.
Bingham watched in slow motion as she fell to the floor. He bent down towards her to check to see that she was dead. Her eyes were closed. Suddenly they opened – and she laughed.

Bingham woke in a cold sweat. This was the third time he'd had this dream in as many days. The act of the kill had aroused him - until Eleanor opened her eyes. But she was there - every time he fell asleep. He had not experienced this with any other of his kills. Thinking about the day he took Eleanor's life, he lay in his bed, with the early dawn beginning to make itself known through the dirty, tatty green sheets that masqueraded as curtains.

After a long search, he had found her retirement home in the sleepy Northamptonshire village of Willoughby, tucked away in a secluded terrace of cottages on the outskirts of the village. The only access was by a dirt track and most of the terrace was hidden away in a small, but dense, copse. If you didn't know the cottages were there, you would never be able to find them. An excellent location opening up all sorts of possibilities for her demise, he had thought.

Once found, Bingham kept a watch on her and formulated a plan that would not arouse the suspicion of the neighbours. He told the neighbours that he was taking his 'Aunty Eleanor' away for a holiday and that they could not tell her, as it was a surprise. They agreed not to let on. Fools, he thought.

Bingham walked up to the cottage opened the little green picket gate and on up to the front door, where he knocked. The door opened quickly, but only as wide as the door chain would allow.

'Yes, who is it?' Eleanor asked.

'Hi, Mrs Smyth. It's Bingham, Bingham Tyler.'

'Who?'

'You know, Bingham! You put me and my step-brother and sister in a foster home many years ago.'

He tried not to let the anger in those words show to Eleanor.

'I was passing through the village.' he continued, with what he hoped was charm, 'and found out you lived here from the postmistress, so I thought I'd come and say hello and see how you are.'

'Oh,' Eleanor thought for a moment.'Yes, Bingham. Yes, I remember you now.'

He heard the chain being removed and was inwardly smiling to himself. The door opened fully and Eleanor invited Bingham into her house.

Eleanor had never been a tall woman, but to Bingham she now stooped slightly and appeared quite frail. He smiled again to himself, knowing that this heavy responsibility he felt he had was going to be easier than he thought.

'Come in, Bingham, have a seat,' Eleanor said with a smile, as she showed Bingham into the living area.

Bingham quickly glanced around the room taking in the number of exits, location of the furniture, stairs and kitchen. He sat down facing the kitchen door.

'Would you like a cup of tea or something?' she asked.

'Yes, that would be very nice, thank you.'

Eleanor went into the kitchen. Bingham watched her as she made the tea.

'So, Bingham,' she said, as she shakily brought in a tray of tea, 'Tell me what you've been up to in all these years.'

'Well, Mrs S,' he started. 'You know that I wasn't the best of foster kids–' He gave her a big smile.

'Yes, I know, you did have a few problems, as I recall.'

'Right, well, I did manage to get myself in with a nice family eventually and they settled me down.

'Or thought they did.'

'Yes, as I can see. That's a nice suit you're wearing. Are you doing well in your job?'

'I am, yes.'

'What do you do?'

'I'm a surveillance expert for the police.'

'My, my, that sounds exciting.'

'Not really, spend most of the time looking at surveillance videos and the like.'

'Well, you have come a long way. The last thing I expected from you is to see you working for the police.'

'Well, I don't actually work for the police. The company I work for is contracted to them.'

'Oh, I see, doing what?'

'We provide surveillance equipment to them, that sort of thing.'

'Aren't you going to tell her that you've been sacked from the job and put in the nick?'

'Quiet!' Bingham said, as an aside.

'Sorry?' Eleanor asked, with a frown.

'No, it's OK, but it has its ups and downs. But, you know, the pay is quite good.' Bingham carefully took a sip of his tea.

'So, what are you doing in the village?' she asked.

'I was just passing through. Can't tell you a lot really, wouldn't be right.' He winked at her.

'Oh,' she said, as she tapped the side of her nose. 'I think I understand.'

'Do you go out a lot?' Bingham asked, after a short pause.

'No, no, not at my age. Some of the neighbours pop in to see me. Check that I'm OK. I'm not as agile as I used to be, you know.'

'When does your neighbour come in and see you?'

'Everyday, but she's away at the moment– won't be back for a couple of weeks.'

'Better for you then... perhaps.'

'No, my arthritis puts a stop to me doing things,' added Eleanor.

'Yes, I seem to recall you were always up to something or other. Have you suffered for long?'

'About ten years, I suppose.'

'You take the right medication, do you?'

'Yes, I have loads of pills for various ailments, but when you get old that happens, I'm afraid.'

'Well, I hope I don't get old.'

'We all do, Bingham, we all do. Part of life.'

'And death.'

'Yes, indeed. Do you want some more tea?'

'Thanks.'

'And what about something to eat? Look at the time,' she said, glancing at the clock on the mantelpiece above the fireplace, 'can I make you a sandwich or something?'

'Don't go to any trouble on my account, Mrs S.'

'No trouble at all.'

She got stiffly up out of her chair and walked into the kitchen.

'Let me help you.'

Bingham followed Eleanor into the kitchen. He stood just inside the kitchen door, waiting for his moment. Eleanor removed some cheese and spread from the fridge. She smiled at him and said, 'Do you want to get the bread for me? It's in the bread bin in the corner.'

Bingham walked across the kitchen and removed a loaf of bread from the bread bin.

'You're taking too much time over this.'

'Be quiet.'

'Sorry, did you say something, dear?' Eleanor asked.

'No, no.'

Eleanor was standing with her back to Bingham. The opportunity he had been waiting for had finally arrived. He walked up behind her and put the bread on the side next to her. He then grabbed her with one swift movement, putting his left arm around the front of her shoulders and just under her chin. With his right hand he took hold of her head and swiftly snapped her head to the right, instantly breaking her neck. She never felt a thing. He let go of her and her body slumped to the floor.

'Well, you deserved it,' he said to her, 'Leaving me alone with no friends, no family.'

'What are you going to do now Bingham?'

'Don't worry, I've thought it all out.'

'I'm sure you have.'

Putting on a pair of rubber surgical gloves, Bingham picked up the frail, lightweight body from the floor and took her to the top of the stairs in the cottage. At the top of the stairs, he threw her down. She came to rest at the bottom of the stairs, lying limply against the wall, her head slumped forward.

'That'll do. Looks like an accident then, doesn't it?' he said out loud to himself.

Walking down the stairs, he removed a small webcam from his pocket and set it up on the top of the TV. He had disconnected any tell-tale lights, so nobody would know the webcam was permanently on and being streamed live into his apartment. He removed a tablet PC from his pocket, checking that the camera worked.

Bingham then spent time methodically trashing the cottage. He wanted it to look like a burglary that Eleanor had interrupted.

He opened the unlocked back door in the kitchen. With a towel, so nobody could hear, he broke the glass on the kitchen door and spread the glass around, so the point of entry could be found.

Finally, he removed a small piece of paper from his pocket. He looked around for somewhere to put it. Carefully removing it from the plastic bag, he placed it under the lamp by the telephone. Just leaving enough of it visible, so that someone could find it.

'Why are you giving yourself away?'

'Because I need to let people know who did this and to bring Jimmy out in the open, so I can do the same to him.'

'You are a fool.'

'Am I?' he questioned himself.

Chapter 4

Bingham Tyler was a twenty-seven-year-old computer geek. He was grey, gaunt and emaciated from habitual drug use. His long, prematurely receding, black greasy hair lay limp around his neck and shoulders.

After thinking about Eleanor Smyth some more, he climbed out of his pit. He looked around his 17th floor apartment. If he was alive forty years ago, he thought, this place would have been the penthouse suite of a prestigious and well-known local hotel chain. Now, however, it wallowed in the town's red light district, an ugly grey concrete building, more reminiscent of a tower block and had few redeeming features. He couldn't believe that the local council had bought it for social housing and then won an award for original thinking.

He thought about how he had managed to get himself into this position. If his childhood hadn't been emphasised by the murder of his mother eighteen years ago and then being bounced from one foster parent to another as a difficult child–he scoffed at that idea – life may have been a little more tolerable.

It was only the last couple he was fostered with, John and Claire Partridge, who had any understanding of his needs. They found he excelled in computer science and everyone thought that this was where his future was. That was until his foster mother went away, when he was seventeen.

The social ping-pong between foster carers and the disappearance of Claire Partridge was the final straw for him–he recognised that– but the streak of violence that he had managed to subdue reasserted itself afterwards. But by concentrating on what he was good at – developing technologies and violent computer games –

he kept himself away from people that he wanted very little to do with anyway, until he met *her*. His mind was awash with thoughts of his childhood and early years trying to work and become a member of the human race, blaming everyone but himself for his situation now and in the past. He had learned to feign being 'normal' in his early teens and been seen by some as a charming extrovert, but he tired of that persona very quickly.

Bingham rubbed his face and his arms red raw with his latest injection marks and bruises. He walked slowly over to his array of stolen or acquired surveillance equipment. Covert wireless video cameras disguised as normal household items and Global System Mobile voice activated bugs –dial the SIM card in the unit and listen to the conversation. Laser and WiFi transmitters he'd installed on what used to be the rooftop garden of the hotel, allowed him to watch his prey with impunity. He was able to hack into most of the CCTV surveillance equipment that watched over the town and any computer system connected to the web.

Still in his early morning stupor, he remembered he was glad that he had spent time in the computer laboratories at school, using his developing charm and wit with the young female teaching assistant. He found that he seemed to have a good head for computer algorithms and programming techniques. And hacking into the teaching assistant's home computer and activating her webcam without her knowledge, allowed him time to indulge in his own sexual fantasies. He was constantly amazed that he seemed to have little interference in what he did with his computers.

Sitting in front of his bank of TV and computer screens, he murmured, 'I don't want to live in such shit.'

'I know Bingham, you won't be here for much longer, think of that.'

'If it wasn't for that bitch of a so-called girlfriend screwing me out of all my money and everything I own and that copper for nicking me, we wouldn't be here, would we?'

'No, we wouldn't.'

'I hate women and I hate coppers, particularly Jimmy Kingsfield.'

'I know, I know.'

'Women are all nothing but tarts. They all need putting into slavery where they belong.'

'What do you see them as then?'

Bingham swung around in his big brown faux leather chair. The only part of his apartment that resembled anything like clean was the area around his computers. The rest of his flat was poorly kept and sparsely furnished.

'Tools, nothing but tools –to do my bidding,' he answered.

'But they may not want to do YOUR bidding.'

'I don't care –they will, if I force them.'

'What about those women who work outside this shithole then?'

'What about them? They wanna walk the streets and give blow jobs or get shagged by any John that comes along, that's their look out –and I'll use them and abuse them at my leisure as well!'

'I still don't think you are a very nice person, thinking that Bingham.'

'Well, that's tough!'

'Don't you have any conscience about what you do?'

'Conscience! What the fuck has conscience go to do with it? I don't give a fuck about conscience! Nobody gave a shit about me –why should I give a shit about them? Anyway, I have you, don't I?'

'John and Claire looked after you; they worried about you all the time.'

Page 46

'Yeah, and looked what happened to them after she went away.'

'I wish you would just listen to me occasionally. I am, after all, your voice of reason.'

'Yeah, really?! Well, you're doing a fucking brilliant job.'

Bingham walked over to the window of his apartment and looked down onto the street below. The area around his apartment block was poorly lit. The public house opposite used to do a better trade when the hotel was in its prime, but was now run down. The only customers were those who worked outside, usually accompanied by the next John.

'Look at them –hanging around on street corners, waiting for the next desperate twat to come along –talk of the devil…'

A big silver Mercedes had drawn up to one of the girls on the street. Bingham adjusted the camera he had trained on the street and went back to his workstation, increasing the gain on the microphone antenna.

'Can I interest you in something?' he heard the girl say to the driver.

Bingham watched.

The girl got into the car and it drove off.

Bingham smiled.

'I know where you're going,' Bingham mumbled to himself. He accessed the camera fitted in the Mayorhold Car Park ground floor and watched as the big Mercedes drove into the car park and stopped in a corner of the parking area.

Bingham watched and smiled.

'This is better than TV –Bingham's bonking channel,' he said out loud in amusement. He watched as the girl was clearly giving the driver of the Mercedes a blowjob.

Bingham laughed.

'You're enjoying that mate, aren't you? So am I,' he said, as he himself became more aroused. He realised that his recent reoccurring dream made it more inevitable that he would need to violently take one of the girls below.

'I can't understand why I'm not attractive to girls?' he mused.

'Well, if you tidied yourself up you might have a chance.'

'Thanks. I think I'm OK.'

'But you're not OK, are you? Look at you –you're a junkie and a violent junkie at that! It's no wonder that people don't want anything to do with you.'

'It's only since I got screwed in that court case.'

'Yes, because the real you was revealed –all those friends who thought you were a great guy, realised now how you duped them all these years. Is it any wonder…'

'I didn't know that the bitch would take me to court, did I?'

'Oh, come on Bingham, you fucking raped her and threw her out of a window. How did you not expect to go to court?'

'OK, I realise that I made a mistake.'

'A mistake.. a mistake? What the hell sort of world do you think you live in?'

'Stop shouting at me.'

'You need someone to shout at you.'

'Nobody ever listens to me, I'm virtually invisible to everyone.' Bingham said, a little dejected, in an attempt to change the subject.

'I will seek my revenge on the people who put me in this position, particularly the bastard that got me kicked out of my one and only job. I have a plan for him and I am close to making it a reality.'

Silence.

'What - got no comment on that then?'

Page 48

Silence.

Bingham's wiry frame was sustained on high-energy drinks, junk food and more than the occasional shot of cocaine or methamphetamine - 'Ice' as his dealer called it. The constant use of methamphetamine made sure that his face and body were covered in sores, blisters and track marks, where regular injections had collapsed some veins, making it difficult for him to shoot up. Some of the sores had even turned septic.

'You don't look good, Bingham.'

'I don't care! I have more important things to worry about.'

'When did you last go out?'

Bingham pushed his hand through his greasy hair, rubbing his face and thinking. 'I can't remember. I have everything here that I need.'

'But you only get it delivered. That's not good – you're losing your social skills.'

'Ha! Social skills? You're havin' me on. I never had any fuckin' social skills in the first place!'

'We could help you to get better socially, you know.'

'Who's we? No. I need time to plan for the destruction of Kingsfield.'

'Not really happy about that.'

'Well, that's tough, then, isn't it?'

Bingham turned once again to his surveillance screens and watched the recording he'd made of the police, who were working in the cottage, with interest.

'Well, what do you think about these two here, then?' he asked, pointing at one of the screens in front of him.

'What about them?'

'Don't you think that they are a bit too happy, considering they are at my crime scene?'

'Why? Just because you're not you mean?'

Bingham didn't respond to that comment. He remained transfixed at the eight monitors he had in front

Page 49

of him, watching what was happening in the little cottage Kingsfield and his team were in.

'Just because your relationships don't work out doesn't mean to say that their marriage won't.'

'But,' Bingham said, leaning in closer to the screens, 'no marriage survives this day and age, does it?'

'It only survives if you try. They are.'

'Bollocks!' pointing to Kingsfield on the screen. 'He got me kicked out of my one and only good job.'

'Rubbish, it was your own fault –he was only doing his job.'

'Yeah and if I hadn't been banging that cop tart, he'd never have found out.'

'Possibly, but why did you show her all this stuff, other than to stroke your own ego?'

'I didn't fucking think she'd go and tell 'em, did I?'

'What did you expect her to do, particularly after that last time you fucked each other?'

'I knocked her about a bit, but she deserved it.'

'What? Because she appeared here unexpectedly and found you out? You amaze me, Bingham, you fucking amaze me. You know I don't like you when you treat women that way, like that prozzy you treated badly last week.'

'She deserved it as well.'

'Why? Just because she wouldn't take it in the head?'

'Yeah, I pays my money and I takes my choice.'

'You really piss me off, Bingham. Grow up!'

'Never.'

'Well, there's not much hope, then, is there? Women are not put on this Earth for you to do what you like with. And all because you're angry about your own life.'

'Yes, I'm angry at my pitiful existence and I'm going to do something about it. I have a few plans that will achieve my revenge. And ultimately, my acceptance back into society.'

'Yes, but was it not Confucius, who said, 'if you embark on a journey of revenge you should dig two graves?'

'Well I have no intention of dying –I can be sure of that.'

'We'll see, shall we?'

Bingham leaned back in his chair, cracked open another can of high-energy drink and dropped a rock of crack cocaine into it. It bubbled fiercely for a couple of seconds, before he downed half the can.

Bingham's disastrous relationship with Jessica gave him some prison time for GBH. He thought that she deserved it. Women should be put in their place occasionally, as he explained to the female magistrate. Needless to say, she sent him to prison for six months.

Bingham returned his gaze to the screens in front of him in time to see Kingsfield leave the cottage with his wife. He froze a frame where Kingsfield and his wife appeared to be looking directly into the camera and smiled.

'I'll wipe the smile off your fucking faces,' he seethed at the TV screen. 'I've got some fucking plans for both of you.'

He wanted to know everything about Kingsfield, everything, anything to discredit and reduce his world to nothing. Bingham continued to mumble to himself,

'Yes, I plan, must get on with my plans. I will see to you and your tart of a wife, you mark my words.' At that he raised his can to the images on the TV screen.

Bingham had nothing but contempt for Kingsfield. He remembered that Jim Kingsfield brought his one and only good job to an end after just a minor mistake on his part. He would still have a job with 'Polserv' –a technical support company that provided surveillance equipment to the police service when needed –if it wasn't for him.

Page 51

Bingham had been a shining light in the company, seemingly able to get into any computer system he wanted and manipulate data, which he mainly did in secret for his own dark ends.

His mistake was to let the policewoman who he was trying to have a proper relationship with, see how he did it. They were still looking for her, because she had disappeared before the court case. There was no case to answer, so the Crown Prosecutor withdrew the case. Excellent result, thought Bingham.

He opened another tin of drink.

There was a loud bang on the door, suddenly followed by a shout of 'Police! Open the door!'

'Shit, shit, shiiit.'

Desperately trying to dispose of the drugs on the top of his desk, there was a loud crash, as the door burst open and further multiple shouts of, 'Police! Stay where you are!' Within seconds the flat was full of uniformed police officers, followed by a detective that he seemed to recognise.

'Bingham Tyler?' asked the Detective

'Yes, what is the meaning of this? You can't just come bursting in here without a warrant.'

'This ain't America, mate, and yes, we can,' the Detective retorted.

'Just piss off out. You have no rights here.'

'Bingham Tyler, you are under arrest for rape and assault causing Grievous Bodily Harm. You do not have to say anything but, it may harm your defence, if you do not mention when questioned something that you later rely on in court. Anything you do say will be given in evidence.'

'You've got nothing, you fucking twat –this is all a load of bollocks.'

He spat in the face of the Detective, who calmly wiped his spittle away with the handkerchief that he took from his pocket.

'You can add assault on police to that as well.'

'Fuck you,' Bingham shouted, as he was led out of his flat.

'Wanker,' the Detective mumbled under his breath. 'OK, everyone, let's see what we can find.'

Chapter 5

Two days after the murder investigation had begun at the cottage, Heart was in Kingsfield's office, perched on the corner of his desk with a black coffee in a plastic cup he'd got from the coffee machine in his hand.

The small, drab, blue eggshell-painted office was only big enough to take two medium sized desks that had seen better days. Kingsfield had managed to squeeze in two extra soft covered blue chairs he had nicked from the training room to put in front of his desk. At least those who did come to his office didn't have to stand, he thought. There was a long metal-framed window behind Kingsfield's desk, which had been permanently sealed, so it wouldn't open. It took the sun all day, so in the summer his office was like a sauna. And the tatty cream blinds didn't do anything to stop the heat getting in. Kingsfield had been told that his office was only temporary. That had been two years ago.

'So, where are we with this?' Kingsfield asked Heart. Kingsfield was sitting in the chair in front of his desk. He sat forward and rubbed his face with both hands. The last two days had been frantic, like the start of most murder enquiries. He was also hacked off that the Detective Chief Superintendent hadn't given him the manpower he needed for the investigation. So, once again it looked like it was going to be down to him and Heart with a little help from anyone else he could round up. He glanced at Heart, waiting for a response.

'Short answer boss, nowhere yet. We have actions outstanding to hunt down witnesses and take statements. SOCO are still at the cottage, so it'll be a while till we get any info coming out of them. And because it was so rural, we're not getting much info from the press release.'

'We get *anything* from the press?' enquired Kingsfield.

'Nope, other than what are we doing about it –you know, normal shit you get from them on a quiet news day. What really intrigues me is this cryptic note you found underneath that lamp. As if she was trying to tell us something.'

Heart got up from his position on the edge of the desk and sat down in the other chair opposite Kingsfield.

'Yeah, I can't understand that either. It would be nice if we had some sort of clue to point us in the right direction, cos at the moment, we're just pissing in the wind.'

There was a tap on Kingsfield's open office door. The small portly frame of Detective Chief Superintendent Colin Marland barged in, without any acknowledgement from Kingsfield.

'I don't expect you two to be sitting around the office on your arses. Shouldn't you be out on enquiries?'

'We're just collating what little information we have on the cottage murder, Sir. So we know where to go and what to do. Make best use of the limited time and resources we have in this investigation,' remarked Kingsfield, with more than a hint of sarcasm in his voice.

Kingsfield was not a particular fan of Marland and quite obviously Marland was not a fan of him either. Trying to keep enough distance between the pair of them to reduce this sort of interaction was going to be difficult, to say the least.

'Don't you get narky with me,' Marland drawled in his thick Derbyshire accent. 'I told you yesterday that we're short of manpower for yet another suspicious death enquiry. Happen you'll want me wipe your backside for you, just get on wee it.'

'Did you come here for a reason?' Kingsfield tried to keep the irritation out of his voice. It didn't work.

'Get off your high horse, Kingsfield. Chief wants you at his briefing in thirty minutes, so look sharp.'

Kingsfield nodded. Marland turned and walked out of Kingsfield's office, slamming the door behind him.

'What a tosser!' exclaimed Heart. 'Been promoted five ranks higher than his capability.'

'Six actually, if you include Police Cadet!' Kingsfield grinned, got up from the chair in front of his desk and went around to the other side and stood looking out of the window.

'OK, Dave, where were we?'

'I was about to say that the Department for Work and Pensions, they took over from the DHSS, are looking into the murder victim, Smyth for us. They found some of her archived case notes, which they've sent up from some storage place in Gloucestershire - but they don't hold out much hope that they can be any use. They have been very helpful though. Apparently she had a good reputation, even in her retirement.'

'That's good, then. What are these documents –do we know?'

Kingsfield thought for a moment, then said, 'hopefully, they'll lead us somewhere?'

Heart nodded. 'Hopefully – yes. Apparently her main job was finding foster places for children and had a good reputation for placing kids with the right family. She got a couple wrong, but I suppose she couldn't get it right all the time.'

'Mm, OK, but look, Dave, I don't want this to turning into a dead-end. See if we can blag someone else from another team to look at some of the outstanding actions and get a handle on this note we found under the lamp.'

'OK, I'll ask Stevens. I don't want to give up on it just yet. I think it's the key to the whole case.'

Heart was the sort of detective that didn't generally give up on something and Kingsfield thought that sometimes Heart was a like a dog with a bone when he got his teeth into a case.

DC Winston Okenewu tapped on Kingsfield's office door, which was still closed after Marland had left. Kingsfield waved for him to enter. As usual, Kingsfield thought, Okenewu was immaculately dressed in the dark-grey pin-stripped suit with a blue shirt and matching tie.

'What's up, Win?' asked Kingsfield.

'You wouldn't believe who we've just locked up!'

'Enlighten us,' Kingsfield said, glancing at Heart.

'Well, you know that weird, geeky little guy you had kicked out of PolServ a few years back?'

'Who can forget him? Bloody psycho, if you ask me!' Kingsfield exclaimed.

'Well, he's in the cells.'

'Oh, what for?'

'Rape, GBH…'

'I knew that little twat would come again, so to speak,' retorted Heart.

'How did he manage that then? Didn't think he was capable,' said Kingsfield.

'A sex worker outside where he lives made a complaint against him.'

'How did she know him? Or is that a silly question?' said Heart, turning in his chair to face Okenewu.

'Apparently, she says she's had him before and he was violent towards her then, but she never complained —only this time he broke her jaw. He's well known for it among the other sex workers apparently.'

'Perhaps I'd better go and 'talk' to him,' Kingsfield said, rubbing his hands in what appeared to be delight at the thought.

'No, it's OK, boss, we don't want you hanging him upside down out of the window again, like last time.'

'Ah, that's a pity.'

'Oh, and we're doing him for assault on police, as well.'

'Why?' asked Heart

'He spat in my face when I arrested him.'

Kingsfield noticed that Okenewu brushed something unseen from the arm of his jacket after he said that.

'Fair enough,' said Kingsfield and Heart in unison. Okenewu turned to leave the office.

'Let me know when you charge him and I'll come down,' repeated Kingsfield

'OK,' said Okenewu, leaving.

'Don't you go getting yourself involved with this character, Jim…' Heart warned Kingsfield, as he finished the last dregs of his, by now, cold coffee.

'I know, I know –he's just bit of a thorn in my side that's all. You know –unfinished business and all that.'

'Yes, well, as I said –don't get involved, Jim, that's all I'm saying. The idiot is trouble, you know that.'

Kingsfield simply nodded to Heart as turned to leave.

'I'll get what team we have together for a briefing – 'bout half an hour?'

Looking out of his office door into the Incident room he suddenly asked, 'who's the uniform?'

'Oh, that's young PC Prentice. Remember Andy Prentice? Inspector? Retired a few years ago.'

Yes, I remember him,' replied Kingsfield, as he moved to sit down behind his desk.

'It's his lad. Been in about four years, still enthusiastic about the job! Chris, I think his first name is. He's been doing a little task for DC Stevens.'

Kingsfield nodded and sat down at his desk in deep thought, not about the case they had just been discussing, but the disappearance of his friend Stephanie Parker, which was still an open case. A case he had not thought about for quite some time, until Okenewu mentioned Bingham Tyler.

He recalled that his friend and colleague, WPC Stephanie Parker, had simply vanished some years ago. He had known Stephanie since she came to the station as police cadet on his shift when he was a probationer. He also remembered the first night she was out on duty with him and Doreen Miller, coming across a murder on the De-Senlis Estate.

Over time it was apparent that the discovery of the body, and the circumstances she had found herself in, had had a deep and lasting effect on Stephanie's psyche. She seemed to become extremely promiscuous, very attractive to a lot of young coppers when it was common that most policewomen seemed to be stone-faced and rather robust in stature. But Stephanie frequently appeared at work smelling of drink, which was hushed up by the shift, until it couldn't be kept quiet any longer. They sent her off to the police rehabilitation centre at Flint House and after a considerable rehabilitation, she returned to the shift, finished her cadet rotation, went off to training school, where she did very well, and resumed normal duties to finish her probation. It seemed that she had turned herself around from whatever dark place she was in. Kingsfield had seen her occasionally – she'd remained in uniform when he transferred into CID.

But he had become deeply concerned for her when she told him that she was Bingham Tyler's girlfriend. She said she'd met him at a bar and told her that he worked for 'PolServ' and was 'a bit whizzy' with computers and other technical stuff.

At that time of course, Kingsfield had no idea who he was. It was only after a few months and after several jobs involving 'Polserv,' Tyler and himself that Stephanie had visited Kingsfield's office one morning with numerous bruises on her arms, face, and legs. She told him that Tyler had violently assaulted her the previous evening. She'd turned up late for a date at his apartment, unexpectedly, having been delayed at work. They'd argued about what he was doing with his own surveillance equipment. It was clear to Parker that Bingham was virtually hacking into the lives of everyone he had a grudge against –manipulating data, blackmailing his prey, mostly women, for his own ends.

It was then Bingham told her that he was the little boy with the shoebox at the murder of his mother, who she had had to sit with after they had been taken from the house. Bingham also told her that he had deliberately targeted her –he had wanted her ever since that time. She told Kingsfield that she was mortified to find out and had not realised who he was until she told him.

As a result, Kingsfield had begun a covert operation (with the full cooperation of 'PolServ') that had lasted six months. When Bingham was arrested and charged with offences that ranged from fraud, rape, assault, blackmail and unlawful interception of communications under the Regulation of Investigatory Powers Act, WPC Parker seemed to have dropped off the end of the world. She didn't appear as a witness to give evidence against Bingham, so the rape and assault part of the case was dropped by the Crown Prosecutor.

Kingsfield, a Sergeant at the time and the Investigating Officer in charge of the case, had quite plainly made a deep and resentful enemy of Bingham. He remembered in the Crown Court when Bingham was taken down. Bingham indicated to Kingsfield that he was coming after him by making a chopping gesture across his throat. Bingham served three out of his five year sentence. Kingsfield thought the sentence was pretty lenient and that that he should have got something far more severe.

The one thing that troubled Kingsfield was the fact that Parker, a police officer, had failed to turn up to give her evidence on the charges that directly related to her. This was something he was determined to resolve.

He knew that Parker very much played the dumb blonde with the big boobs, but Kingsfield knew that this persona was the wall she had built to hide her insecurity in coming to terms with that first murder and the other serious incidents she was expected to attend as a police cadet. Sending police cadets out operationally thankfully doesn't happen now, Kingsfield thought.

But Parker's persona quickly got her the reputation as the 'station bike' - anyone could ride it. And despite him warning her about her recklessness several times, she seemed to be in a continual downward spiral that could only end badly.

A subsequent high profile search and media campaign for Parker had not revealed any leads. There'd been no CCTV of her anywhere, no use of credit or debit cards and her bank accounts had not been touched. And she hadn't been seen since. Kingsfield was highly suspicious of the fact that Bingham could have disposed of her, but he could never prove it.

Even when Bingham was arrested eighteen months later for assaulting another girlfriend, Kingsfield had not been able to get to the bottom of Parker's disappearance. Despite turning Bingham's seedy dive upside down, looking for evidence that he knew he was never likely to be found, Kingsfield was convinced it existed somewhere.

Chapter 6

Kingsfield was brought around from his thoughts by Heart, tapping on his open office door and standing in the doorway.

'Managed to cobble together a team of sorts, so they're ready when you are boss.'

'OK, give me a minute.'

Kingsfield collected himself, putting all thoughts of Stephanie Parker temporarily out of his mind. He focussed on the current murder victim, and then strode out of his office into the briefing room. He sat on the desk at the front of the room and signalled for Heart to carry on.

'Right, everyone, thank you, thank you. We listening, Stevens?' Heart called as he addressed his junior officer. The room fell silent.

'Now as you all know, our victim was a seventy-year-old woman, living on her own at Copse Cottage, Willoughby, part of a row of semi-detached cottages, situated at the end of a small track on the outskirts of the village. Locals tell us that she was quite active and regularly seen around the village, although she kept herself to herself. We know that she was a social worker with the DHSS —as it was then. She retired five years ago, when the local office was re-located. She was found here.'

Heart pointed to a large TV screen, showing a plan of the cottage. 'At the bottom of the stairs, with her neck broken. At the moment we don't know whether this was due to the fall or whether it was broken by the intruder.'

A hand went up at the back of the room.

'Yes Stevens, what?'

'How do we know that the fall was not just an accident, Sarg?'

'If you let me finish, Stevens, I'll tell you.'

'Thanks, Sarg.'

Stevens looked at his colleague, smiling and leaning back on his chair, so that the chair back was up against the wall.

'You stay like that, mate, and your chair's going to go over,' whispered Fred, Stevens' portly colleague. Stevens just smirked at him.

'When you've both finished, I'll carry on,' Heart said to them both. Stevens sat up.

'Although we're still waiting for the post-mortem results, the view is that it was either a burglary and she interrupted the intruder or that they were looking for something specific.'

A hand went up. 'What now, Stevens?' Heart said tiredly.

'Do we know what they may have been looking for?'

'Stevens, if you kept quiet and stop interrupting, you'd get the whole story as we know it, then you can ask questions.'

'Right-o, Sarg.'

A chuckle went around the room at the banter between DC Stevens and his Detective Sergeant.

'Now, where was I, before being so rudely interrupted?' Another chuckle around the room. 'Right, something specific. We believe at this stage that the intruder was looking for a document or other papers of some sort. What we did find, which appeared to have been hidden, was a piece of paper –a note –under a table lamp near the stairs.'

Heart pointed to the location on the screen, which now showed an overall view of the scene.

'We don't believe it was put there by the victim, either before or after the incident. She was probably dead by the time she got to the bottom of the stairs. We are at a bit of a loss as to how it got there, so we'll assume for the time being that she put it there well before the intruder got into the house.'

'Perhaps the intruder put it there to take us off the scent? Or perhaps she put it there deliberately, so we could find it and point us in the direction of her killer?' It was Stevens again. Heart shot a glance at Stevens that indicated he was not amused at being interrupted for a third time, although Stevens did have a fair point.

'Now,' Kingsfield stepped up. 'I know that some of you have not been allocated to this enquiry, but we need to know as much as we can about this woman's past, so we need to look at all her work files from the social. And as you are so keen, Stevens, we'll get you and your 'opo' to sit and go through this lot.'

Kingsfield tapped a pile of archive boxes that had recently been delivered.

'I am convinced the answer is in here, so we'll see where it leads.'

He tapped the boxes once again.

Stevens looked at the pile of boxes, not looking too amused about the task. He turned to Fred, his work partner. Fred was an overweight Detective Constable, in a brown leather jacket and dark crumpled trousers – a throwback to the 1980's, when he joined CID.

'This lots going to take forever,' he muttered to him.

'That'll teach you to interrupt then, won't it?' Heart said.

'OK, Sarg, point taken, no need to rub it in.'

But Heart knew that Stevens was good at picking stuff out by reading files and case notes. He'd once tasked him with a particularly nasty cold case after his transfer into CID. Due to Steven's diligence it ended in a conviction, which would have seen him on the fast track, if he'd just stop taking the piss out of everything.

He was certain that if there was anything in these boxes, Stevens would find it.

'OK,' said Kingsfield, 'Dave will hand out your tasking, so you all know what you're doing. Any work needs to cited under Operation Juniper. Off you go. We have a murderer to find.'

The room dispersed and Kingsfield went back to his office with Heart in tow.

'You look concerned, boss?' Heart said as they walked back into their office.

'Yeah,' Kingsfield rubbed his hands through his thick brown hair and stared out of his office window. He thought for a moment, then turned to Heart.

'That idiot Win has got downstairs concerns me.'

'Why?'

'It's just that we never got to the bottom of his case and where Parker disappeared to.'

'That was a long time ago. You don't think this is connected, do you?'

'Mm, I'm almost convinced of it. She was his girlfriend for a while, you know, until she realised who he was.'

'You're not trying to convince yourself that he was involved in that one, Jim?'

Kingsfield simply continued looking out of the window without responding

'Another hunch?' questioned Heart

'Mm,' Kingsfield turned back to Heart.

'Anything else then?' Heart asked.

'Yeah, do me a favour, will you and just look into this Tyler guy for me? Rattle some cages –see what falls out.'

'OK, but I think you're barking up the wrong tree.'

'Humour me.'

Kingsfield turned to look at Heart as he left the office.

'OK, you're the boss.'

Kingsfield got that same feeling he had at the cottage, that meant he was even more convinced that things were not quite right. If he could just put his finger on it. Perhaps a word with Bingham might shed some light on his worries. He decided to find out and headed across the open station forecourt into the custody block.

The custody suite at Kingsfield's nick was only a satellite to the main lock-up, which was in the centre of town. It only had half a dozen cells and was constantly buzzing with activity. Kingsfield noted that PC Prentice had brought in another prisoner.

'What's this one for then, Prentice?' he asked.

'Real big case, Sir… Shoplifting in Sainsbury's… I get all the good jobs, you know.'

'Well, we all have to start somewhere,' grinned Kingsfield.

He then turned to the Custody Sergeant as he was finishing with another 'customer.'

'Need a word with Tyler,' said Kingsfield.

'Official interview?' asked the Custody Sergeant.

Kingsfield didn't reply. He indicated for the Custody Sergeant to go to his office. Kingsfield went behind the desk and followed him in. 'I won't be a minute.' he said to his colleague at the other end of the desk, who was dealing with a particularly truculent prisoner. He nodded.

In the office, the Custody Sergeant said, 'I can't just let you have a word with a prisoner in the cells, like you used to, Jim.'

'I just want to ask him one question, that's all.'

'I'll have to put it on the custody record.'

'Yeah, I know, come on Brian, two minutes, max.'

'I'll have to come down there with you.'

'Good man.'

'Don't know about that! You don't half cause some trouble, don't you?'

'Yeah… with a capital T,' Kingsfield smiled.

Brian went with Kingsfield to the cells. He opened the main heavy iron gate to the cell block and walked down a small corridor with the cells situated on the right. They stopped at the end cell and Brian opened the heavy oak door with equally heavy steel keys that jangled like Jacob Marley's chains. The door swung open.

'Well, well, well –look who we have here!'

Bingham had been sitting on the wooden bed against the corner of the wall. The cell stank of a mixture of dried urine and sweat.

'It's OK,' Brian said, turning to Kingsfield. 'We had a drunk in here for most of the night last night, not had a chance to fumigate.'

A brief smile passed his lips.

'Yeah,' Bingham said, sarcastically, 'I get to sleep in all the good places. What the fuck do you want?' he added, addressing Kingsfield.

'Let's calm down before we start. We just want a quick word,' said Brian.

'Not talking to you, am I? Talking to this twat here.' Bingham indicated Kingsfield.

'Still no way to talk to either of us, is it?'

'Or what? You gonna lock me up?' Bingham said derisively.

'Now look, Bingham, I just want to ask you one question.'

'Well, I ain't gonna answer. I've got nothing to say to you, other than that I have plans. Shut up, will you, I'm not talking to you. I'm talking to my mate, Jim.'

Bingham started to mumble to himself.

'Is he…?' Kingsfield looked at Brian, questioningly and gave a circular motion with his finger around his temple.

'Loopy? Yes, I think so, but the forensic physician wouldn't section him.'

'Pity.'

'Bingham, you listening to me?'

Bingham stood up and walked towards Kingsfield. He held his ground. Bingham stood so close to Kingsfield, that when he spoke, he could smell his stale breath. 'You, copper, are gonna die-ey! Die, Jimmy boy, die, die, DIEEEEE.'

He jumped back and sat down.

'Yeah right, what's your next fantasy?'

'Mark my words.'

Kingsfield could see that Bingham's pent up anger was just bubbling away under the surface and ready to explode.

'OK, then, so there won't be any harm in you telling me where Stephanie Parker is, then?'

'Oooh, haven't you found your copper TART?' Bingham shouted at Kingsfield, standing up again and moving towards him. Brian stepped forward and pushed him away from Jim. 'Touch me again and you go on my list, Sergeant Brian.'

'So, where is she, then?' repeated Kingsfield.

'Dead, for all I care! Not seen her since you fuckin' banged me up, have I?'

'Funny, she didn't turn up for your trial.'

'Yeah, funny that, obviously knew what was good for her.'

'Really? You put her off, then?'

'Might have said something.'

'Said something or did something?'

'You think I've done her, don't you?'

'Yup, I do.'

'Well, you'll have to fuckin' prove it then.'

'Oh, I will, one way or another, I will.'

'Not if I fucking kill you first.'

With that Bingham lunged at Kingsfield, but was held back by Brian.

'SIT! - DOWN!' The Sergeant commanded.

Kingsfield indicated for them to leave.

'Not going to get much more out of him. Are you sure he's not on something?' asked Kingsfield, as they walked down the corridor, back to the charge room.

'Got it in for you though, hasn't he?' Brian said.

'Seems that way, but I just can't understand why.'

Jim thanked Brian before leaving the custody suite, heading back to his office.

Chapter 7

Making his way quickly back to his incident response vehicle with his hot char grilled burger and highly salted chips, PC Chris Prentice got into his Ford Focus patrol car. The burger and chips sat enticingly on the passenger seat as he drove back to the police station for a late refreshment break. The smell of the food filled the car, overwhelming his senses and thankfully masking the smell of his last prisoner, a regular town centre drunk, who always smelt of fish and known locally as 'Grimsby.' Prentice resisted the temptation to eat some of the chips as he drove, which were sticking out of the top of the packet. He knew that it would not display the right image if members of the public saw him stuffing his face with chips as he was driving. In this day and age somebody was bound to lodge a complaint, take a photo, or upload it to some social-media site –as if they didn't have anything better to do, he thought to himself.

Arriving at the police station, he drove into the yard. Prentice parked up and went inside to the police canteen in the basement towards the back of the station. The canteen relied on artificial, bright and over-illuminated lighting. There were only a few basement windows, which, as far as he could make out, had never been cleaned, and were almost black from years of neglect.

'Ten four refreshments, Echo 44,' he called into his airwave radio. Normally he would just send his status in text form to the control room, but for some reason today it was not working. The system was 'down' he was told at the start of his shift, so they had to resort to old-fashioned radio procedures, which he had learned from his dad, retired Inspector Andy Prentice.

'Roger 44,' came the reply, then, 'nip in and see me before you go out again, couple of little jobs for you,' the radio controller added. The police station was one of the few stations left that had its own control room. Lucky, Prentice thought, as most of the others in the County had been centralised in a move that was seen to save money. Inwardly he smirked at that notion. Actually, it made operations worse, for the unseen controllers had no local knowledge when it came to directing units to incidents –something he had suffered from only recently, when he went to help out on another Division. Still, at least his central station's control room had a stay of execution for the time being. And this, he thought, could only be a good thing for the town.

Prentice walked into the canteen and plonked himself down in an overstuffed, dark brown and heavily stained easy chair –a chair that had seen more than its fair share of life. Some of the stuffing was slowly making its way out of the back and the left armrest, but by all accounts it was considered to be the most comfortable, particularly if you had just spent four hours patrolling on foot around the town centre. Prentice was glad he didn't have to do that any more. He flicked the television on using the remote and settled back to eat his 'snap,' as he called it. The TV was on the news channel. He left it on that, but didn't really take much notice of it. As he began to eat his burger, he casually browsed through an ancient copy of 'Police Review.'

There were no other officers in the room. It seemed that it wasn't all that long ago when the whole shift had refreshments together. He missed that, he realised –and he also realised that actually he had been lucky to get this far into his break without being called for a job.

As incident response vehicle driver, he was first shout for all the emergency calls that came in – something he relished. But he wasn't the only IRV driver of course. Still, it did seem that he spent his time doing most of the work. Mind you, he was only twenty-three and young in service. He needed all the experience he could get, so his dad always told him.

Of course, the peace of his refreshment break was soon interrupted. He'd just taken another bite out of his burger and was savouring that char grilled taste when the telephone on the wall in the corner of the canteen invaded his senses with its shrill, 'answer me now' tone. He tried to ignore it, taking another quick bite from his burger. He was determined to get most of it down his neck before being forced to answer the phone. He stuck a couple of chips in his mouth, as well, for good measure. He knew what was about to happen next. Just once, just once, he thought, it would be nice to actually finish his snap and not run the risk of getting a stomach ulcer, like most of his older colleagues!

The phone stopped ringing, only to be followed by a private call on his airwave radio. Although the new national airwave radio system for the police was really good, he thought, the problem was that an officer could speak privately to another officer without going through the main control room and therefore could never be left alone. He already knew who was calling.

'Yes, Gerry. What is it?'

Gerry was the regular controller on the shift, a retired copper with thirty plus year's service, so he knew what he was talking about.

'You can't fool me into thinking that you're not in the canteen!'

'I could've been on the bog or something.'

'But I know where you are, all the time. Isn't this new radio system great? Of course, in my day we only had unreliable VHF radios.'

'Alright, alright! Can't a man have some peace? What've you got for me?'

'Sorry mate, but a Grade One has come in.'

Prentice knew that it was his responsibility to attend all 999 emergency calls, but he just wished for once he could be left in peace to eat!

'OK, I'll come and see you for details.'

'Roger, see you in a minute, then.'

The tone on the radio indicated that the call had been terminated.

Stuffing the rest of his burger in his mouth, Prentice left the canteen, belching loudly, taking the stairs two-at-a-time, heading for the station's control room.

Chapter 8

Janet ran as fast as she could out of Fulborough Wood. She was out of breath and Tigger, her golden retriever, was panting, his big pink tongue hanging out the side of his mouth as he looked up at her as if asking what the hell that was all about? She stood on the path opposite the wood waiting for the arrival of the police. She'd made a frantic 999 call on her mobile, after the grizzly discovery she had made. It had upset her more than she expected.

Fulborough Wood was more a copse than a wood, in the traditional sense. It was probably less than an acre in size and was the remains of what used to be part of the Fulborough House estate. The edge of the wood closest to the road was enclosed by a six-foot high sandstone wall, some of which had fallen down over the years. It was dense with tall Ash, Birch and Elm trees, some of which were over twenty feet high. Clearly, the estate did not maintain the area and it was well overgrown, but many people used the area to walk their dogs.

Janet didn't walk her dog in the wood that often. She looked down at Tigger and rubbed his head and ears as she waited for the police. Tigger moved closer to her and sat down, waiting for his next instructions. Janet was a lover of TV crime dramas, but she never thought she would end up in a real one herself. The light was fading and there was a distinct chill in the air, she realised. She hoped that the police would arrive soon.

'Perhaps they will need me to give them a statement?' she thought. 'Let's see. How do these things work? They'll get the pathologist out to see if the body was dead and how it died. Some grumpy old detective will arrive and shout instructions at everyone, while trampling all over the crime scene without any of those white or blue suits on,' she continued. 'Then they'll cart the body away in a nondescript black van and the pathologist will do a post-mortem - or autopsy as the Yanks call it. Exciting. Perhaps they'd let me help them, like Miss Marple?' she wondered.

The sound of the police siren wailing in the background bought Janet back to reality, making Tigger bark. This, she then realised, was a real dead person, not some TV show –somebody had taken their life and that was sad. Janet pushed her collar length black hair out of her face and then pulled her jacket tightly around her. She stuffed her hands in her pockets as her initial excitement faded. Tigger sat patiently at heel.

The police car came to a stop in the lay-by opposite the entrance to the wood. Janet peered into the car looking at the driver. He's a bit young. I'd have thought they might have sent someone a bit older. They say that if policemen start looking young then you must be getting old, she thought, as she watched the young PC get out of his car.

Prentice, got out of his patrol car and walked towards Janet and Tigger. 'Wonder what he thinks of me standing here?' she thought. She acknowledged him with a tiny wave of her hand, which was still stuffed in her pocket. 'Mid-thirties, spinster, probably,' answering her own question.

'Hello,' Prentice said to Janet. 'I'm PC Prentice. I understand you have found something suspicious in the woods?'

'Er… yes, I think it's a body in a shallow grave.'

'Oh, and how did you come by that, then?' Prentice enquired, with a bit of suspicion in his voice.

'It was Tigger here,' she pointed to her dog, 'who found it really. Wouldn't come away from it, just kept barking. I went over to see what the fuss was about. He does it sometimes. Barking down rabbit-holes, if he sees some movement, being a retriever and all that.'

'Do you walk in the wood regularly?' asked Prentice. Janet noticed that he made an adjustment to his utility belt, while searching for his torch.

'No, we don't walk here that often –it's been ages actually,' replied Janet, nervously.

'I see. Would you like to show me where it is then?' he said, addressing the dog and rubbing his head. Tigger vigorously wagged his tail at the attention from this new human.

Janet stifled a giggle at the policeman talking to her dog. She tried to remain composed, although now that the policeman was here, she felt even more upset about it all. Prentice looked at Janet.

'Let's go and have a look then shall we. How far in would you say?' he asked Janet.

'About 70 yards.'

'Can you put Tigger on a lead, please?'

'Oh yes, sorry.'

Janet produced a small lead and choke chain from her pocket and attached it to Tigger. She watched the policeman retrieve his torch from his belt and they all entered the wood. By now, the light was almost gone, so Janet was shown the way by his torch light in front, like a cinema usher used to lead the way.

It's like being led into my worst nightmare, Janet thought, as they made their way up the footpath. After walking for about fifty yards on the well-used path into the woods, Janet indicated that they needed to leave the path and head towards a clump of trees with some bushes underneath them. Tigger was straining on his lead.

'Let him show me,' said Prentice quietly to Janet, who by now, really didn't want to go any further.

'Do I have to go in further?' she enquired.

Prentice turned to her. He could see that she was upset.

'No, it's OK, you can wait here. Just point out to me the area where you saw the body.'

She indicated the clump of bushes under a circle of small trees.

'Give me the lead and –what's his name again?'

'Tigger.'

'OK, me and Tigger will go and have a look.'

Chapter 9

Prentice took the lead from Janet. They walked on a few feet. Tigger got agitated and started barking at the clump of bushes. Prentice knelt down on the floor and indicated to Janet to take her dog, which she did quickly, then retreated to a safe distance.

Prentice shone his torch under the bushes. He saw that there was an obvious disturbance in the ground that the bushes had concealed. Leaves were covering what was essentially a hollow. The dryness of the ground had compressed the soil to reveal a definite elongated ellipse under the trees. Prentice wondered why it hadn't been discovered before now.

He realised that this would be his first discovery of a murder victim and he tried to think about everything he was taught at the training school about murder scenes. 'Don't disturb anything. Identify a route in and out to the scene. Remember what you touched. Gloves – shit no gloves on,' he thought. Prentice quickly extracted a pair of latex gloves from the personal protective kit on his belt. 'What risk is there to me doing this. Contamination. Don't contaminate the scene!' His mind was racing. Part of him wanted to retreat and comfort the witness –what was her name? God, he hadn't asked her. Never mind. Later. Stay focused, Prentice. Focus!

The light had totally gone now. The twittering of the birds in the wood had fallen silent and so had Tigger. He was sure that the witness could hear his heavy breathing and probably see the sweat in the small of his back. He could certainly feel it. 'Come on. Get a grip man. Focus!'

Prentice slowly crawled his way under the bushes and carefully moved some of the leaves and earth aside. As he did so, he revealed the skeletal upper part of a right arm. 'OK, that's enough for me, better get the big boys in,' he said to himself.

He retreated from the bushes, stood up and retraced his steps back to the witness and saw that Janet was crying.

'I'm sorry,' he said, 'but yes, you have found something we need to take a closer look at. Let's go back to my car where I need to call the detectives. Are you OK?'

'No, not really,' said Janet sobbing, but relived to be leaving the wood. 'I don't think I'll be coming back here soon.'

Prentice took Janet by the arm and took the dog lead from her. They walked slowly back to the road.

'Do you have a vehicle here?'

'No, I live in the houses just down the lane about half a mile.'

She waved her arm in the general direction of her home.

'Do you have anyone to come and collect you?' enquired Prentice.

'No, I live on my own.'

'What about any other family close by, to come and sit with you?'

'No, they all live away.'

'OK, come and sit in the car for a minute. I need to take some details from you. Sorry, what's your name?'

'Janet.'

'OK, Janet, let's sit in my car then and I'll call this in. I'll just get your basic details from you for now, but the detectives will want a full statement at some time.'

'What about Tigger?' she said. 'I can't put him in your car –he's all dirty.'

Prentice almost replied it didn't matter, thinking of everything that had been in the back.

'Well, perhaps if we leave the car door open, he can sit with you?'

'I could send him home?'

'Does he know the way then?' Prentice said, smiling at her

'Oh, yes,' and with that she instructed Tigger with a sharp 'home, boy.' Tigger began to trot off home, watched by Prentice and Janet.

'Amazing animals, dogs,' he said in passing.

'Yes, they are and he is a treasure and my guardian.'

Prentice noticed that Janet was still a bit tearful.

'Are you OK?' he asked again.

'Yes, I'll be OK, thanks.'

She sniffed. Prentice produced a packet of travel tissues from the glove compartment of the car and gave them to Janet.

'Thank you,' she said, trying a smile.

Prentice called in the details and waited for the detectives to arrive. He could not leave the scene, of course, but he told Janet that he would drive her home when he was released from the scene. She didn't mind waiting.

'No good stewing about it at home, alone.' she thought to herself.

Kingsfield was the first to arrive on scene. He occasionally crewed up with younger officers working in the town for two reasons, one to keep his hand in and know what was going on in the town and two to see how the younger officers were working. He was already mobile, when the call came in. 'Two bodies in three days –this isn't going to do the figures any good,' he thought as he arrived at the scene.

'Stay in the car, please,' Prentice asked Janet, as he got out to greet Kingsfield.

Unlike some other DI's, who tended to treat uniforms as just plods, Kingsfield knew that some of them would make good detectives one day or provide the information needed to do a good job. His brief meetings with Chris Prentice hadn't given him a chance to make his own assessment of him, but by all accounts he was a good copper in the making. Meticulous in his work, so Kingsfield was sure the scene was in good hands.

'Chris,' Jim said, 'what have we got?'

''Bout 70 yards in, body in the bushes, shallow grave, covered in leaves. Not moved much, other than to confirm the presence. Noted my way in and out. The rest is up to you, Sir. Entry is marked with a traffic cone.'

'Good job. Better than shoplifters from Sainsbury's, eh, Chris?' he smiled.

'Yes, but I've still got to deal with him when I get back to the nick –as soon as you release me, obviously, Sir.'

'Yeah, job's not finished till the paperwork's done, part of the bureaucracy of police work, you know. Anyway, any witnesses?'

'In my car. She's a bit shaken up, only lives up the road in the houses just around the corner up there.'

Chris pointed to a row of house in the distance.

'She was walking her dog, when it went bonkers at the trees –and the rest as they say. Said I'd take her home when you've finished with me. Lives on her own.'

'Do you think she'll be OK?'

'I think so, Sir, yes.'

'Well, I'll get an FLO to visit her when we get her statement. Make sure you tell her that later.'

'OK, Sir, I'll tell her.'

'Right, better go and have a look then.'

Chapter 10

The scene of crime circus, as Chris Prentice thought of it, had arrived at Fulborough Wood. Prentice observed that since his arrival Kingsfield had been busy organising his team of detectives and the Tactical Support Unit had also arrived. They were preparing for a methodical search of the wood and the Police Search Advisor Sergeant, known as POLSA, was animatedly talking to Kingsfield as he described the movements of his officers, during the search of the wood.

Kingsfield listened to the POLSA Sergeant who explained that the wood was bordered by a dry stone wall six feet high and only an acre or so in size. It had the obvious signs of once being well kept, but that it had been left to overgrow. Kingsfield recalled from somewhere that the Estate at Fulborough Manor sold off some of its land to pay death duties. The last Lord Fulborough, who had passed away some years ago, had had no interest in maintaining it and left it abandoned. The current Lord Fulborough was far more interested in his collection of fast cars than worrying about a small piece of woodland on the edge of his estate.

Consequently, Kingsfield saw some of the wall had either fallen or had been broken down. Now, the local kids came to play, lovers came to make love, owners used it to exercise their dogs –and murderers came to bury their dead, it would seem. Kingsfield raised an eyebrow at that thought, as the POLSA sergeant finished briefing him.

Now though, as the SOCO officers went about setting up crime scene tents and lighting, a large area of the wood had been designated a crime scene and cordoned off by Chris Prentice with a large roll of 'POLICE - DO NOT CROSS' tape.

As Kingsfield began briefing his own detectives, another unmarked police car turned up and parked behind Chris Prentice's patrol car. DS Heart and DC Stevens got out of the car and walked towards Kingsfield.

'Where have you two been, then?' enquired Kingsfield.

'Sorry, boss, got a bit delayed with some other stuff, got here as quick as we could,' replied Stevens.

'Yeah, a likely story. As you are late for my briefing, you can go with Prentice and take the witness back home - and while you're at it, you can start knocking on some doors when you get up there. Get a feel for what we might be dealing with.'

Stevens' shoulders visibly slumped –he hated door-to-door enquiries. 'Still, won't be late next time,' he thought.

Heart also looked a bit put out, but he acquiesced and politely agreed with his DI. They wandered over to Prentice's patrol car and as they got in, Stevens said, 'so Chris, where you taking us?'

'Less than a mile up the road, Clive,' Prentice replied.

Prentice pulled out of the lay-by he had been parked in, as Stevens stared out of the vehicle towards a group of SOCO officers. He tapped on Prentice's shoulder.

'Hey, Chris,' he said, 'what do you call a group of SOCO officers?'

''Scuse me?' replied Prentice.

Stevens repeated the question.

Heart, butting in, asked, 'this isn't one of your silly jokes, is it, Clive?'

Stevens looked at Heart and smiled. 'OK, OK, come on then, Clive, tell us all.' Addressing Janet in the front passenger seat, he said, 'You'll have to excuse my partner here, he thinks he's the force joker!'

'Oh, that's alright,' Janet replied. 'I suppose it lightens the mood,' she added.

Stevens was like a puppy wanting someone to play with him and desperate for an answer of some sort. They rode in silence, thinking. Finally Prentice piped up -

'Well, Clive, come on, you need to tell us. You can't call them a murder of SOCOs, can you? Because it's a murder of crows. So, what's it to be?'

'A DNA of SOCO's,' Stevens proudly announced.

'No, sorry, Clive, that doesn't work. A DNA of SOCOs? No, no definitely not. What do you two in the front think?' Heart asked.

Prentice thought for a moment, then 'what about a microscope of SOCOs?'

'Mm,' Clive said, 'it has possibilities.'

'Can I make a suggestion?' Janet asked.

Prentice looked over at her and smiled, 'if you want to,' he said, with a big grin on his face.

'OK, what about a fingerprint of SOCOs?'

'By jove,' Stevens said, in a mock upper-class, Pygmalion-type accent, 'I think she's got it. Yes! A fingerprint of SOCOs. Yeah, like it. Well done, well done!'

He clapped her lightly on the shoulder. Janet simply turned to Stevens and gave him a weak smile. They drove the rest of the way in silence, with Stevens mumbling to himself about his fingerprint of SOCOs.

When they arrived at Janet's house, Tigger was waiting patiently on the door step.

'There you are,' turning to Prentice, she said, 'home safe and sound.'

'Great, you have him trained well.' Prentice replied. 'Come on, then, you two in the back, start knocking some doors like the DI said. I've got a prisoner cooling off in the cells I need to get back to.'

'OK, OK,' Stevens said, 'don't remind me.'

They all got out of Prentice's patrol car. Stevens buttoned up his new tweed jacket, to protect him from the evening chill, as they both slumped off towards the first house in the row.

***

Kirsty Kingsfield had arrived at Fulborough Wood before the two detectives and was getting out of the SOCO incident van, in a fresh SOCO suit, as Heart and Stevens left the scene. She gave a little finger wave to her husband, who walked over to her. He gave her a peck on the cheek. She smiled in acknowledgement of such public intimacy. Jim returned the smile.

'Are you coming up to the scene with me?' she asked, as they both began walking towards a group of SOCOs preparing to move into the wood. They talked as they walked.

'No, I've been up there and I want to preserve as much of the scene as I can. God only knows who's been trampling through it.'

'OK,' Kirsty said. 'Have you looked at the remains?'

'Briefly – all skeletal, I think.'

'Well, in that case we'll need to take away the soil the remains are lying on, as well.' Kirsty stopped and adjusted the hood on her SOCO suit.

'Right. I'll tell the senior SOCO.'

'See you later then?'

Kirsty joined a group of SOCOs ready to move towards the scene and noticed Stevens staring out of the window of the patrol car that she saw was just leaving.

'What are they staring at?' she called to Kingsfield, as she walked towards the group.

'If Stevens is involved,' Kingsfield called, 'its bound to be something he thinks is funny.'

Kirsty acknowledged Kingsfield with a wave of her hand, as they entered the wood and disappeared into the darkness. Flashlights bouncing around all over the place, they moved towards the white lights ahead, which indicated the location of the victim. Their grim task had just begun. It was going to be a long night.

Chapter 11

The following morning in her pathology department, Kirsty sat behind her desk trying to concentrate on sorting through her emails. She had a large cup of black coffee in a 'keep calm and carry on' mug. With only a couple of hours sleep, the coffee went someway to keeping her partially awake. She sat back in her chair and rubbed her tired eyes. Looking around her office, she concluded that she really needed to make it her own. Her position as the senior forensic pathologist had been given to her after the retirement of her friend and mentor, Professor William Blake. She had inherited his over-spacious office and, up till now, she had not had the time or the inclination to transform it into something closer to her own style. There were still dark shadows on the wall, where Blake's many certificates and photos had sat for a good number of years, making the walls look grubby and dark.

She sighed heavily and returned to looking at her computer screen, when the mortuary assistant, Anton, tapped on the door and came in. Anton was a 5' 6' short-haired, Polish immigrant, who had come to the UK to study pathology on a cultural exchange programme and decided to stay. He was young, formal and respectful of his new boss, whom he admired greatly –not because she was his boss, or that she was a pathologist, but because he couldn't understand why such a job would want to be done by a woman.

'Morning, Anton,' Kirsty said, now tapping away at her computer.

'Morning, ma'am,' he replied. 'The remains brought in last night have been prepared for you and are in the old post-mortem room.'

'OK, thanks.'

Anton turned to go. 'Oh, and your husband is downstairs, as well,' he added, as he left the office.

Kirsty logged off her computer and collected her smart card from the keyboard, 'OK then, let's go do this.' She followed Anton out of the office and caught up with him in the corridor.

'Have the police shown any indication of being able to identify who the remains belong to, Anton? Or is it going to be down to us?'

'No, ma'am, not at the moment. The police are still working on that one.'

'OK, thanks.' She paused, 'Anton?'

'Yes, ma'am.'

'You don't have to call me ma'am all the time. I'm not the Queen.'

Anton made a slight adjustment to the bright yellow tie he was wearing, thinking.

'No, ma'am.'

They walked on and entered the lift, travelling down to the ground floor in silence, although Kirsty thought that Anton wanted to say something, but he simply adjusted his tie again. Eventually he spoke up.

'What would you like me to call you then, –ma'am?'

'Well, Dr. Kingsfield or just Kirsty is fine.'

Anton nodded his head.

When they walked into the PM room, Kingsfield and Heart were already gowned up. Kingsfield acknowledged his wife by bowing deeply. 'By your command, ma'am.'

Anton looked at Kirsty. 'Why does your husband call you ma'am then, –ma'am?'

Kirsty took Anton by the elbow to one side of the room and whispered, 'because he thinks he's being funny and he's been watching 'Battlestar Galactica' on the telly.'

Anton stifled a laugh. 'Ah,' he said, 'the eccentric British!'

Kingsfield cleared his throat. 'Er, I heard all that.'

'You were supposed to,' Kirsty said turning towards her husband.

'Yes, OK, OK. Shall we get on with it then?'

'Patience, sweetie, patience.'

Heart, who had been standing quietly next to Kingsfield, remarked, 'do you to ever stop taking the piss out of each other?'

'Nope –leads to an exciting relationship.'

'Mm, can't last forever.'

'Probably not, but I'll have a bloody good try,' Kingsfield smiled at Heart.

Kirsty looked at the remains on the post-mortem table in this, the hospital's oldest post-mortem room. She recalled that the traditional ceramic slab in front of her had been saved from destruction during building works in the 1970s. The infirmary had been built in the 1800s and the hospital decided to keep it for historical reference, under a project to retain the hospital's long history. She remembered looking at the historical archives in the hospital's boardroom that showed a hospital on the site since 1794, after moving from a house in George Row, opposite All Saints Church, in 1793. Now covering forty acres, it had maintained a steady throughput of the dead, dying and injured ever since. Although not generally used for day-to-day post-mortems, today on it lay the skeletal remains removed from the shallow grave in Fulborough Wood.

Kirsty moved to the side closest to her and Anton, digital camera in hand, moved to the opposite side of the table. The two detectives moved to the head of the table, where they stood, silent, watching Kirsty and Anton work.

She examined each piece of the skeleton with meticulous care, making sure that every scratch, bone striation, fracture and what little remained of tissue and clothing were all recorded.

The examination itself took a few hours and by the end of it, Kirsty had a fairly good idea of the cause of death. She had been able to identify that the victim was female. The murderer had somehow managed to break the pelvis and there was damage to the hyoid bone, indicated that the victim may have been strangled.

'I find this strange,' she said to her husband.

'What's strange?' Kingsfield queried.

'The way the pelvis has been broken. See, this break here is an anteroposterior compression fracture, commonly called an open book fracture.'

Kirsty demonstrated by opening the pelvis like a book, 'This indicates that pressure had been put on both sides of the pelvis at the same time, enough to break it, which accounts for the breaks at the sacroiliac joints, here.'

'What, a heavy weight like a person or something stronger?'

'Well, I suppose it could have been done by a person.'

She showed Kingsfield by pointing to the pelvis again, 'but the break is fairly clean, '

'It must have been extremely painful,' Heart said.

'Well, yes, it would have been. The pelvis is a cradle for a lot of important organs, flooded with nerves and blood vessels. She would have been in excruciating pain.'

'Could this have been done during a rape, for instance?' Kingsfield asked.

'Never seen such damage, but in the right circumstances it might be possible. But the body would need to be on something not very wide, like a...' she thought for a moment, 'gymnastic bar, or a bit bigger. It is very difficult to break a pelvis - a lot of determination needed.'

'And the strangulation?'

'Could be part of the sex, −autoerotic asphyxia, deprive the brain of enough oxygen and the feeling of pleasure caused by hypoxia can be enough to stimulate an orgasm. It's seen predominantly in males using a ligature to hang themselves to get a better hard-on. Some women are aroused by strangulation the same as men. On the other hand it could have been just a strangulation, probably with bare hands, −if ever strangulation is normal?'

'Yes, but what you are saying points to a violent struggle, nothing normal about it at all,' Heart said.

'You're right, Dave,' Kirsty replied. 'Whatever happened here was brutally violent and she would not have stood a chance. She would have died in extreme pain.'

'So, what type of person could we be looking for?' Kingsfield asked.

'Violent psychopath probably. Woman-hater, perhaps. And to do this sort of damage with no conscience about what he's done. We'll assume it's a he, unless the killer is a female Russian shot-putter from the 1970s,' she added trying to lighter the mood a little.

'Well,' said Kingsfield, 'this puts us in a different ball-park.'

Turning to Heart, he said 'we need to get an ident on this woman soon as we can.'

'I'll send some DNA off for testing and try and find some dental records. But in the meantime, we'll have to wait,' said Kirsty.

Kirsty turned to Anton. 'Can you box up the remains and put them away safely, Anton?'

'Yes ma'am, er –sorry –Dr.' Anton smiled, nervously.

All three of them left the post-mortem room, removing their gowns as they did so, leaving Anton alone. They walked down the long, dimly lit corridor, back up the stairs to Kirsty's office, where the conversation continued.

'OK,' said Kingsfield. 'What about our first victim, Eleanor Smyth? Have we confirmed it's her?'

'Yes, the lab re-constituted some finger prints from her decayed hands and have confirmed that it is her.'

'Anything more on the cause of death?'

'Broken neck, as we first thought. No other evidence of foul play, but she didn't do it when she fell down the stairs, that I can tell you.'

'Why?' Heart asked.

'Break's in the wrong place.'

Kirsty went over to the light-board and retrieved some x-rays from a cabinet. She stuck them on the board.

'See this break here?' She pointed to the screen that clearly showed the head detached from the body at the C7 vertebrae.

Heart and Kingsfield looked at the screen. They both nodded.

'Well, too low –would have expected it to be a bit higher.'

'So, we are saying that someone broke her neck, then placed her at the bottom of the stairs?' Kingsfield asked.

'That,' Kirsty said, removing the x-rays from the light-board and putting them back in the large envelope she took them from, 'is down to you, sweetie. You're the detective, not me.'

She gave him a quick peck on the cheek, as they left her office, leaving Kingsfield and Heart to ponder on what they had just heard.

But to who, they both wondered, belonged the skeletal remains of the young woman, who had died in such agony?

Chapter 12

Across town, DC Stevens had spent most of the night ploughing through DHSS files on their first murder victim, Eleanor Smyth. He'd been at it for many hours. He leaned back in his chair, stretched, removed his reading glasses and rubbed his eyes.

Getting up from his desk, he walked across the major incident room to the permanently on coffee machine. The lights in the room were off, but there was the anticipation of sunrise beginning to burst through the windows. The room was silent, all but for the quiet, almost imperceptible hum of computer hard drives, as they downloaded the morning network update.

He filled his Homer Simpson mug, that proudly stated 'the last perfect man,' with his usual thick black coffee, threw in four spoons of sugar, briefly stirred it with the nearest spoon he could find and, depositing the spoon back where he found it, turned to go back to his desk, –only to be startled by DS Heart standing behind him.

'You been here all night, then?'

'Shit, Sarg, don't do that. You could have had hot coffee down your nice clean, white shirt.'

'Well, you must be tired, if you didn't hear me come in.'

'Yeah, well, I have been here all night. I'm sure you can't even remember when you last pulled an all-nighter.'

Heart laughed. 'Not as long ago as you think. OK, then, find anything?'

'No, not found anything remotely connected to our murder enquiry.'

'What, nothing?'

'Nope, nada, zilch, nillsville.'

'OK, you better go home then and come back a bit later.'

Stevens started to walk back to his desk. 'Nah, nearly done now, want to get it out of the way so I can get back to some real detective work.' He was laughing as he walked back to his desk.

'Alright then,' Heart said, 'You go when you're done and I'll keep it sweet with the boss.'

'Thanks, Sarg. Oh, did you hear that the DI went to the cells and saw Tyler, who Win arrested the other day?'

'Yeah, I heard. He'll get himself into trouble again, if he does that too often.' Heart replied.

'No, I'm sure the boss knows what he's doing,' Stevens said, as he poured himself back into his chair. Putting his glasses back on, he resumed reviewing the files, as Heart left the room for his own office.

***

When Bingham was finally charged and released from custody, he returned to his flat and made sure that 'they' had not trashed his place. Muttering to himself, he wandered in circles around his apartment, as the computers rebooted.

He was angry, –angry at getting arrested, angry that the tart had complained about him and even more angry that he had had to talk to Kingsfield in the cells.

Angry, angry, angry. Bingham punched at the wall, as his computer screens lit up.

He had placed his wireless surveillance camera high in the trees at Fulborough Wood. As the cameras came on-line, he opened the live feed. Bingham just stared at the screen. He could not believe what he was seeing. The picture he saw was a hive of activity. He screamed at the screen, 'how the fucking hell have you found her?'

'This is not good.'

'Don't you think I know that?' Bingham replied.

'It's only a matter of time before they come looking for you again.'

'Don't you think I know that, as well?'

'What are you going to do then?'

'How the hell should I know? If you'd fucking shut up for five minutes, I might be able to think straight, for once, without you banging on in my ear all day.'

No response.

'Sleep talking, again?'

'How can I do that, Bing?'

'Because you're a scheming bastard, that's why.'

'What have I done? How can you accuse me?'

Bingham was even more annoyed now. He picked up a drink tin, found it empty and threw it at the wall. He went over to his fridge and opened a new one.

'Did I leave anything to trace back to me?' he questioned himself.

'Time will only tell. Remember Locard's principle, 'every contact leaves a trace.'

'Yes, yes, I know. I'm not stupid! Psychotic probably, but not stupid. Just go away.'

'You know I can't. I need to show you what you don't want to see, who knows what you do is wrong and abhorrent.'

'You don't have to get involved. In fact, I would prefer it if you never speak to me again. Shit! Just piss off will you!'

'You just don't like the fact that the body you hid has been found.'

'Yeah, knowing the coppers and their forensic puppets, they are bound to find out who it is and sooner rather than later.'

Bingham looked at the screen again. He could see that there was a big police presence at the wood. What was he going to do now? His twisted mind turned over the options. Do nothing and wait? Try and find out how much they know already by hacking into their computers? Discover who found her and dispose of them just for sheer spite and his enjoyment? The easiest option would be to do nothing. Perhaps they wouldn't find any evidence that could be traced back to him - after all it was five, six or seven years ago. He couldn't remember now, but no, he took the easy option, which was unlike him and decided to wait and see.

'Just wait and see I think,' he repeated to himself.

***

Stevens sat for a further hour at his desk, as more of his colleagues appeared for work. Most of them were taking the Mickey out of him for staying overnight. He was just about to give up as he threw another file back into the box. It caught the pile that was left for him to read. Most of them fell to the floor, spreading papers and other documents all over the place.

Swearing profusely at his clumsiness, he began to pick up the files, knowing that tiredness was getting the better of him. As he continued to gather up the files off the floor, he saw a photograph sticking out of one of the folders. None of the other folders he had looked through had any photos in them, so this one drew particular attention.

Picking up the photograph, he saw that it featured the murder victim and three children, ages ranging from five to fifteen, he estimated. They were clearly photographed in front of Stonehenge. He turned the picture over to see if there was any notation - and was stunned into silence. He checked the front of the folder, as with all the others it only had a reference number. He read the reference number in big bold numbers at the top right of the folder: 1515-498.

'Bloody hell!' he exclaimed.

Getting up quickly from his chair and pushing it back into the desk behind him with a loud crash, drawing the attention of others in the room, Stevens strode over to Kingsfield's office. Kingsfield was sitting at his desk reviewing action messages.

'Boss, you gotta see this,' he said, handing Kingsfield the photograph. 'Look at the back.'

Kingsfield turned the picture over and read the back.

'Stonehenge, 1994, Me, AG, CG, BT.' Then in small writing at the bottom right of the picture, the numbers '1515-498'.

'Well, I'll be—' started Kingsfield. 'What's in the rest of the file?'

'Don't know. Not looked at it yet.'

'Right, you go back and go through the file with a fine toothcomb. I think we can call this a breakthrough. Well done, Stevens.'

Stevens turned to leave Kingsfield's office, to be met by Heart coming in after hearing the commotion. Stevens walked back to his desk, bowing as he did so to his colleagues, who either ignored him or threw empty plastic cups and some sarcastic comments at him.

'He is a dork, sometimes,' Heart said, smiling as Kingsfield handed over the picture.

'Yeah, I know, but the boy's done good this time. Look.'

Kingsfield showed him the reference on the back.

'Yes, he has. Do we know who the kids are?'

'No, but I want Stevens to go and find out. Somebody must have a further record or know something about this.'

'OK. He was complaining about not doing real detective work, so we'll see how he gets on with this, eh, boss?'

'Exactly,' Kingsfield replied. But he was looking deeply at the photograph. Something in him didn't like what he was seeing: there was a certain familiarity, he thought, about the kids in the picture.

Chapter 13

Later the same day, Jordan was waiting for the arrival of Mr and Mrs Porter at the hospital mortuary. He sat in his patrol car in the reserved space, writing up his pocket-book, when there was a tap on the passenger side window.

As he had been there for a few minutes without the engine running, the persistent drizzle had caused the car to steam up. He could not quite make out who was knocking on the window. He opened it slightly to see Dr Kirsty Kingsfield looking into the car and holding a large pink golfing umbrella.

'You waiting for me?' she asked.

'No, Doc. Come to do a road death identification.'

'Oh, the Porter boy?'

'Yeah.'

'Who's coming?'

'I think just the Dad, but I'm not sure.'

'OK, you coming in?'

'Yes, thanks. I'll be just a minute or so.'

'Right, I'll put the kettle on then. I know how you traffic boys like a cuppa,' she said, smiling.

'That'd be great. Not had one all day, thanks,' Jordan said, returning the smile.

A few minutes later, Jordan left his car and went into the mortuary. The main entrance had a set of blue double doors that opened out onto a wide corridor towards the cold room, situated on the left of the corridor. It was about the size of two cricket pitches laid side by side and hadn't seen a lick of paint in at least a decade. Ahead of him was a large set of lift doors, big enough for a hospital trolley to transport the body to the PM room on the first floor. The strong smell of hospital disinfectant hit him as he walked in. 'I couldn't work in a place like this', he thought, shuddering, more from the chill of the mortuary than anything more esoteric. Most of the technicians look as pale as the corpses they work on. Still, if you work with the dead without any natural light – and there wasn't any here, –you're bound to take on that jaundiced look he had seen on so many technicians in the past.

He joined Kirsty in the general office situated to the side of the main mortuary entrance. The office was impersonal and utilitarian. Grey drab walls, poor lighting and only functional, uncomfortable furniture to sit on.

As Jordan walked into the general office, Kirsty handed him a coffee. He knew Kirsty vaguely – he'd met her a couple of times before, when dealing with road deaths of a particularly suspicious nature. Generally post-mortems for road deaths were done by a pathologist and not one who specialised in forensics. He also knew that she was Jim Kingsfield's other half and only recently married. He could tell –she still had that 'new love' spring in her step.

'So, anything special about this fatal?' Kirsty asked Jordan taking the offered cup from her. As he did so, Anton walked in and Kirsty told him that his drink was on the table. Jordan knew Anton and acknowledged him as he entered. Turning back to Kirsty he replied to her question.

'No, not really, no. The only thing is that this lad is the son of an Ex-Detective Chief Superintendent, who left the force a few years ago. No, we think at the moment it was a case of too much alcohol, but we'll wait for your team to answer that one.'

'I'm sure we'll get some answers for you once we have done our thing,' she replied. 'Anyway,' she smiled, 'I must get back upstairs and carry on. Nice to see you again, Jake.' She turned and left the room. 'How good is that?' Jordan thought, that the Senior Forensic

Pathologist would take time out to make coffee for her staff and stay and chat, unlike the other guy who wouldn't give you the time of day. And far more attractive as well, he thought, as he watched her disappear out of the office.

A few moments after Kirsty had left, the buzzer for the relatives' entry at the side of the building went off.

The relatives' room, to the left of the entrance with the office on the right, was a little more inviting than the main mortuary. It had its own private entrance and up-lighters around the wall provided brighter lighting. Soft comfortable chairs were provided for the family and vases of plastic flowers adorned shelves around the room, in the hope of making the room less impersonal.

Anton who had been sitting reading the paper, got up and answered the buzzer. Mr Porter had arrived. Anton opened the lock and, turning to Jordan, indicated that he would fetch and prepare the body.

He left without a further word or an acknowledgement from Jordan. Jordan went into the visitor's room where he met Mr Porter, who he saw was on his own. They shook hands and Jordan indicated for the bereaved father to sit down.

'Mrs Porter decide not to come?' Jordan asked.

'No, she said that she wanted to remember him as he was, not lying on a cold slab.'

'Yes, I understand.'

They sat in silence for a few minutes, as Jordan completed the paperwork. Breaking the silence, he said, 'I don't think that anything has changed much since you were in the job, as regards to the procedure here.'

'No, there's not much of a procedure to change, really, is there?' he said quietly and clearly subdued about the task that he had been asked to perform here.

'Quite,' Jordan replied.

'When did you last see your son?' he enquired.

'Well, it has been a little while. As I said when we first met, he was due home the day of the accident. He works abroad a lot –in Europe mostly. Got himself attached to the European Commission Joint Research Centre.'

'Oh, what research was he involved with?'

'Last we spoke he said he was researching China's CO_2 levels, been to Beijing, Hong Kong and all over China with a team of researchers.' His voice petered away. 'Doing really well for himself,' Porter's head dropped forward in an effort to remain composed. Removing a handkerchief from his pocket he wiped his eyes. Jordan felt that father and son had been very close.

'Do you know how this happened yet?' Porter asked.

Jake looked at him, thinking that he needed to answer the question carefully. 'At the moment we believe that he may have fallen asleep at the wheel.'

'I see,' Porter replied.

'What about toxicology?'

'We're still working on that,' Jordan replied cautiously. 'Why? Do you think he may have been drinking?'

'Well, I know you'll test for it –and anything else. It's just the detective still in me I suppose. I know I would if I were in your place. You will let me know if you find anything amiss?'

'Of course, yes we will.'

'I don't want to find out at the inquest, you understand.'

'I understand. Did he have a girlfriend?' Jordan asked, changing the subject.

'No, he had a partner who he lived with in Brussels. He was Belgian. They broke up a few months ago,' Porter was about to continue telling Jordan about his son, but there was a quiet tap on the door and Anton entered. He looked at Jordan, simply nodded and left.

Page 103

'OK,' Jordan said to Porter, 'We're ready now.'

Porter got up from the chair he was sitting in, straightened his jacket and rubbed his hand through his thinning, grey hair. Jordan saw that Porter visibly exhaled and was mentally preparing himself, before he indicated his readiness to Jordan. Most who come to do identifications want to see their loved one in a respectable state. It's not as if the dead can see them looking at them, lying there, but Jordan wondered whether it was just a natural way of preparing oneself for the trauma that was about to be faced. He didn't know and probably would never find out.

Jordan guided Porter towards the viewing room, but he needed no guidance. He had made this journey many times as a career detective. Still, his gait this time was not that of a man investigating a suspicious death, but that of a man who was about to identify his dead son.

They entered the quiet area of the viewing room. It was partially sound proofed to give a calm and serene church-like ambience. As they entered Vincent was on a hospital trolley, covered in a white sheet, with the exception of the head and shoulders. On this occasion, however, a towel had covered the right-hand side of the face, away from the relative, to prevent the family from seeing any damage to the face. Vincent's right eye socket and temple area had been severely damaged in the collision. Porter stood quietly for a moment looking at his son. Jordan could see the gathering tears in Porter's eyes and then he asked the question.

'Mr Porter, can you confirm that this is your son?'

Porter nodded and said, 'yes, it is. May I have a few moments alone?'

'Certainly.'

Jordan and Anton left the viewing room, leaving Porter with his son.

Porter stood looking down at Vincent. The gathered tears began to stream down his face. His shoulders hunched forward and he openly cried for his son. After a few minutes he wiped away the tears with his handkerchief and tried to compose himself before he left. An impossible task. Whoever looked at his face would see the blotchy skin and bloodshot eyes as tell-tale signs that he had been crying –but he didn't care.

He bent over his son, stroked his hair and lightly kissed his forehead.

'Good-bye, Vince,' he said quietly, under his breath. Then he stood up straight, turned and left the room.

Chapter 14

The rain was pounding on the roof of Rosie Jordan's Mini Cooper as she drove into the car park of Gaffney International Haulage. Based on the Round Spinney Industrial Estate on the outskirts of Northampton, she had been working there as the human resources manager since her marriage to Jake. Jordan had wanted her to leave, but it was a family business and she told him that she felt that she owed her allegiance to it.

Rosie's sister, Elizabeth, and her husband, Adam Gaffney, had never turned up at Rosie and Jake's wedding. And that, quite plainly, was the elephant in the room as far a Jordan was concerned. He had never met his brother-in-law, who was a rotund, flushed faced man by all accounts, with thick black receding hair and signs of a once-large trucker's belly.

Gaffney was passionate about making his haulage company a success, saw himself as a decent businessman and was in good standing with the local branch of the Road Haulage Association, of which he was a past chairman. The company had a fairly good reputation and he managed to generally keep it under the radar of the Vehicle & Operator Services Agency (VOSA) and the Police. The company had had a couple of run-ins with the law, as most companies do from time to time, but only as a result of what Gaffney called some 'rogue drivers' he employed one year.

Lizzie, as she preferred to be called, couldn't give a stuff about the company and had no interest in it, so eventually Rosie took over her role as Human Resources manager. Rosie had no idea as to how her sister spent her days and had little communication with her, if any at all. She did know that she was very good at spending the company profits, something that both she and Adam had had words about in the past. Neither did Lizzie take much interest in her husband and hadn't done so for a good five to six years. Rosie frequently spoke of her disappointment to Jordan, about her sister's life and her husband, but she soldiered on working for him in the hope that things might get better.

Rosie parked her car in the space provided for her outside the main office building. She had been pre-occupied with the constant arguments she'd been having with her husband about his work, so she was not in a particularly good mood.

In the first floor office, Adam Gaffney was standing looking out of the window, holding a cup of strong coffee, the smell of which had permeated his medium-sized, plain, white walled office, which was dotted with the occasional pictures of his trucks. His eyes wandered around his rectangular shaped office, with the door in the centre of the room. A large landscape window covered the outer wall. Furniture in the office was sparse, with a large old and battered oak desk at one end and a small modern conference table at the other, surrounded by six green and silver conference chairs. A totally unco-ordinated office as Rosie remarked on more than one occasion, he thought. He turned his attention back to looking out of the window, over his haulage yard and watched Rosie drive into the car park. One of his smaller curtain-sided trucks was just leaving.

He watched Rosie get out of her car and run to the entrance, trying to cover her head with her coat, so as not to get her hair wet.

Gaffney smiled to himself, put his cup on his desk and went downstairs to meet her at the front door. There was nobody in the office other than him, now the truck had left his yard. The two arrived in the foyer together and he helped her off with her coat.

'You look even more gorgeous with wet hair,' he said jokingly, with a broad grin.

'Just behave, will you, Adam? Can I at least get into the office before you start with your innuendos.'

She returned his grin. 'Some of us come to work for, ah, what is it? Yes. Work!' she exclaimed. 'And a lot of it I have to do today, thank you!'

She smiled at him again, and sashayed off down the corridor. As she did so, she received a slap on her rump.

'Later then,' Gaffney said mockingly. Watching her walk away down the corridor, he recalled that he had always been particularly impressed by the way the clothes she wore highlighted her slender figure.

Rosie and Gaffney had been having an affair for about six months - an affair which came about purely by accident. Rosie was working late one evening when Jordan was at work. Adam had been 'stood up' by Lizzie after he'd arranged a meal at a local restaurant. Lizzie said he'd never told her about it, but he knew that he had done so days before.

So Adam invited Rosie to dinner instead. It started off innocently enough. There were no preconceived ideas, but over time the two grew closer and one thing led to another. They both needed someone to talk to about their domestic situations, they were available, they worked together and it was obvious that things would get intimate in time. They revealed to each other that they both had a passing attraction between them since their first meeting. Neither seemed to be worrying about the fall-out from their affair they knew would come some time –all they wanted was each other's company.

Gaffney went back upstairs to his office, finished his coffee and started reviewing his drivers' rotas. As a driver himself, he liked to keep up with the day-to-day goings on with his drivers. They understood him and he understood them, so he had a pretty good relationship with the majority of his regulars.

An email pinged into his account. He looked at the name that came with it. It was a name he had not seen or heard of for a very long time. The message simply read,

'We need to talk. Soon!'

It was signed simply, 'Cynthia.'

Before he replied, Gaffney knew he would need to give some thought to his response, but he would more than likely end up complying with the demand. The arrival of the email made him think of his early life in foster care and the death of his mother.

His life in care was lucky, he realised later, after finding out about the trouble his step-brother, Bingham, kept getting himself into.

Adam was put with foster parents, who later formally adopted him. He always knew that he had to make something of his life. He saw so many of his contemporaries end up either in prison, drug addicts or just in the rut of unemployment and social benefits. He was determined that that wasn't going to happen to him. He did well at school, found an interest in transport and started as a driver in a small local haulage company.

But the spectre of his mother's death in 1994 always followed him like a dark cloud. He never saw the person who did it and the police assumed it was her current boyfriend, but he knew better. He knew that it wasn't him, but he did know that the argument they were having sent him, his sister and Bingham upstairs to their safe place in the cupboard. It wasn't until they were found by the policeman and the police-woman that they realised that something had happened to her. They all went to her funeral, of course, and he understood what had occurred, but he was upset that the police never found her killer or brought anyone to justice. Nobody saw anything –or so they say. He was sceptical about that, but what else could he do at that age? 'Too late to do anything about that now,' he thought.

He got up from his desk and went over to a locked filing cabinet in the far corner of the office. Unlocking it, he opened the bottom drawer, which revealed a number of smaller boxes. He removed one of the boxes and searched through it, until he found what he was looking for.

The faded photograph of his sister and his step-brother, along with the social worker, brought back all those terrible memories. At least his adopted parents gave him the education and stability that he needed, he thought.

The photo showed the siblings standing in front of Stonehenge, the day before they were all sent off to their different foster parents. The social worker, Eleanor, had looked after them that day. He remembered that it was a good day. The sun shone and even Bingham was on his best behaviour. There were no arguments between him and his sister and they all played happily around Stonehenge, even Eleanor joined in. She was desperately sorry that they could not have found foster parents who could take all three of them. Consequently, the three children were scattered across London and the Midlands and told never to contact each other.

Soon after they were settled in their first foster homes, Gaffney was contacted by Eleanor who passed on details of where his sister, Cynthia, was living. Eleanor told him that if ever anyone found out she had passed the details, she would probably get the sack. But she felt that it was only right he and his sister should know. Gaffney asked Eleanor whether she had told Bingham where they were. She told him that he was having some difficulties settling in with one particular family, so there was no guarantee where he was going to end up. So, no she hadn't. Gaffney was happy with this. He didn't want to see him again –ever.

Unbeknown to Eleanor, Bingham had managed to somehow extract information about the whereabouts of both his step-brother and his step-sister. Over the years he had maintained a distant watch on the goings on of his so-called step-family, but never contacted them directly. Bingham knew that one day he would need both their services and had kept information about their lives on one of his many computers.

As Gaffney considered what to reply, in a different place Bingham read the email sent to his step-brother– and smiled.

Gaffney sat down and stared at the photograph.

'Why does she want to get in touch now?' he thought, 'after all these years?'

He'd not heard from Cynthia for years. Only when her marriage fell apart did she contact him. In the one meeting he had with her, she was in a pretty awful state and he wasn't very sympathetic towards her. He remembered telling her to pull herself together and sort herself out and by all accounts it appeared that she had. Bingham, his step-brother, on the other hand, he had not seen hide nor hair of since they split up. And a good job too, he thought.

He didn't have any feelings for either Bingham – no surprise there–or for his sister, but the mere fact that he was looking at the photograph was emotionally draining. He needed some fresh air to think, so he lit up a cigarette and headed outside.

Chapter 15

Gaffney sat in a quiet little tearoom just off Fish Street, in Northampton town centre. It was small, secluded and had all the hallmarks of a business in decline. Poor uneven melamine tables with blue-check plastic tablecloths populated the café, of which only three were occupied with single men drinking out of large white mugs. Plastic chairs, generally four around each table, of which there were no more than a dozen, just managed to fit into the public area. The café was decorated with magnolia and mottled, pale green walls and gingham drapes around the room at picture rail height. Gaffney thought that it would have been more fitting in the 1960's than the twenty-first century. Despite its ancient façade, the food and drink was generally passable and he'd chosen the place knowing that it would not be noisy or heaving with latte-drinking girls who do lunch. The front door stood open in an attempt to invite people in.

He'd arranged a face-to-face meeting with Cynthia. Not that he wanted to meet her at all, he thought, but she had sounded desperate when he'd eventually decided to call her.

He thought about the last time he had seen her, following the visit to Stonehenge, while stirring his large mug of coffee.

'Are you going to drink that or stir it to death?'

He looked up and saw Cynthia standing in front of him. He removed the spoon from his coffee and placed it on the table before looking at her directly. 'Why are we here, Cynthia?' he asked tersely.

She noisily pulled the chair out opposite him and sat down. Raising her hand and snapping her fingers, she tried to attract the attention of the young waiter. He ignored her.

'You have to go up and get it yourself here.'

'Perhaps you would oblige, then?'

'What do you want?'

'Fruit tea, please, any flavour will do.'

Adam went to the counter and ordered the drink from the waiter. 'We'll pay at the end,' he said, as he walked back to the table. A few moments later the waiter, who Cynthia had snapped her fingers at earlier, brought her tea over and almost threw it at her with a Neanderthal grunt.

'Nice place you've picked to meet me, after all these years.'

'It's out of the way and there's never much passing traffic.'

'Yeah, I can see why,' she replied, giving the waiter a stare.

'Come on then–what's the panic?' He tried not to sound irritated, but it didn't work.

'Have you seen the local press or TV over the last few days?'

'No, I tend not to keep up with the local news or nationals for that matter–don't have the luxury.'

'You've not heard about the murder in Willoughby, then?'

'I've heard about it, yes–just another murder as far as I can see.'

'God, you always were a bonehead! How you manage to run a business is beyond me.'

She leaned closer and lowered her voice. 'Who do you know who lives there?'

'I have no idea.'

'Come on, man, think.'

'No, nobody comes to mind.'

Page 113

'Willoughby–Eleanor?' She said irritatingly and waited for the penny to drop. 'Ah, recognition,' she thought.

'Eleanor, yes. What about her?'

'She was the one that got murdered, been there a few weeks before they found her apparently.'

'Really?' Adam sat quietly for a moment, taking in the news.

'It can't have anything to do with us. The last time I saw her was when she told me where you were being fostered.'

He posed the question, but immediately knew the answer. It had everything to do with them.

'We can't just let this go, Adam. We have to go to the police.'

'Why do we need to go to them? They won't have us on their radar. Besides, if anything, they'd have been on our tail by now.'

'How do you know they're not already?' She looked around the virtually empty cafe to see if she could pick out 'The Feds,' as she preferred to call them.

'They're not in here with us,' Gaffney exclaimed. 'Why are you so paranoid about them Cynthia?'

'I don't know. I just don't like authority. You of all people should understand that.'

Cynthia squashed the teabag against the side of the cup with a spoon, and then removed it, slapping it in the saucer.

'What about him?' she said scathingly, referring to their step-brother. 'Have you heard from him?'

'No, and I don't expect to.'

'Why not?'

'Because he's not been in touch since we were separated.'

'But he's our step-brother.'

'So?'

'So, he's bound to get in touch sooner or later.'

'Why? He probably did her anyway. You know what he was like as a kid–got his rocks off killing every living thing he could find and thought it was a joke.'

'You don't think..?'

'I wouldn't put it past him.'

'Do you think he'd come after us?'

'Nah, no reason to.'

They sat in silence for a few moments more, while they finished their drinks. Gaffney started fishing around in his inner jacket pocket. He produced the faded photograph of them at Stonehenge.

'Have you still got this?' he asked, as he showed her the photograph. She took it from him and stared at it hard, then threw it back at him.

'No,' she said. 'I destroyed it,–the way our lives were destroyed by the murder of our mother–and being split up didn't help either.'

'What do you remember about that night?'

'I remember being ushered out into a police car and never seeing our mother again, if that's what you mean.'

'I was thinking about it the other day that's all,–after you sent me that email.'

'Brought it all back, did it?' Cynthia said, irritated.

'Yeah, it did. What's the matter with you anyway? You wanted us to meet. There's no reason for you to get irritated with me.'

'Sorry, but I'm worried that this is all going to come flooding back. You know, 'the feds' will dig into everyone's lives.'

'But there's no reason for them to contact us, as I said before.'

'But it's bound to happen. It's bound to come back at us like a runaway train and hit us full pelt when it does.'

'Why should it?'

'Because…'

Page 115

'Because what?'

'Because all along I have known that the police suspected one of us for doing our mother.'

'God, Cynthia, don't be so melodramatic! Is that all you're worried about?'

Cynthia didn't reply, just turned away and looked around the cafe, not meeting Adam's eye.

'Are you trying to tell me something,–something that you know… or think you know?'

Still looking away, Cynthia took a big sigh and said, 'you know as much as I do if you think about it.'

'I'm sorry, Cynthia, I don't know.' Adam was becoming more and more exasperated by Cynthia's attitude. 'I don't know what you mean. Explain it to your thicko brother.'

He moved to try and catch Cynthia's eye, so that she would look at him. She turned back slowly and stared at him for a moment.

'Look,' she said, 'we both know that we saw Bingham with that carving knife in his hand. We both know that mum had argued with him all day about all the dead stuff he kept in that shoe box. So what else can you think? He did it, Adam. I'm certain of it.'

'You don't know that.'

'Yes, I do, because I know what he is capable of, remember?'

Cynthia rolled up her sleeve to reveal the scar across the top of her arm.

Adam glanced at it and remarked, 'that was an accident and you know it.'

'Mm, I'm not so sure it was. I'm sure he was a trainee psychopath back then–God only knows what he's like now.'

Cynthia sighed, sat forward, stretched her neck and rubbed the back with her hand. She wanted to move away from talking about Bingham and the past.

'You don't know how many times I've wanted to get in touch with you, Adam, but didn't want to be rejected by you not answering my calls. I've had enough rejection in my life.'

'Just because we were sent to different foster homes didn't mean to say that we had to stay out of touch or not contact each other.'

'But I wasn't allowed to, Adam. They said it wasn't good for my emotional stability.'

Cynthia made a speech symbol sign with both hands as she used the phrase, 'emotional stability'.

'I don't think that's what Eleanor would have wanted, for us to stay apart. She did give us our contact details. Even though she shouldn't have done.'

'But we are different people now, Adam.'

'Are we really? Just because we went to different foster parents and brought up in different ways, doesn't make us different here.' He indicated his chest. 'We are still the same people, as we were when we were kids. We are still brother and sister. What would our mother say if she saw us like this, on our first meeting in twenty years?'

'Why did they force us apart, then, Adam? Things could have been so much better for us had the two of us stayed together.'

'Look, Cynthia, they made the decision for whatever reason, when we were really too young to understand. It was all new to us. We didn't know which way to turn and they said we would be better on our own. Whether they were right or wrong is neither here nor there. There is nothing to stop us being brother and sister now.'

Cynthia looked down at her cup and, while still looking at her cup, she said,

'Adam, I realise I am not a nice person. I know that. I seem to have inherited our father's arrogance and flawed superiority.'

'Yes, I saw that when you sat down,' he smiled for the first time.

'We didn't do ourselves any favours when we were growing up, did we? Fighting each other all the time, while our parents, as we know now, were falling apart themselves.'

'Yes, we did fight a lot, didn't we?' he chuckled. 'But I'm all for an easy life now. Having to put up with you and the idiots I grew up with, I learned to let it wash over me.'

'You can't be that laid back, surely? You're a businessman.'

'Yeah, a little, but business is different and I have learned to be a bit more hard when I need to be. I do need to be a bit harder than I am sometimes, so Rosie tells me.'

'Sorry, who's Rosie?'

'Rosie is my, er, well - you know.'

Cynthia looked quizzically at him. 'Didn't I see in the papers some years ago that you married an Elizabeth somebody?'

'I did. Rosie is her sister and I've already said too much and dropped myself in it!'

'So, let me get this right,' said Cynthia. 'You married Elizabeth and her sister is your bit on the side?'

'That's about it–yes.'

'Mm, typically male.'

Adam shrugged his shoulders.

'Does she know?'

'Who?'

'Elizabeth.'

'I think she may have her suspicions.'

'Dangerous waters you are in brother. Have you prepared yourself for a fall?'

'Maybe, maybe not.'

'So naive.'

'Let's change the subject, shall we? What about you?'

'What about me? Look–' she said, indicating her portly form. 'I've turned into middle aged, over-weight, domineering old bag. Adam, I just want to know what we are going to do about him.' She indicated the third boy in the picture. 'What if he contacts us all of a sudden? I don't want him contacting me. He was a horrible boy.'

'Well, let's cross that bridge if and when we come to it, shall we?' replied Gaffney, 'We don't need to do anything at the moment.'

'So, what are you going to do then?'

'I'm not going to do anything other than go back to work. You are going to go back to whatever you do and we'll take it from there.'

Despite being brother and sister, Gaffney realised they had never really got on together. Their early years growing up on a run-down council estate did nothing to bring them closer. In fact the situation was only made worse when their father died a year after Adam was born and their step-father was eventually sent to prison for life.

Cynthia seemed to have taken on an arrogant air of superiority, whereas Gaffney was far more tolerant of his situation and resolved to work to get a better life. It was difficult and sometimes his state of mind was thought to be a bit suspect by his social workers. But when they saw that he had made something of himself and almost became a model child under the guidance of his foster parents, Social Services looked upon him as a success.

The crisis had brought them into contact with Eleanor Smyth, whose job it had been to help ensure orphaned children were found reasonable foster homes. The photograph of the day trip to Stonehenge had been a treat organised by Eleanor before they all got split up. She had told Cynthia that she thought they should have stayed together, but unfortunately it wasn't her decision. She had the photo taken of them all, so they would not forget each other. As for their step-brother both Cynthia and Adam felt that he could rot in hell. A despicable child, they all thought, even – secretly – Eleanor. He had no manners, no courtesy, was self-centred, shameless and tried to dominate. And with a mouth like a drain, even at nine years old, other kids in the neighbourhood tended to give him a wide berth.

Cynthia finished her tea, wiped her mouth with a paper napkin and got up from the table.

'Well,' she said, 'if the Feds come calling, I won't be saying anything about us.'

'If the police do come round,' Adam remarked, 'they probably already know. Anyway, I don't think they'll find us–they have no reason to.'

'Yeah, well. We'll see, shall we?'

She moved to leave and turned to the young waiter, who she saw was moving towards her. 'He's paying,' she said to him, indicating Adam, as he got closer. The waiter looked at her with contempt, grunted and walked back behind the serving counter, taking a couple of sideways glances at her as he did so.

Adam remained seated as Cynthia left the cafe. Finishing his coffee, he rang Rosie, paid for the drinks on the table and left just a few minutes after his sister.

As he walked back to his car, Adam thought about what Cynthia had said about their step-brother. 'He does have the bottle to kill someone, but would he really do that to Eleanor, after all she did for us?' he wondered. 'What advantage does it give him? Nobody worried about what happened to us, after all. He has no reason, unless there was some other motive?' Adam pondered, as he continued to walk back to his car. He looked up at the sky–dark clouds were gathering, ready for another downpour. 'Will it ever stop raining?' he thought.

Chapter 16

'Stevens!' Kingsfield shouted from his office.

'Boss?' came the response.

'Get your arse in here.'

Stevens quickly left his desk and scurried into Kingsfield's office.

'Made any progress on that photo yet?' he asked.

'Getting there, boss. Waiting for a call from one of the Department for Work and Pensions managers. Hopefully they will be able to give us a bit more info on the picture. Apparently, it was taken the day before the three got moved to separate foster homes.'

'Nice of her to take them out for the day, I suppose.'

'Yeah, indications are that she didn't want them split up. They guy on the phone said there was a comment in her report. They're sending that over with the info about the picture.'

'Why wasn't it already in the file then, all this extra info?'

'The guy didn't really explain that –they seem to have numerous files for her for some reason.'

'Is that good or bad, I wonder?'

Stevens made no comment, assuming that Kingsfield was thinking out loud. Kingfield sat back in his chair and took a slurp of coffee out of a now cold mug. Thinking. Stevens waited patiently for the next question.

'Mm. OK. How long have you been waiting for a response from this manager?'

'Couple of days.'

'No, far too long.'

'I'll ring them, again, then?'

'Better still, get yourself down to their offices and speak with him or her and do a bit more poking around while you're down there. I'm sure they must be able to come up with a bit more for us.'

'OK, you want me to go down to 'The Smoke' then?'

'Is that where you're getting your info from?'

'Yeah, the local office put me onto their archivist, who works down there.'

'OK, take Win with you.'

Kingsfield saw that Win Okenewu was approaching his office from the other side of the incident room. He tapped lightly on Kingsfield's office door before entering.

'Where we goin' then, Stevens?' he asked him.

'Road trip down to 'The Smoke.''

'Excuse me?'

'London,' Kingsfield said. 'My old man used to call it 'The Smoke.' Didn't think anyone used it anymore.'

'Why 'The Smoke'?' asked Win

'Something to do with coal fires and fog, I think,' said Stevens.

'You got something for me then, Win?' asked Kingsfield.

'Well, I took that photo you wanted enhanced, aged or whatever, told the techies what you wanted to do and they said they'll look into it.'

'By when?'

'Later today by all accounts. Not as long a process as it used to be. Anyway, they've got a new piece of software they're itching to try out.'

'They'll let you know when it's done, then?'

'Yes, guv.'

'Right, call me as soon as you get a response from them.'

Okenewu nodded and walked out of the office with Stevens.

Kingsfield got up from behind his desk and walked out of his office into the main incident room. He clapped his hands, bringing to attention everyone in the room.

'Right, everyone, listen in. We need to get some movement on the Smyth murder. A new line of enquiry has opened up, thanks to Stevens.'

Kingsfield smirked at the thought that Stevens wasn't there to take his normal bow.

'We need to see if we can ID the kids in this photo.'

He put a copy of the image on the big screen and turning to his Detective Support Officer sitting at a desk to his left, said,

'Jill, I need you to do some research for me–Internet, records office, other than what we've already got, that sort of thing.'

She nodded.

'Frank.'

He pointed to the Detective Constable at the rear of the room. 'Use some of your Social Work contacts to get some info about foster home protocols now and back then.'

'Sure, Boss,' Frank replied.

'Have we got any ID on the second victim yet?'

Dave Heart pitched in at this point, from his desk in the corner of the room.

'We're still waiting for a positive ID, through DNA and dental records. We only know from the PM that it was a woman in her 20s.'

Kingsfield's heart sank. 'Wasn't Stephanie Parker in her mid-twenties?' he tried to remember.

He acknowledged Heart's comments.

'OK, back to work, everyone.'

Turning, he walked back into his office. His thoughts had returned to Stephanie Parker's disappearance. It was beginning to bug him again, just like when it all kicked off at the start, he thought. His relationship with Parker was purely platonic, not that he didn't find her attractive or anything, but simply because having to mentor her when she was a cadet and he was only a young probationary officer, he didn't feel that it was right taking advantage of his friendship with her. And he thought that Parker herself was grateful for that. He knew that intimacy with her would change their relationship forever and what they had was far more productive on so many other levels other than a quick shag.

He knew, of course, that many had taken advantage of her naivety and he even noticed a change in her demeanour after the Hazelrig Close murder. But that never changed his attitude or friendship for her. He remembered that she told him that she confided in him far more than her other 'conquests', as she called them.

The discovery of the body in Fulborough Wood has to be Parker, he thought. The age fits, the timescale fits, so he really needed to open her enquiry again. Not that it was ever closed of course—these things never are—but if new information or evidence comes to light they are usually resurrected. From his point of view, it would never be closed until he had all the answers. Whether his boss would understand was a different matter however.

'Sod this,' he mumbled to himself and walked out of his office. 'I'm going upstairs to see the boss,' he said to Heart, as he walked past him towards Marland's office. Heart acknowledged him with a nod.

The floor above Kingsfield's office and the incident room held a suite of offices for the Senior Investigating and Deputy Senior Investigating officers, along with support staff and occasionally Silver Command. Detective Chief Superintendent Colin Marland's office was in the corner of large open-plan suite. Marland was a high flying detective who'd been imported from another force to take command of the Major Incident

Team. As the commander of this unit, he was the forces' Senior Investigating Officer for all major crimes within the county.

By police standards he was a short man, standing at only five feet, five inches tall. In his mid-forties, he had taken on the spare tyre that most men in their mid forties succumb to when they don't exercise.

However, his appearance was more Chief Executive than detective, with a clean cut, grey pin-stripe suit, perfectly fitting and a red silk handkerchief in the top of his jacket pocket.

The only thing that marred this ensemble was the brightly coloured Mickey Mouse tie that he was wearing. His collection of bright ties had become somewhat of a legend amongst his peers and other officers. A trademark he had no intention of doing away with just because he was the force SIO, he'd commented once.

As he entered the command floor, Kingsfield could see that Marland's office door was open. Normally a good sign, thought Kingsfield. If it were closed he wouldn't even have bothered. Kingsfield didn't see Marland as a career detective like him, so his priorities were a little different from everyone else's on the team. He could be brash, argumentative and suffered from 'little man' syndrome, being under the standard height for most coppers.

Marland waved him into his office, before he could knock.

'Just about to call you, Kingsfield,' Marland boomed as he sat signing off some papers on a desk that looked far too oversized for him.

'How are we doing with the Smyth murder?'

'If you came to the briefings every now and then, instead of sitting on your backside, you might find out,' thought Kingsfield, but instead, he said, 'We have a couple of new leads that Stevens is on at the moment.'

'Stevens. Ah, ee's the joker, supposedly?'

'Yes, supposedly,' Kingsfield responded, uninterested.

'But I have come to see you on another matter,' he continued.

'Oh and what might that be?'

'A cold case that I was working on, which I think may be linked to this murder and which I think we need to look at again–a re-investigation of the evidence.'

'Do we now? And 'ow do you come t'that conclusion?'

'Just a hunch.'

'Yeah, well, I've heard about your hunches, Kingsfield. They get you into trouble, don't they?'

'Not all the time, no!'

'Ah but they do. All the time apparently. Detective work is not about 'unches any more Kingsfield.'

'I would beg to differ, Sir,' he replied.

'Well, you would, wouldn't you? So tell me, what's this 'unch you 'ave?' Marland gave a brief, wan smile at Kingsfield.

Sitting on Marland's desk was a glass jar, full of bright yellow coloured sherbet lemons. Marland took the top off the jar and popped one in his mouth, not bothering to offer one to Kingsfield. He sat back to listen to Kingsfield, with his arms behind his head in a pose of superiority.

'Tosser!' thought Kingsfield. He cleared his throat before speaking.

'I think the body we found in Fulborough Wood is connected somehow - don't know how yet - but I think it may be the same killer.'

'Don't tell me you think we have a serial on our hands?' Marland smirked at Kingsfield.

'Yeah, definitely a tosser!' thought Kingsfield.

'No, I didn't say that. I just think that they may be linked.'

'What evidence 'ave you?'

'None, at the moment.'

Marland sat forward.

'So, you want me to re-open a case, just because you think there may be a connection with the Smyth murder? Do you take me for an idiot?'

'Well, yes!' thought Kingsfield.

'No, not at all, Sir. I thought that I would do the courteous thing and tell you of my suspicions. If you don't want to listen, so be it. But I will be investigating it further.'

Kingsfield could see the pink hue rising from Marland's thick neck up towards his cheeks.

'Will you now?' Marland growled. 'Unless you can bring me new evidence, I will not entertain you going off on one of your 'unches –we don't want another witness paralysed for life.'

'Ouch… that hurt,' thought Kingsfield

'I think that last comment is unfair, Sir. You have no knowledge of the incident so don't have any damn authority on the subject.'

Marland harumphed.

'Well, I want to hear no more about it. Just get on with the task of finding the real killer of Smyth, instead of dragging up old cases that we're not likely to solve any day soon.'

'That is what I plan to do, Sir. I also think the remains are that of a missing WPC.'

'Any DNA to prove that?'

'Still waiting.'

'There you are, see, jumping to conclusions, before any real evidence. Who is this missing pee-wee anyway?'

'Stephanie Parker.'

'Never heard of her.'

Kingsfield snapped at that remark.

'No, it was before your time here, happened while you were wending your way around other police forces on promotions.' Kingsfield was becoming even more irritated by Marland's apparent dismissal to everything he was saying.

'Careful, Kingsfield.'

'Well, with respect, Sir, we might get something done if you were to take an active part in our investigations and look at the unsolved ones we have on our books from time to time. That is your job after all, isn't it?'

'One more word and I'll stick you on for insubordination, Kingsfield. Just get back downstairs and do your job, before I lose my temper even more.'

'Detective work is about detecting,' Kingsfield resisted, 'and detecting is about working what I call hunches or gut feelings. Any 'D' worth his salt will tell you the same.'

Marland got up from behind his desk and walked around the front of it. He stood in front of Kingsfield, who towered over him. Kingsfield felt like patting him on the head like a pet. He smiled to himself, while Marland entered into a diatribe about modern detective work, which Kingsfield did not bother to pay attention to.

'… And I want some results on this case quickly – it's bad enough with one dead body on our hands let alone finding another one. Or do you want me to put someone else on the case? … Are you listening to what I am saying Kingsfield?'

Kingsfield turned on his heel to walk out of his office.

'Do not walk away from me,' growled Marland.

'I'm going to do my job – Sir!'

Just for one moment Kingsfield thought that Marland might come out of his office after him, but instead he stood there, steaming.

'I'll keep you apprised,' Kingsfield said, as he left the office.

'Don't test me, Kingsfield.'

Kingsfield kept walking.

'Kingsfield!' Marland called.

'That went well, then?' Heart said, having arrived upstairs on the command floor himself. He stepped in line with Kingsfield, as he walked out of the office.

'I thought so,' Kingsfield smiled. 'Synex hasn't got a fucking clue about detective work, really he hasn't.'

'Synex?' queried Heart.

'Yeah, gets up your nose and stays there for eight hours.'

***

Having returned to his haulage yard, Adam Gaffney was staring out of his office window. It wasn't a particularly picturesque view across his yard and other parts of the industrial estate, but at least he could see some green in the direction of Overstone, in the distance when the weather was clear. Today it was not clear and even for the last few days, the weather had been murky and not very inviting. Coupled with the fact that two of his thirty-eight tonners had managed to get tyre blow outs on the M1 and the M62 yesterday, both of which were on the drive axles, it had cost him a fortune in new tyres and one of the trucks lost the wheel fender as well. All expensive commodities to say the least.

He sat back in his tatty high back chair with his feet up on the radiator on the wall behind his desk. He was going over his conversation with Cynthia. 'Was I a bit harsh on her?' he wondered. She was, after all, his sister and although all three of them had been told not to communicate, he couldn't help feeling that, in hindsight, it was probably the wrong thing for the social services to tell them to do. He also thought that she didn't look well. She had put on a lot of weight, as she herself pointed out. No longer the slim sixteen-year-old that she was when they were kids. He had no regrets about being split up and he thought that she didn't either. It was only his step-brother that kicked up a fuss, vowing all sorts of revenge on everyone for dragging him from his real home. At only nine, nobody listened to him anyway. But he seemed to have far more intelligence than he should have for his age. Adam had no intention of getting into contact with him now that they were both adults–and he hoped that his step-brother felt the same way about him.

Adam started biting his nails, a habit he had managed to wean himself off when he got into a stable home environment–a habit that only manifested itself when he thought of the trauma that had occurred back in 1994.

***

By the end of the afternoon, Kingsfield was still sitting in his office. He'd been out on a couple of enquiries with Heart, none of which had come to anything. He was frustrated and angry that things were not going well. He'd had a stand-up row with the DCS, which didn't help matters. So he felt more than frustrated–he felt depressed and needed a drink.

He was moving to put his coat on, when Win came into the office with an envelope.

'You off home then, guv?' He asked.

'Yeah, had enough for today.'

'You'll want to see these first, I think?' Win said, opening the envelope he had brought with him. He took out three photographs and the original. The three photos were of the three children, all of which had been altered to make them look as they were aged into their twenties and thirties.

'These are the people with Eleanor at Stonehenge?'

'Yup.'

'Do we know who they are yet?'

'Two of them we don't yet, but–' Okenewu handed Kingsfield the third photograph and said, 'who does he remind you of?'

'Tyler!' Kingsfield exclaimed.

'My thoughts entirely.'

'Good job, Win,' Kingsfield said. 'Good job. You all sorted for London tomorrow with Stevens?'

'Yes, all arranged, but whether I can take a day of Stevens' piss-taking is another matter.'

They chuckled and agreed.

'You see me when you get back with any info you dig up. Great job with the photos.' Okenewu put them back in the envelope and left them with Kingsfield, leaving him alone in the office. Kingsfield looked at the picture of Tyler again.

'Bingham Tyler!' he said aloud. 'I've got you now, you little shit.' It was the perfect end to a shitty day, he thought.

Chapter 17

Jim and Kirsty Kingsfield both had days they would prefer to forget. And this was one of them. Although happy about the breakthrough, Kingsfield was still troubled by the photographs that Okenewu had brought him just before he left the office. They were spread out on the large occasional table in his apartment. Kirsty was troubled by the identification of the unknown remains she had in her mortuary. She never liked having the disinherited reclining in her morgue. Both had set about to try to put the recent events behind them for one evening, but it was difficult for them.

Kingsfield liked to cook. He didn't feel that he'd ever make Masterchef, but nevertheless he found that it took his mind of the day's work, to take time to prepare a good meal when he'd had a bad day. Kirsty on the other hand, preferred to spend time luxuriating in a hot bath, with aromatherapy scents. This evening was no exception.

Sitting at their kitchen table, Kingsfield served up a spaghetti bolognese, with garlic bread and a good Italian red–Montepulciano d'Abruzzo. Kirsty sat at the table with anticipation, smiling and watching her husband fighting with the spaghetti as he tried to get it on the plate for her.

'Oh, still too much starch on the pasta–sorry.'

'Hey, I'm not complaining. If I made it, it probably wouldn't look like spaghetti at all,' she giggled.

Once he'd finished serving, Kingsfield sat down opposite her. They clinked glasses and tucked in. Kirsty made appreciative comments about her husband's cooking but noticed that he seemed pre-occupied.

'Penny for them?' she asked.

'What? Oh no. It's nothing really–work stuff, you know,' Kingsfield replied, twirling spaghetti around his fork, thinking, 'I just wonder how you do it that's all.'

'Do what?'

'Post Mortems, Autopsies, whatever you prefer to call them. I know we've had this conversation before, but that body found in the woods is bugging me.'

'Well, PMing skeletal remains is easier for me than it is for you trying to find out who it is.'

Kirsty sat back in her chair and took a sip of wine, watching her husband. 'I think it's more than you're telling me though.'

Kingsfield sighed and leaned forward, putting both elbows on the table, leaning over his dinner, the fork dangling loosely from his left hand. He looked straight into his wife's eyes and held the look for a moment.

'God, you are gorgeous, did you know that?' He gave her a wide smile.

Leaning forward, she returned the smile and poured herself more wine, 'Don't try and change the subject. So, what's bugging you?'

'Don't really know whether I want to talk about it over the dinner table,' he said.

'It's OK. We're grown adults.'

'Right,' Kingsfield said, leaning back in his chair, 'tell me about decomposition?'

'You want to talk about decomposition at the dinner table?'

'You said we were grown adults–perhaps you can't stomach it, then?' he laughed.

'No, no, I can take it.'

'I bet you can,' he said with a wink.

'Don't be cheeky. OK, human decomposition–generally accepted to be five stages. When we die and the heart stops pumping the blood around the body, gravity takes over and it rests in its lowest point –

lividity. After several hours rigor-mortis sets in. The body temperature acclimatises to its surroundings, cells begin to break down and the digestive tract produces gasses–oh and it smells, too. How are you doing?'

'Yes, fine, I'm still listening,' Kingsfield said sucking a long piece of spaghetti into his mouth.

'Second state is where the body bloats up and releases its gasses, then it begins to decay, loss of fluids, maggots appear, the smell is even worse –still OK?'

Kingsfield nodded.

'The advanced decay process is the end and the ambient temperature will determine how quickly it gets to this stage. Body fluids may stain any soil and could actually kill vegetation in the area.'

'Ah, that's why there was little greenery around our victim in the wood, so the overgrown bushes would be further away from the body; otherwise we might have found her earlier.'

'Yes, that's a possibility, it certainly accounts for the tent-like overgrowth we found. Anyway, the last stage is where the body becomes skeletal and dries out. But there may be a problem. There is something called adipocere, commonly called grave wax, or mortuary wax. This is a waxy substance that forms on a decaying body in wet and cold conditions. It sometimes allows parts of the body to be preserved. There was research done some years ago on the skeleton of a child that had parts of its brain preserved for three hundred years. I am surprised that we didn't find any on your body in the wood, if she had been there from the start. It would certainly be the right conditions for it to form. And that, sweetie, is the potted history of decomposition. Now, I'll be asking questions later, so I hope you took notes.'

She beamed at her husband, who by this time had finished his dinner and was sitting back in the chair with his arms folded and listening intently to his wife.

'So, what do I deduce from all of this information– that she may have been moved there at a later stage or that she's been there all the time?'

'But you still look… perplexed… no sad, there is a sadness in your eyes.'

'Is there? Well, I just can't imagine Stephanie's body being there all that time and we didn't find her,' Kingsfield admitted.

'You know who she is then?'

'I have my suspicions, but that's all they are until you can get me the proof from DNA.'

'Who is she then?' Kirsty questioned.

Kingsfield explained to her that Stephanie Parker was a WPC who went missing five years ago, after failing to turn up to a Court case involving one Bingham Tyler – 'who just happens to be in one of the photos on the table over there.' He waved casually towards the table in the front room. 'Despite a national search for her and lots of media coverage, we never found her. I think he did her in because she was to give evidence against him after he raped her.'

'Yes, I seem to recall something about it now, but it's a bit drastic, killing off a witness, isn't it?'

'Probably, but he is erring on the side of psychopathic, so I wouldn't have put it past him.'

They both got up from the kitchen table and went to sit on the sofa, Kingsfield collecting a large cognac and a cigar on the way.

'Look, I'll try and get them to put a rush on the DNA, then, if you think it would help, but I can't guarantee anything,' Kirsty suggested. She wrapped her silk dressing gown around her and sat down on the sofa where her husband joined her. She snuggled up against him, tucking herself up under Kingsfield's right arm. He began nonchalantly to caress her.

'What's this WPC to you anyway–why so interested in her?'

'She was a police cadet when I was a probationer. We were both on the same shift, based at Mere Way, before they closed it as a police station. When she finished her initial training she came back on our shift, but I noticed that she had changed and I put that down to the first operational shift she did, with Robyn Miller, God rest her soul, and me. We went to a murder in Hazelrig Close. It was her first shift, her first body and her first murder. Surprised she stayed in the force really after that, but she did and I've got to admire her resilience for that, but she became, well, promiscuous would probably be the best way to describe it.'

'I would hardly believe that seeing a dead body would turn anyone promiscuous.'

'No, but I think it went someway to changing her outlook on life in general. She was only seventeen, after all.'

'Mm, I suppose the mind works in strange ways.' Kirsty said sleepily.

Kingsfield pulled heavily on his cigar, while warming the cognac in his hand. He suddenly sat forward, jerking Kirsty awake.

'Well, I'll be…'

'What?'

'A light-bulb moment, sorry love, but I think I know who the other two in the photograph are. I've been such an idiot. Too concerned thinking that the remains in your morgue was Parker, to see what's been in front of my face ever since Stevens found the photo.'

'So, who are they then?' asked Kirsty.

He stared at the photograph of Tyler, trying to put his thoughts in order. 'Right, these two here,' he said tapping the original photo, 'are the children that we recovered from the Hazelrig Close murder back in 1994.

Why the hell didn't I realise this earlier? I've been racking my brains thinking about where I had seen these kids before. It wasn't until just now that it's all come together, but what does it all mean?'

'What do you mean?' she replied, sleepily.

'What relevance do these pictures have to the Smyth murder?'

'Perhaps they don't have any relevance.'

'My hunch is that they do, but I have so many questions and not enough answers.'

Kirsty was a little more awake now.

'So, what other questions do you have then?' she asked.

'OK, we know that the reference number on the back of this photograph, here.' Kingsfield showed her the rear of the photograph, as Kirsty sat up and he continued, 'was identical to the reference number found at her murder scene. You were there when we found it.'

'Yes, I remember.'

'Well, we also know that these three children were sent to foster parents after the murder of their mother. Their mother was the only family member. Nobody else came forward anyway to help with that enquiry back in '94. We also know that the murder of the mother is also an open cold case.'

'What—nobody was convicted?'

'Nope, we assumed back then that it was done by her current boyfriend, who we never found.'

'Not her husband or partner, then?'

'No, he was already inside serving life for killing two ambulance men, when they came to his aid in a street brawl.'

'Nice man, then.'

'Yeah, right. But we digress. If this photo identifies the killer, which one is it? Bingham Tyler is somehow related to these two. And having talked about Parker, it has become even more apparent now, that they are all connected. I think I need to talk to these other two, the brother and sister. I've sent DC Stevens down to the DHSS archive to try and find out more about them. Social Services are a bit reluctant to divulge their names and I can't remember them – unless – unless I put them in my first pocket book. Social won't divulge addresses, as they were fostered or adopted and the records are closed, but I'll put even money on Tyler for the Smyth murder.'

'What, you mean 'like father like son?''

'Precisely.'

'But what if it's one of the other two who did it and the question is obviously why they did it? Will you get the details from DHSS records eventually?'

'Oh, yes we shouldn't have much difficulty. I think they were reluctant to email stuff to us, but once Stevens gets down there to London, I'm sure he'll come up with the goods.'

'OK, so, how does this reference number get found in a fairly conspicuous place at Smyth's cottage?' Kirsty asked.

'That is the sixty-four-thousand-dollar question, my dear, but my gut instinct tells me that it was him.'

Kingsfield tapped the picture of Bingham Tyler.

'But there is no other evidence to prove it.'

'Have you had any SOCO results from the cottage passed to you?'

'Well, I spoke to the SOCO manager when he came to collect the prints of Smyth –he alluded to the fact that the only prints that were found were hers. They think that the killer either wiped it clean or wore gloves.'

'What about the piece of paper with the reference number on? Has that been checked for prints?'

'I assumed so.'

'Don't you think you ought to find out?'

Kingsfield went silent for a minute.

'Mm,' he said. 'I'll get Dave to check on that in the morning. Kirsty snuggled down further on the sofa.

After a few more minutes contemplating and not coming up with any further answers, Kingsfield decided that the best place to be was in bed with his wife. He became aware of the mood music that had been playing in the background, Michael Bublé singing an old Frank Sinatra classic.

He felt Kirsty's warm body stir next to him, which tended to melt away all thoughts of work and distract him at the best of times. He decided that they both needed to be in bed. He stubbed out the last of his cigar, downed the rest of his cognac and scooped Kirsty up in his arms. She opened her eyes briefly, smiled up at him and closed her eyes, snuggling closer to him.

He carried her into the bedroom and set her down gently upon the bed. On doing so, her dressing gown fell open to reveal the perfectly formed, smooth, unblemished body he had come to adore.

They made love twice and by 2am fell into a restful and contented sleep, the day's troubles having been washed away.

Outside, the CCTV camera had been pointing towards the bedroom of the Kingsfield's apartment. Bingham had been watching.

Chapter 18

Bingham drove up to the secluded terrace of cottages on the outskirts of Willoughby village. He drove along the dirt track that revealed the hidden terrace behind a small copse of Ash trees. This is so well-hidden, Bingham thought, that if you didn't know the cottages were there, you'd never be able to find them. All the better for the plan for her he had formulated over months of observations. Lulling the neighbours into a falsehood about his Aunty Eleanor.

He opened the small green picket gate and walked up to the front door, where he knocked. The door opened quickly.

'Come in, Bingham, have a seat,' said Eleanor.

Bingham quickly glanced around the room, as he stepped over the threshold into the cottage. He followed Eleanor as they walked through the lounge into the kitchen. She offered him a seat at the small kitchen table. He went to sit down, but Eleanor turned her back to him as she went to fill the kettle with water.

He moved up behind her and grabbed her with one swift movement, swiftly snapping her head to the right, instantly breaking her neck.

Bingham watched in slow motion as she fell to the floor. He bent down towards her. Her eyes opened. She laughed.

By now Bingham was used to this recurring dream. Every time he had it, the longer it lasted. The more detail was added, but it still disturbed him. He knew that it shouldn't concern him, of course. He had done this sort of thing before and had not had this same reaction. But it was never right. It never happened like he saw in his nightmare - what about the talking? What about the tea?

Not right. Not right. He looked at the clock. 4am again. Always 4am.

'*It will always be 4 o'clock, until you admit your guilt to the police, Bing.*'

'Don't you ever sleep?'

'*You sleep, I sleep—you're awake, I'm awake—it's just how it is.*'

Bingham got up from the pit that was his bed and walked, naked, into the kitchen and got a caffeine drink from the fridge. He cracked the can open and took two big swigs of the sweet liquid inside.

'*Is it no wonder you cannot sleep drinking this stuff. It only wakes us up.*'

He leant against the fridge, ignoring the voice in his head. He thought about what he had observed in the Kingsfields' apartment no more than two or three hours ago. But there were no prostitutes on the street below his apartment to vent the sexual urges he'd had while watching the two of them in bed. Smiling to himself he walked over to his computers and replayed last night's events in Kingsfield's apartment.

***

The following morning Kingsfield was refreshed and in a buoyant mood. As he walked across the back yard towards the door of the police station, Dave Heart was coming in the pedestrian entrance. He'd been out for an early morning jog and they arrived at the back door at the same time.

'Well, you look like the cat that had the cream,' Heart said to Kingsfield as he passed his warrant card over the card-reader.

'You could say that,' Kingsfield grinned. 'Win gave me a photo at the end of play yesterday. Have a guess who one of the kids in that photo is?'

'It's Tyler. I know. Win left a copy of all of the photos on my desk before he and Stevens went off to London.'

'Our first real lead,' commented Kingsfield.

'Doesn't mean to say he killed her,' replied Heart.

'No, but I'd put money on it. I also discovered, because I've been an idiot, that the two others in the photos were the kids we picked up at a murder in '94 - my first murder as it happens, when I was a proby.'

'So, do you think that they are all in it together, then?'

'That I'm not so sure about, but they are worth checking out, don't you think?'

'So, do we need Stevens to stay down in London then, or shall I recall them?'

'Well, we need their addresses so no, leave them to it for now.'

While they were talking at the door, Heart became a doorman for the other uniformed officers coming and going from the station. He indicated for Kingsfield to step into the station.

As they stepped further in and closed the door, Kingsfield said, 'by the way, that note left under the lamp at the Smyth cottage, the one with the same reference number, you know?'

'Yeah, what about it?'

'Have we had it checked for prints and DNA?'

'I'll have a look when I get upstairs. I can't see that they wouldn't have checked that. Any reason why?'

'No, Kirsty brought it up last night when I was looking at these bloody photos,' Kingsfield said, as he waved the brown envelope with the photos inside he had been carrying.

'I'll give SOCO a ring and let you know.'

Heart peeled off towards the changing rooms. 'I'll see you upstairs in a minute.'

Kingsfield was already bounding up the steps two at a time towards his Incident Room. Heart watched him go. He knew he'd seen that look on Kingsfield's face before and it was never a good sign for him–or anyone else for that matter. After showering, Heart went up to the incident room, making a quick call to SOCO as he went. Walking into the incident room he went to Kingsfield's office. He wasn't there.

'Anyone seen the DI?' he called out to the office. Some officers looked up and shook their heads.

'Fred, you seen the boss?'

'No, not this morning.'

Jill was entering the incident room, as Heart asked the question.

'Where's the DI off to in a hurry?' she remarked.

'Why, have you seen him?' asked Heart.

'Just seen him high-tailing it out of the back-yard, as I was coming in,' she said.

'Oh fuckin' hell, he's off on one of his crusades again! He'll be the death of us all,' said Heart, shaking his head. 'Fred, get a car and I'll meet you downstairs. I think I know where he's gone.'

Meanwhile, Kingsfield was threading his way through the traffic at St. Peters Way in his grey CID BMW. He wasn't making much headway with the meagre blue lights fitted to the front of the vehicle. Despite being lit up like a Christmas tree, drivers had no idea he was approaching. He didn't want to use the sirens, but in the end, to get through the traffic he didn't have much choice. He used them sparingly as he left the roundabout and shot up Gas Street, towards Mayorhold car park. Much better when we had the old 'Kojak' lights, he thought, as he acknowledged a driver that had given him some space.

He drove up the hill towards the town's red light district and Tyler's apartment. As he got close, he killed the lights and coasted slowly to a stop in front of the main entrance. Strange, he thought, that this used to be the best hotel in town. As he got out of his car, he glanced upwards to where he knew Tyler's apartment was. The sky above the apartment block had turned to a marbled grey, threatening even more rain. Kingsfield shuddered and buttoned up his jacket. Pushing through the double doors of the main entrance, he made his way to the lifts. Luckily, they still worked.

He knew that Tyler's apartment was on the seventeenth floor and entered the lift when the doors pinged open. A disembodied metallic voice informed would-be passengers that they were on the ground floor. He stepped into the lift and was nearly knocked out by the stench. He hit the button for the 17th floor and the doors closed.

'Lift going up,' the metal voice intoned.

Kingsfield looked around the lift. It was the standard aluminium metal box. All the trappings of grandeur had been removed. The carpeted floor had been replaced by thick marine ply that had years of dirty footprints on it. Half the walls in the lift were also covered in the same thick plywood with various pieces of graffiti written or spray-painted on. In one corner, human urine and excreta, and in the other corner someone had left a 'pavement pizza.' 'I'm glad I don't have to travel in this shit everyday,' he thought.

Suddenly, the lift stopped. Silence from the voice. The door didn't open. He pressed the button for the seventeenth floor again. The lift stayed still and then the doors opened without warning. He found that he was on the fifteenth floor. He stepped out of the lift and found the stairs, no problem making the last two floors on foot, he thought assuming that the left was faulty.

If he could catch the madman today, that would be a big bonus.

'He still doesn't know we're onto him and that is the biggest advantage,' thought Kingsfield. Varying emotions were running through Kingsfield, as he made his way up the several flights of stairs. He disliked Tyler, ever since he put him away when he was a Detective Sergeant. The guy was not human, in his opinion, and a total lunatic. The thought of putting him behind bars again was pushing the adrenaline into his body, as he made the seventeenth floor.

Gathering himself before he entered the corridor to Tyler's apartment, he reminded himself that professionalism was the name of the game here. He knew only too well that his hot-headedness earlier in his career had gone against him. But he knew he wanted this bastard and jeopardising any court case by being rash was not on the agenda today. But he knew that would be difficult. This man had been an embarrassment to the police service when he worked for PolServ, an embarrassment to humanity and, above all, a thorn in Kingsfield's side for far too long.

He entered the hallway with the intention of surprise, as knocking on the door first was not going to be an option. The hallway was littered with discarded fast food wrappings, empty beer bottles, cans and anything else that the occupants of the block couldn't be asked to put in a bin. Kingsfield shook his head in despair. The stench of the lift had followed him into the hallways - or was the smell just so powerful that it stayed up his nose? He didn't really care at this stage. All he wanted was Bingham Tyler.

He knew that Bingham wouldn't have had the door fixed from the previous raid and he was right. As he approached the door, he could see that it was slightly ajar.

He carefully removed the straight-handled retractable baton from his belt and held it hidden in his right hand, ready to use. If he extended it now, the sound would give him away.

He pushed the door open.

It creaked.

He winced.

He took one step inside.

He heard a voice.

'Did you really think that you were going to surprise me?' Bingham shouted to Kingsfield. 'Look up and smile, Jimmy-boy!' Kingsfield looked up and saw a camera was looking right at him. He gave a brief, unconvincing smile at the camera.

'I knew you were coming when I stopped the lift on the fifteenth floor. Worn you out has it, those last few flights?' Tyler said.

'In your dreams,' Kingsfield muttered and took another step forward into the apartment. He extended his baton. No point in hiding it now.

'Come on then, Bingham.' Kingsfield called. 'Where are you, you little shit?' Kingsfield made his way down a small length of hallway that opened up into the main apartment. He saw a door to his left. 'Was that a shad…' But before he could finish that thought, Bingham was on him. Wielding an old cricket bat, Bingham swung it at Kingsfield's knees. With a crack he brought Kingsfield down, but not before Kingsfield struck out with his baton, sending Bingham's wiry frame sprawling across the floor into a waste-bin. Bingham quickly recovered and picking the bin up, threw it at Kingsfield. Kingsfield dodged out of the way and went for Bingham before he was fully off the floor, knocking him down and into the kitchen area of the apartment. Bingham quickly got up and ran at Kingsfield, screaming like a banshee. Kingsfield blocked Bingham's uncoordinated blow. He struck a blow to Bingham's chest, sending him sprawling back towards the kitchen. Kingsfield ran at him again, but this time wasn't quick enough to get out the way of a large and heavy, dusty saucepan that Bingham quickly wrestled from the rack it was standing on. It crashed into Kingsfield's head and he dropped like a stone. Unconscious.

'Ah! Ah! See, not so big now, are you, copper?' Bingham spat the words out onto an unconscious Kingsfield.

'You gonna do him, then?'

'What!'

'Look, he's unconscious, prime time to do what you've always planned.'

'No, not the right time. I want to do him in my time, not his.'

'But he's there, Bing, at your mercy.'

The sound of sirens approaching in the streets below stopped the conversation. Bingham searched Kingsfield's pockets for his car keys. Finding them, he ran out of his apartment, before the other coppers arrived, collecting Kingsfield's baton as he went.

'Must get away from here. Gather my thoughts.'

'But he's there, Bing, look!'

'No, my time, my time, my time–so shut up!'

Holding his head as he ran out of his apartment, he headed for the service lift, down to the street.

Chapter 19

The service lift door slid open and Bingham ran from his apartment block towards the rear of the building. Running around to the front of the building, Bingham pressed the key-ring remote to identify Kingsfield's car. The car finally identified itself with a blip, blip and flashing of the indicators. Getting into the car and heavily out of breath, he started the engine, threw the car into gear and screeched out of the car park. He gunned the accelerator, as the car catapulted wildly into the street, nearly colliding with a woman crossing the road and causing another vehicle to move quickly out of the way to avoid a collision. He roared down the hill towards St. Peters Way and up the London Road, out of town.

Unbeknown to Bingham, DC Fred and Heart were heading towards him in the opposite direction.

'Come on, Fred, step on it. We don't want a dead DI on our hands as well.'

Fred accelerated the battered CID Peugeot down the London Road, turning towards Tyler's apartment, blue lights and sirens blaring. Heart was in the passenger seat and pointed ahead.

'Look, there's the boss' car, coming towards us. Slow down.'

As the car got closer, he could see that Kingsfield was not the driver. The BMW drove past with Bingham in the driving seat. He gave Heart a one-fingered salute and laughed.

'Shit – shit! Where the hell is the boss, then?' he asked the question out loud, but didn't expect an answer. Heart got his airwave radio from the inside pocket of his jacket and alerted other units to look out for Kingsfield's BMW.

Arriving at Tyler's apartment, they abandoned their vehicle under the canopy and ran towards the lifts. Fred pressed the button to call the lift. It seemed to take ages.

'Come on…come on…' shouted Heart, punching the lift button two or three times. As if that was going to get the lift to them any faster. He considered the stairs, looked at Fred and then discarded the idea, as the lift finally arrived.

Getting into the lift, they hit the button for the seventeenth floor, but it stopped at the fifteenth.

'Great,' remarked Heart, 'Looks like we're gonna have to run the rest of the way.'

DC Fred just looked at Heart, who gazed at his oversized belly.

'You can run if you like,' Fred exclaimed.

Heart cast an eye over Fred.

'Just think of this as the start of your new exercise regimen,' Heart said with a smirk.

'Yeah, right… come on then.' Fred said with resignation in his voice.

The overweight Fred had to push himself up the last flight of stairs. With him breathing heavily, they both entered the apartment.

'You really need to do some more exercise,' Heart remarked to Fred, who was now wheezing behind him, standing bent over with his hands on his knees, trying to catch his breath.

Fred just waved Heart forward, unable to speak.

Heart found Kingsfield coming round on the floor of the kitchen.

'Where is he?' he croaked to Heart.

'Nicked your motor and cleared off.'

'Bollocks.'

Sitting up with his back against the wall, Kingsfield groaned.

'You should have waited for us,' Heart said quietly to Kingsfield.

'Yeah, well, you know me.'

'Only too well, Jim. Jesus man, he could have killed you.'

'Well, he didn't, did he?'

'Not this time, luckily for you. Anyway, we've circulated your motor, so hopefully someone will pick it up.'

'OK,' said Kingsfield. 'Help me up.'

Fred arrived in the apartment, still a bit out of breath and helped Heart to get Kingsfield to his feet. 'Let's have a look round while we're here,' he said, still a bit unsteady. 'There must be something of interest we can find?' continued Kingsfield, rubbing his head.

'You need to go to hospital. That was a nasty clunk on the head you got, if he hit you with that–' Heart pointed to the saucepan on the floor by Kingsfield.

'No, I'll be fine.'

Heart and Fred started to have a look round Bingham's apartment. Fred looked at all his surveillance equipment and sat down at the workstation.

'Blimey,' he said. 'What's he want all this stuff for?'

He shook the mouse on the mouse-pad and all the screens burst into life. Password protected.

'Not gonna get into these in a hurry,' called Fred.

Kingsfield walked over to the monitors. Fred was sitting in Bingham's big chair. 'Most people usually write their passwords down somewhere. Fred, have a look around, see if there's anything obvious.'

Fred looked at Kingsfield. 'Yeah, boss, but he ain't normal, is he?' Fred started to rifle through draws and cupboards in the area of Bingham's desk.

'I can't see that a twat like Tyler would write a password down either. He is quite bright you know,' remarked Heart.

'But the bloke's unstable,' said Fred, still rummaging through draws. 'Goodness alone knows what's going on in that twisted head of his. Ah ha, this look promising!' Fred found a small red index book and flicked through it. 'Mm. Not much here,' he mumbled to himself. 'Could be a variety of combinations.' He started trying combinations of words he found in the red book.

While he did that, Heart and Kingsfield continued to look around the apartment, Kingsfield still rubbing his head occasionally. After a few moments of silence wandering round the place and searching through what little stuff was lying around, they both ended up in the kitchenette area.

'What's the problem with you and this guy, anyway?' enquired Heart.

'Oh, it's a long story, Dave,' replied Kingsfield, while opening and shutting kitchen cupboards.

'He must have some reason why he wants to do you?'

'It was a difficult case and a long time ago it seems. I don't suppose most detectives worry about the criminals they bang up in jail. They certainly don't worry about them coming after them when they get out. That's more the stuff of movies.'

'So, what is it then–are you worried about him?'

'Nah…' replied Kingsfield, unconvincingly.

'Don't believe you, Jim–this guy seems to be capable of anything, despite his geeky looks.'

'Then I have every confidence in you being able to protect me,' he smiled.

'What, like I did just now?'

'Well, you got here, didn't you? A bit late–but you got here,' he grimaced as he rubbed his head again.

Heart was still not convinced that Kingsfield would come up with the goods, to tell him what was going on with him and Tyler. He pushed again. 'I still don't understand why he has a vendetta against you –I need to know, Jim, if you want my help.'

'OK, OK.' Kingsfield sat down on the kitchen stool. To Heart the simple reaction he got from Kingsfield sitting down made him look deflated and tired.

'I have two reasons why he is the way he is,' Kingsfield began. 'One, I put him away for a few years for rape, wounding and fraud. He is a violent man by nature, despite, as you say, his geeky looks. He certainly intimated to me when they took him down that he had every intention of coming after me when he got out.'

'Surely, you didn't think that he would make good on that threat? If we thought that about all the crim's we sent down, we'd all be protected 24/7.'

'No, of course not, not at the time, but what really pissed me off was what he did to Steph Parker.'

'Ah, the missing policewoman.'

Kingsfield went on to explain the circumstances of her disappearance, the attempted rape, the failing to turn up at court to give evidence and the ensuing nationwide search.

'So, you think that he's after you because you sent him down?'

'No, not only that. I did lose him the only decent job that he had with 'PolServe.' And he only got that because of Parker's recommendation about his ability to use all this equipment he's got right here.' Kingfield waved his arm in the direction of Bingham's surveillance kit that Fred was still working on.

'Well, losing that job was his own fault. Can't see that he can blame you for it. He was using it for his own ends. His own criminal ends, I might add,' said Heart.

'I know that, you know that, but he obviously doesn't accept it, does he? Hang on. I've just had a thought. If he is so adamant that he's going to get me somehow, perhaps that has translated to his computer passwords?'

Page 153

Kingsfield got up from his stool and walked over to Fred at the computers.

'Here, Fred, try this password.'

'What password?' asked Fred.

Kingsfield wrote down a password in his notebook and showed it to Fred.

'Really, you want me to try that?'

'Can't hurt, can it?' said Heart, as he joined the other two.

Fred typed in the password - KINGSFIELD. 'Nope, that didn't work.'

'Try the I's as ones,' suggested Kingsfield. Fred typed.

'Nope, still no good.'

'OK, try this one.' He spelt out the name of his wife.

'No, still no good. But, let me try this.' Fred typed in K1R5TY. 'Bingo, not that inventive really, now you come to think about it.'

'One of your better hunches,' said Heart to Kingsfield. 'Well done, Fred, now let's have a look at what he's been up to.'

On the screens in front of them Kingsfield and Heart found surveillance on Kingsfield's apartment, a haulage yard, the wood where the second body was found and Eleanor's cottage.

'Why would he be watching Fulborough Wood?' asked Heart.

'More to the point, why is he watching my bloody apartment?' responded Kingsfield.

'Same reason he wants to take over your life, I suggest, but the wood?'

'Perhaps he wanted to know when she was found? I can't understand what advantage it would give him to know.'

'Still doesn't answer the question as to why? Maybe he just gets sexual satisfaction knowing that she's there,' suggested Heart.

They both stood there in silence for a moment, flicking through Bingham's computers.

'You think that the body we found in Fulborough Wood is Parker, don't you, Jim?' Heart interrupted the silence that had fallen across all of them.

'I'd rather not say at this stage. Let's say that I have my suspicions.'

'OK, but don't go putting all your eggs in one basket. It may not be her.'

'I assume we're still waiting DNA results?'

'Yeah, I'll see if FSS can put a rush on it, now we've found all this crap. Jesus, he's a fucking perverted bastard.'

'OK. Let's get SOCO and the tech boys in to tear his hard drives apart. Why the hell wasn't this stuff removed when we raided the place?'

'We only wanted to arrest him for rape and assault. I suppose that Win thought there was no need,' said Heart. Kingsfield leaned forward and pushed a few screen buttons with the mouse again.

'He is into everything, even the nick. Look.'

Kingsfield brought up the view of the front and rear of the police station where they were based.

'He knew I was coming for him, watched me leave, followed me through the town's CCTV system,' Kingsfield continued to scroll through the pictures of various places Bingham had an interest in. Fred had moved to another desk with more computers and more surveillance equipment and started looking through those, as Heart continued to search the apartment.

'Er… boss,' Fred, said gingerly. 'Perhaps you should come and look at this? I found some recordings under a file named JKK'.

Page 155

Fred was watching an apartment window. The playback zoomed in. Kingsfield came to Fred's side and saw that it was a recording of him and Kirsty in bed - and not asleep.

'Go help Dave,' Kingsfield said quickly. Fred did as he was told. Kingsfield filled the chair Fred had decamped from and began to go through the file named JKK. There was a recording of him at the Smyth crime scene with Kirsty and recordings of him in his apartment and leaving and entering the police station. As he continued to look at all Bingham's recordings, he became acutely concerned for his wife. If Bingham had it in for him, then clearly it followed that he would have it in for his wife as well. If he did try to make good on the threats he made to him while he was in the cells a few days ago, perhaps he needed to order some protection for her. But he knew that if he did she would only refuse it. He took his mobile phone out of his pocket and called Kirsty. There was no answer. He called the mortuary. He was told by one of the technicians that she was doing a PM, but would pass on a message to her. At least he felt a little better knowing that she was at work and surrounded by her colleagues. He resolved to speak to her as soon as he could.

'He really has got a down on you, Jim,' Heart said quietly behind him. 'You need to be careful. Psychos like that are unpredictable. I can only think that it is going to end in tears for both of you.'

'It will not be me, I can assure you, Dave.'

'Well, just be careful, OK?'

Kingsfield nodded. 'Yeah, OK. Come on, lets get out of this place. Seal it up.' Kingsfield left the apartment with Heart, leaving DC Fred to arrange and wait for the SOCOs.

'I'm concerned, Dave,' Kingsfield said to Heart as they entered the lift on floor fifteen.

'Oh, about what?'

'Tyler, you're right, he is out to get me–he said as much when I saw him in the cells, but I thought it was all bluster. But seeing all that stuff in his apartment makes me very concerned, not for me, you understand, I know I can look after myself, but Kirsty – that's another matter.'

'What do you want to do about him and Kirsty?'

'See if you can get one of the surveillance team to keep a guard on Kirsty – but don't make it obvious – and get an All Ports Warning out for Bingham.'

'Roger that,' Heart said, as they got to their car.

Chapter 20

Bingham parked in the Holcot country park on the Pitsford Reservoir causeway. The car park was empty, other than one Land Rover parked in the corner. Bingham could see what he assumed was the owner walking his dogs. Pitsford Reservoir is the main water supply for Northampton town. The persistent rain during the summer had filled it almost full. The water lapping at the edge of the car park was calm, with a light northerly breeze. The waters looked dark, like Bingham's current mood. He parked in a secluded area between some trees, so as to try not to draw attention to himself.

'How the hell did he find out about me?'

'Because you want to be found, my friend. You said as much when you placed that note in Eleanor's house. It was a cry for help.'

'No, I don't think so.'

'Yes, you want to be found out, Bing. This vendetta been going on for far too long. Just give it up!'

'Never, never!'

'It will be your death, Bing.'

'No, no, no, no,' he screamed, banging the steering wheel with both hands. 'I will see him dead! I will see him dead, if it's the last thing I do.'

'But it probably will be.'

'I don't care. I will have my revenge, I swear it!' he growled.

Bingham started the car.

'I must dump this car–the whole fucking police force will be looking for it. But where?'

He thought for a moment and then he knew exactly where.

'I will have to bring my plans forward.'

'What plans are these?'

'I had intended to steal a truck from my idiot stepbrother, but I'll have to move things forward now.'

Although he hadn't seen him since they were split up as children, he had kept up with what his step-brother had been up to and had quietly kept some surveillance on him over the years. Bingham left the country park and made his way to his step-brother's haulage company.

Driving out of the park, he turned right towards Holcot village, through the village and out towards the main Northampton to Kettering road. At the roundabout, he turned right back towards Northampton. He drove through Moulton, hoping that he would not come across a police car. He thought that by this time they must all know that he'd stolen Kingsfield's car. He managed to get to the Round Spinney interchange without detection and onto the Industrial Estate, where he knew his stepbrother had his haulage yard.

He abandoned the vehicle between two parked up semi-trailers, in the yard of Gaffney International Haulage. As he got out of the car a driver approached him.

'You can't leave that there, bud!' the driver shouted. Bingham ignored him and continued to walk towards the main building. He needed the truck to complete the plan that he had formed in his mind to defeat Kingsfield.

'Hey you!' the driver ran up towards Bingham. 'Hey, I'm talking to you.'

'Fuck off,' Bingham shouted. The driver went to grab his arm, but the baton Bingham held in his other hand, that he had wrested from Kingsfield, extended quickly and swung round on the driver, hitting him in the neck and shoulders. The driver, off balance and caught by surprise, fell backwards onto the floor.

Bingham ran towards the main reception and burst through the front door. He went up to the startled receptionist.

'Truck keys!' he demanded, 'I want some truck keys!'

He banged the baton on the reception desk and shouted again, 'Where are your keys?' The receptionist pointed to the transport office. 'Down there,' she said hysterically.

Bingham strode off towards the transport office, as Gaffney was coming out to see what all the commotion was. They met each other, eye to eye.

'Bingham!' Adam exclaimed.

'Truck keys! Now!' Bingham demanded.

'They're all out. You don't think I keep them standing about, do you?'

Bingham swiftly pushed Gaffney and grabbed hold of his arm, pushing it up his back with the baton.

'KEYS!' He shouted even more aggressively into Gaffney's ear. He pushed him further into the office. By this time, other office staff, hearing the commotion outside the office, had backed away into a far corner. A couple of the girls had begun to cry.

'YOU!' He called to the nearest man he could see. 'KEYS, NOW!' The employee looked at Gaffney being held firmly by Bingham. Gaffney nodded to him. The man went to the key-box on the wall and threw a set of keys to Bingham. He caught them in his free hand.

'WHERE IS IT?' He demanded.

'It's the seventeen tonner against the rear wall.'

Bingham forced Gaffney's arm up further up his back, before pushing him at full force towards the man who had thrown him the keys. Bingham turned and ran for the door.

Rosie Jordan was just entering the office as Bingham was leaving and as he violently pushed past her to get through the doorway; she fell hard against the door frame.

Running out of the office building he turned left towards the rear of the lorry park. Seeing the lone seventeen tonne, curtain-sided vehicle parked against the back wall, he climbed the step to the cab. 'This can't be much different than driving those little trucks I was shown on the Peter's farm, all them years ago,' he mumbled to himself. He started the engine and revved it hard. Crashing it into first gear, he drove erratically out of the yard.

Back in the office the transport manager was on the phone. They'd dialled 999 and had informed the police that one of their vehicles had been hi-jacked from the office. Gaffney walked over to his transport manager. Rubbing his right arm, he asked his manager to give him the phone, which he did. Gaffney informed the police that the hi-jacker was his stepbrother and gave them his name.

Jake Jordan was sitting on an observation position near to the football stadium when the call came in about the hi-jacking at Gaffney International Haulage. 'Rosie,' he thought. He made a note of the registration mark of the truck and told control that he was making his way to the premises of Gaffney International.

When he arrived he went to reception, but before he did so he saw that the stolen police BMW had been parked in the lorry park. He went over to it to confirm, then radioed in its location.

A few minutes later, Jordan got a call from Kingsfield.

'Jake, you found my BM?'

'Yes, Jim, it's in the lorry park at Gaffney International.'

Both Kingsfield and Jordan had worked together in the past when they were both based on the same uniform shift in the town centre.

'OK, don't leave till I get there. I'm on my way.'

'Do you want it checked out first?'

'No, it'll be OK. I know who's had it.'

'Yes, your man, Tyler, has hi-jacked one of their trucks.'

'Right, get your guys looking for him and the truck, but be careful. He is a dangerous man.'

The radio beeped as Kingsfield terminated the call.

Chapter 21

Jordan walked into the offices of the haulage company and was directed to the transport office by a traumatised receptionist, who was being comforted by another female member of staff. As he walked into the office, he was taken aback by the sight of his wife in an embrace with Gaffney. She had her back to the door, so did not see him enter. Perhaps, he thought quickly, this was why things had not been good at home recently. He thought back to the recent arguments. He must however keep calm and remain professional. He would deal with his wife later, he thought.

'Adam Gaffney?' Jordan enquired.

'Yes, that's me.'

Rosie recognised her husband's voice and pushed herself swiftly away from Adam, turning towards her husband. He could see that she was extremely embarrassed, but before Jordan could say anything else, Rosie introduced him to Gaffney.

'What has happened here?' he enquired in a professional manner. He did not make eye contact with his wife, who could see that he had rumbled what was going on between Gaffney and her.

'Shall we go up to my office?'

'Yes, let's,' retorted Jordan. He locked an accusing eye on his wife and she averted her gaze, as he left the office with Gaffney.

Gaffney explained to Jordan the circumstances of Bingham's visit.

'What is this man Bingham to you or this company?'

'To the company –nothing. To me, he's my step-brother.'

'Is he usually this aggressive?'

'Don't know. I haven't seen him for twenty years. Didn't like him as a kid, if that helps.'

'Really? Why did he come here, then?'

'I have no idea.'

'Why does he want one of your vehicles?'

'Don't know.'

'Do you care?'

'Not really, no,' bristled Gaffney, 'as long as I get my truck back.'

Jordan wanted to ask how long this man had been having an affair with his wife, but he thought better of it. And looking at his slicked back hair and the size of him he wondered what she saw in him.

'So,' asked Kingsfield, who had arrived while Jordan was questioning Gaffney. 'you have no idea why he would want to come to your office after no contact for twenty years?'

Gaffney turned to talk to Kingsfield, 'as I said, I have no idea.'

'You didn't keep in touch, then?'

'The family was split up when we were all fostered.'

'You were fostered with Tyler?' Jordan asked.

'Not with him, no, but me and my sister, were told not to contact each other, when we got sent to different foster parents.'

'Why?' asked Kingsfield.

'Don't know—we were too young to ask.'

'Mm, doesn't seem like something the social would do,' Kingsfield replied, by this time he had entered the office completely and was searching his inside pocket. He removed a photograph from a police evidence bag.

'Anything to do with this?' He asked and showed the photograph to Gaffney, who didn't respond. Instead, he opened the top drawer of his desk where he had put the exact same copy of the photo Kingsfield was showing him after he had met Cynthia.

'You mean this photo?' Gaffney showed Kingsfield and Jordan the same photograph.

'Yes. What's it all about, then?' Jordan asked.

'Look, it's a long story and I don't really want to get into it, but he knows–' pointing to Kingsfield.

Jordan looked for an answer from Kingsfield. 'How would you know about this Jim?'

'If I recall, I was at the murder of your mother back in '94. We found you hiding in a cupboard. I think you were thirteen, fourteen –something like that?'

'Fourteen,' confirmed Gaffney.

'So you got split up, sent to foster homes. What about Bingham–where did he go?'

'Don't know and I don't really care. You know what he's like and all this really has nothing to do with either me or my sister. He obviously wanted a truck and thought he could blag one off his stepbrother.'

'Mr Gaffney,' Jordan said, pressing him further, 'I am afraid you are involved, so you don't really have an option, after what has happened here today.'

He looked at Kingsfield. Kingsfield nodded.

'Look, I think it's personal and I don't think it has anything to do with what has happened here today,' said Gaffney.

'I think it has everything to do with it and I'll be the judge of that, after you've filled in a few gaps,' replied Kingsfield, a little irritated. 'Or would you rather discuss it at the police station?'

Gaffney capitulated with a deep sigh and held up his hands in surrender.

'OK, OK,' said Gaffney, offering them a seat at the conference table at the other end of his office. He went to the filing cabinet and removed the boxes he had stored there, the ones he had got the photograph from.

Gaffney related the story of how Eleanor Smyth was assigned to look after them when they were orphaned following the murder of their mother. He explained that it was the Social Services' decision to split them up, when one family couldn't foster them all.

He felt that he was lucky, as the family that took him in were kind, sympathetic and gave him a good education.

'I later found out that Bingham had been sent from foster home to foster home. I think if I remember most of this was reported in the papers when he got sent down for that fraud thing with the police company.'

'Do you know anything about him that was not reported in the papers?' asked Jordan.

'Not really, no. As I said, we were told not to see each other and I didn't want to anyway. But I seem also to recall that his last foster parent was interviewed. They seemed to be good people and appeared to have turned him around from his wayward ways.'

'What did you think of him, when you were children?' asked Kingsfield.

'I thought he was – different, something not quite right up here you know?' Gaffney pointed to his head. 'He was bright, no doubt about that, but he seemed to direct the intelligence he had in the wrong ways – if you know what I mean. Remember the shoebox?'

'I do–but you've not had contact with him since then?' replied Kingsfield.

'No, I swear.'

'Mm… Why am I sceptical about that? You knew he did get a decent education, predominantly with computers and electronics?'

'No, I wasn't aware.'

'What about your sister? Did you stay in touch with her?' asked Kingsfield.

'No.'

'Really?'

'Well, Eleanor did tell each of us where we were. Said she'd get in trouble if her bosses knew. I think she felt that it was wrong for us not to know.'

'Yes, but have you seen her?' quizzed Jordan.

'A couple of days ago, first time in about fifteen years.'

'I see. And why did she contact you now?' said Kingsfield.

'She thought we ought to come and talk to you about us and Eleanor.'

'So, why didn't you?' pressed Jordan.

'Didn't see the relevance and still don't.'

'OK, then. Do you think that Bingham is capable of murder?' said Kingsfield.

Gaffney thought for a moment. 'In all honesty, in his current state of mind? Yes, I do. He never had that many morals even when he was nine. Spent most of his time killing the local wildlife and anything else he could find. We think he got rid of our dog, but could never prove it.'

Kingsfield raised an eyebrow.

'Tell me, Mr Gaffney, just for my personal information, you are married to my wife's sister, are you not?'

Kingsfield shot Jordan a glance. This was unexpected, he thought.

'Yes, I am.'

'Where is she today?'

'God alone knows. She tends to do her own thing.'

'Strange, then, that we haven't met before today?'

'Never had the opportunity.'

'Really? You weren't at your father-in-law's funeral, where we would have met. I just wondered whether you were hiding yourself away for some reason?'

Gaffney became uncomfortable. He wondered where this was going. He knew only too well that he was having an affair with the wife of the man sitting opposite him.

Page 167

'No, not particularly,' replied Gaffney. 'Just one of those things, perhaps.'

'Mm… perhaps?' Jordan replied.

'Is this getting us anywhere?' questioned Kingsfield.

'No, Jim, not for you –but it is for my enquiries.'

Jordan eyed Gaffney, showing a mutual understanding of where both of them stood.

'Let's go,' said Kingsfield, getting up from the conference table. 'Don't go anywhere, Mr Gaffney. We'll need to speak with you again.'

Gaffney nodded and he showed them out of his office. Both of them went downstairs. In the time that Jordan and Kingsfield had been quizzing Gaffney, both Heart and DC Fred had arrived and made some enquiries with the staff. Heart turned to see Jordan coming down the stairs.

'Your missus is in the office down there. Said you'd want to speak to her.'

'No, you carry on, Sergeant. I need to make a move.'

'Oh, OK,' Heart said. Rosie had come out of the office and was standing waiting for her husband to speak with her.

He turned to look at her as he was leaving. He said nothing.

Chapter 22

Having left Gaffney's haulage yard, Bingham drove past the University Campus and down the hill towards Kingsthorpe. He turned right, heading out of town. Bingham knew he couldn't go back to his apartment. He knew that they would be watching. He knew that the police had probably trashed all his kit. He felt blind. He was without his electronic sight, unable to follow or track where any of his 'people', as he called them, were. He did not know what was going on in his voyeur-like world–and he didn't like the feeling.

At the bottom of the hill, he turned right onto the Market Harborough road and continued to drive the hijacked truck north, out of town. As he continued on past Boughton, he noticed a wooded area on his right. There was an entrance just big enough for him to get the lorry through. He turned right off the main road and crashed through the wooden gate. Driving into a spinney he found a secluded area, where he decided to hide and park up for the night. Hopefully, he thought, he wouldn't be found here. He had to play a waiting game, instead of watching.

The evening was drawing in. The clouds had thinned and Bingham looked at the clearing skies, as he crawled into the back of the truck to try and get some sleep. He smiled to himself. 'Mm…' he thought, 'red sky at night, a shepherd's delight. Tomorrow is going to be a good day.'

But his mind wanted to finalise the plan for Jim Kingsfield's death. He felt he was close to achieving his aim. He knew that his adversary would have gone to his stepbrother's yard. He knew that Kingsfield would seriously be looking for him for Eleanor's murder.

'He will indeed,' she said.

He knew that he had to find Kingsfield when he was least expecting it and catch him off-guard. Then he knew what to do. But the paranoia of the day began to draw him into the dark shadows of his mind. His thoughts were becoming more disjointed. Nothing made sense anymore. Fact became fiction. Fiction became fact. What was he doing? What was he to do? What will he do? Revenge was still uppermost on his mind. He convinced himself that once he had rid himself of Kingsfield, everything would go back to normal.

He found some old hessian sacking in the back of the truck and, using it as a pillow, curled up in the foetal position in the back, arguing, rambling to himself. Eventually, he fell into a fitful, haunted sleep. His nightmare returned.

'Come in Bingham, have a seat,' said Eleanor.

Bingham's eyes shot open. 'Where are you?'

'I am here, with you.'

'No, go away! I have enough to cope with, with the other one, not you as well.'

'As you say, Bingham, that's tough, isn't it? You remember what happened? You remember what you did to me? You remember what I did for you as a kid? Do you Bingham? Do you?'

'Yes, yes, I do remember,' Bingham held his head in his hands, shaking it furiously, to get rid of his dream.

'Do you remember, Bingham, that you glanced around my room, as you stepped over the threshold into my cottage. I made you tea and then YOU KILLED ME IN MY KITCHEN.' Eleanor was shouting at him. *'YOU BROKE MY NECK, THREW ME DOWN THE STAIRS AND LEFT ME TO ROT.' Eleanor let him see her rotting.*

'Go away! Go away! Stop it! Stop it!'

'I shall not, until you repent for all the bad you have done–and now you plan to do more!'

'Yes, I will do more and I don't give a fucking shit what you do! You can't hurt me. You're just in my head. You have no power over me. I shall still do as I please!'

'Then I shall remain with you forever!

Bingham watched in slow motion, as she fell to the floor. He bent down towards her to check to see that she was dead. Her eyes were closed. Suddenly, they opened. She laughed. You see… for… ever… Bingham!

Bingham couldn't sleep in the back of the truck, haunted by the killing of Eleanor Smyth. He moved back into the cabin. Deciding he wasn't going to get any sleep, he fired up the truck and drove towards the police station.

'You going to hand yourself in, Bing?' a calmer voice said to him.

'No.'

'I think you should!'

'I think you should go away – both of you.'

'We are your voices of reason, Bing, not that you actually take any notice of me or my new friend, who's with me here now. But we'll still say it anyway.'

'I'll listen to you when you say something I can, or want, to listen to.'

Silence.

'See? Both gone off in a huff now, haven't you?'

Silence.

Tick. Tick. Tick. He looked down at the dashboard. He needed fuel. He saw an all night garage and pulled in. Using Eleanor's stolen credit card, which he had tagged to himself by hacking into her account, he bought both petrol in a can and some diesel for the truck.

'Where did you get that from?' she asked.

''Ave a guess,' was all that Bingham mumbled.

To the garage attendant, he was just another trucker. The attendant didn't even look at the card, as he plugged it into the reader. The new pin number that Tyler had applied to the card worked without question and he left the garage.

Having fuelled up, he parked himself in a lay-by, close to the police station. He hunkered down in the driving seat, cracked open a high energy drink and waited…

***

Kingsfield had been up most of the night. He'd telephoned Kirsty and told her about the events of the day, saying that he was going to stay at work to review the case, looking for something. He didn't know what – he just knew that there was something missing, almost foreboding. Not that he told Kirsty, of course.

He stood staring at the enquiry board in front of him. The board, which took up a sizeable chunk of the incident room wall, was laid out in 'ana-capa' style.

He knew that Dave Heart would have put everything on the board. He remembered training he had undertaken in criminal analysis. He knew that presenting all the case information in this style as a network of events and people all linked together could always provide some answers and take the enquiry in other relevant directions. The Home Office Large Major Enquiry System (HOLMES) took the drudgery out of writing out index cards and putting together all the information–hopefully preventing the SIO from missing anything crucial. He felt that he could see an investigation better, if it was laid out in front of him. That was the way he preferred to work, other than trying to piece together computer printouts. The problem here was that it still presented more questions than answers. 'An enquiry full of

Bingham's handywork with no evidence to prove it', he thought.

Pictures of the two dead women and their locations, facts and photos of crime scenes were staring back at him dispassionately. He'd added the photograph of Bingham Tyler at the end of the line and marked a line between him, Eleanor and Adam Gaffney. Kingsfield added a big question mark from Tyler to the as-yet-unidentified female. He had, in his own mind, come to the conclusion that the woman was Parker, but was reluctant to say anything until it was confirmed. Although Dave Heart was now aware of his suspicions, he preferred to keep it to himself for now.

'All this is because of you, Bingham Tyler' he said to himself and pointing to the picture in front of him. 'What is the reason behind all this mayhem you've caused?'

Kingsfield rubbed his eyes and looked at his watch. 5am. 'This is no good, staring at this wall is not getting me anywhere,' Kingsfield said to himself out-loud. He collected his coat from his office and went downstairs to his car, leaving the station to drive home.

Kingsfield's mind was full of unanswered questions. He needed to piece together the jigsaw to put Bingham behind bars once and for all, but it was all circumstantial at the moment. He was also mindful of the fact that Tyler wanted him –and probably Kirsty –dead. Preoccupied with these thoughts, he drove on.

He realised he was on autopilot, a feeling he remembered having before, but couldn't do anything about it. When he was a young PC on shift, he frequently wondered how he had managed to get back to the section house at 6am in the morning after a week of night shifts. A journey made so often the brain fails to take in anything that is not unusual.

It was not unusual for a goods vehicle to be parked up in a lay-by at that time of the morning and Kingsfield paid no attention to the curtain-sider parked on the opposite side of the road, as he pulled out of the police station.

Kingsfield joined the Nene Valley Way, still some miles from his home. The dual carriageway had little or no traffic on it. He briefly looked in his rear view mirror and caught sight of a goods vehicle some way behind him.

Kingsfield was using Kirsty's old VW Golf, which was not exactly a powerhouse of acceleration or top speed. His Audi TT was in for a service, so he was just taking it easy, in Kirsty's car, trying to put his thoughts in order. He looked in the mirror again and saw that the goods vehicle had got a little closer. In fact, it was a bit too close for comfort on an almost empty road. He accelerated slightly, but the truck kept coming closer and closer behind him.

The closeness of the truck garnered his attention and by now he was fully aware of what was going on. He tried to get a look at the driver, then he saw the name on the front of the truck, 'Gaffney International Haulage Ltd', in his rear-view mirror.

In an instant it dawned on him –Tyler!

'You want to play then, do you?' Kingsfield shouted aloud to his empty car. 'Come on then - bring it on!' Dropping down a gear, he accelerated the little Golf as hard as he could, but was quickly baulked by two heavy articulated lorries, one trying to overtake the other and not doing very well at it.

In the meantime, Tyler's truck had caught up with him and was behind him with its headlights full on, blinding Kingsfield's view in the rear view mirror. The truck crashed into the back of the Golf, pushing it closer and closer to the lorry in front of it. Kingsfield stood on the brakes, but the truck kept pushing. The little Golf was no match for the seventeen tonnes of truck slammed into its rear-end.

The two other goods vehicles were now in the first lane blowing their air-horns and flashing their lights. Kingsfield accelerated past them as best he could. He could hear something scraping on the road behind him. 'Rear bumper probably.' He thought. He decided to take the next exit, where he could have a better chance of getting away.

He took the exit and entered a winding country road. He took a right at the next roundabout, entering a leafy-laned estate. He pulled into an open gateway and waited for the truck to pass. Opening the window of the Golf he listened for the truck. He heard it coming, screaming at full throttle.

He heard it slowing.

He heard it stop.

Kingsfield could see the roundabout through the trees of the entrance where he had stopped. He could see that the driver was trying to make a decision as to which exit to take. He'd decided to take the exit of the road he was on.

'He's bound to see me,' Kingsfield thought, so he slowly reversed the Golf out of the gateway where he had hidden. He knew that if he could race past him it would take him a little while to turn round on such a small road.

As he drove towards the truck, it moved over to his side of the road, so it was coming at him head on. At the last second he managed to swerve out of the way, but the truck caught the rear end of the Golf spinning it out of control. The car's engine stalled. Kingsfield could not get it started. The truck turned round. Thinking that this was not a contest he was going to win, he quickly considered getting out and running for it, but even his athletic frame wouldn't be able to outrun the lorry.

He saw the truck coming towards him. The engine fired up in time for him to move the little Golf out of the truck's way. He began to limp back towards the dual carriageway, but the truck was soon behind him. As he reached the dual-carriageway junction over-bridge, it slammed into the back of the Golf, crash… And again, crash… Then, catching the offside of the Golf, it spun around in the road. The truck hit Kingsfield's car at full speed. He assumed that Bingham was aiming to push the car over the bridge. Kingsfield was helpless to do anything about it. The car was pushed at full force onto the barrier and Kingsfield cracked his head on the 'A' frame as it came towards him, knocking him semi-conscious. The lorry backed off and slammed forward again - crash. And again - crash. Each time crushing and pushing the little Golf harder against the bridge barrier, which was now beginning to buckle under the strain. Bingham slammed into the Golf again. Kingsfield felt the force break both his legs and dislocate his shoulder, sending agonising pain around his upper body. The next and final crash pushed the steering wheel up under Kingsfield's chest, breaking a number of ribs and puncturing a lung. Kingsfield knew he was powerless after that and was finding it harder to breath. With one arm and both legs broken, he knew it was the end and he was sad that his end had come like this. In a state of semi-consciousness, he thought of his wife and his friends. Drifting in and out of consciousness, he finally heard someone walking towards the car.

Bingham got out of the truck with a jerry can in his hand and a big smile on his face. The smile of a job well done, but not quite finished. He doused the car and the truck with petrol. Finding Kingsfield in his vehicle, fighting for breath, Bingham began to laugh. Kingsfield was barely conscious as he walked up beside him.

'Now, Jimmy,' Tyler exclaimed. 'How does it feel to be helpless, just like me when you did me out of my job?'

Kingsfield could no longer answer. He had resigned himself to the inevitable, no matter what happened. He turned his head to see Tyler talking to him.

'Tyler.' He croaked.

'Because, as you said once, I'm a fucking arsehole.'

'No–need - to –' wheezed Kingsfield.

'Oh yes, there is, because I am the fucking winner here. I am the one in charge.

'No, you're not.'

'Shut up! You ain't going anywhere. I'm in fucking charge. I'm in fucking control. But of course, I always have been. I murdered that Eleanor woman, because I wanted you, Detective Inspector,' he hissed.

'So my murder was just to satisfy you're own ends? I'd done nothing to hurt you, Bingham and you used me.'

Bingham tried to ignore Eleanor's voice in his head. 'You know, you have been in my thoughts, in my plans for revenge since you put me away. I am now going to put you away forever, so I can go back to my life.'

Bingham raged on, as he poured petrol over the car and Kingsfield. When he had emptied the can, he threw it away and crouched down by Kingsfield.

'You know,' Tyler said, quietly, as he retrieved a disposable lighter from his pocket, 'I'm going to do something now, something that you want. Do you know what that is?'

Kingsfield slowly shook his head and croaked 'No.'

'Well,' Bingham crouched down and moved a little closer to Kingsfield's blood-smeared face. Bingham whispered, 'you said in your will, that you wanted to be cremated. Well, guess what?' Bingham stood up and feeling triumphant, he boomed 'Fortunately, I am now in a position to grant you your last wish. AND GOD

FUCKING HELP YOU.' Bingham screamed the last few words, lit the lighter and threw it into the car.

Immediately, the car burst into a great conflagration of flame and smoke. Kingsfield's screams did not last long, as the truck that was stuffed into the back of the car also burst into flames. The last thing Kingsfield thought of before oblivion was of his wife.

Tyler walked away from the fire. He didn't look back. He had an expression of satisfaction on his face.

Chapter 23

The traffic car was sitting in the pedestrian area of the high street outside Marks & Spencer. It had been a quiet, uneventful night for the crew, who were about ready to sign off and go home. The high street's early morning calm had been interrupted by the screeching burglar alarm, which echoed around the streets.

Both traffic officers were out of the car. One of the officers was leaning with his back against the car, cap on the back of his head and smoking a roll-up cigarette. The other officer was talking to Chris Prentice. They were all waiting for the key-holder to arrive.

The smoking officer caught a broadcast message on his airwave radio sending units to a serious collision on the Nene Valley Way. He called to his crewmate, told Chris that the alarm was all his and radioed in their attendance to control.

***

Bingham was exuberant –he had done what he had planned. He couldn't believe it was so easy. He had disposed of Kingsfield, his foe! He laughed out loud. As he turned the corner, he looked back towards the great plume of smoke. Several vehicles had already stopped to see if they could help. 'Not a chance,' he thought. This was the happiest day of his life.

'Satisfied?'

'You bet ya!' he said, punching the air with his fist.

'I hope that this is the end of all this trouble?'

'No, I'm only just getting started.'

'You're not doing any more. You have to stop this. This is not you.'

'Ah, but yes, I think this is –this is the real me. I am invincible. I can do what I like and nobody can stop me.'

***

The gates of the traffic department offices slowly swung open and away from Jordan, as he swiped his card across the reader. Driving into the yard, he reversed his patrol car into the Sergeant's parking space and cut the engine. It was 5.45am and he was looking forward to being able to finish at 7am. When he got home after the incident at Gaffney's, Rosie never made any reference to what had happened. He was particularly annoyed about this, but when he tried to talk to her about it, she just stormed out of the house. When the call came asking him to fill the night shift, he felt that, under the circumstances, it was a blessing and was glad to fill it.

Grabbing his kit from the car, he walked tiredly towards his office in the traffic building, yawning as he did so. Getting into the office, he wedged the door open with his kit bag, went into the kitchen area next to the office and made himself a cup of coffee. Walking back into his office, he looked at the pile of paperwork and reports that sat in his in-tray. In fact, all the Sergeants' desks had in-trays full of reports and other papers that were typical of all police forces. 'The pile never seems to get smaller!' he thought. Despite the fact that he was going to spend the next hour and a bit going through this lot, he could be assured that it would be the same size when he came back into work the following day.

Sitting down at his desk and firing up his computer, Jordan got down to trying to clear his paperwork. He unclipped his airwave radio from his jacket and set in on the desk in front of him on a low volume, so that he could just hear what was going on.

He'd only been working for a couple of minutes, when he heard one of his crews, Tango Four, being sent to a collision on Nene Valley Way, involving a car fire. 'Could be nasty,' he thought and turned the volume up slightly. These types of accidents had a tendency to escalate into something worse, in his experience. He continued to work.

Some minutes later his radio burst into life, with an incoming personal call. He answered it.

'What's up, Nick?' Nick was one of the crew he had heard being sent to the car fire.

'Just a heads up, Sarg.' He said. 'This bump has gone pear-shaped.'

'In what way?'

'Well, I don't want to say too much, other than you probably need to get out here to the scene. Car and truck involved.'

'OK, I'll tell control and make my way. Anything else I need to know?'

'Yeah… it's a fatal.'

'Roger–I'm en-route.'

Jordan terminated the call and rang the control room for further information. After that, he got back into his Volvo V70 D5 Estate, hit the blues and powered out of the station. 'Shit.' he thought, the bed and sleep he was hoping for now seemed a long way away. Fortunately, the scene was only across town and took him a few minutes with his blue lights and minimal traffic to get there. Jordan parked his vehicle away from the scene and walked up to his officer.

He saw that his other traffic crew had also arrived and the Collision Investigator was already setting up to take his measurements and photographs. Although the fire service was still damping down, the ambulance had already departed. Even Jordan could see that their services could not help the driver of the car, who appeared to be impaled on the steering wheel and had obviously died an agonising death.

Pork. He could smell pork. That was the over-riding sense that he got as he walked towards the car with his other officer. Others identified different pungent smells when human beings were burnt, but to him he always smelled of pork. 'One reason to become a vegetarian,' he thought. He'd rarely cook bacon at home, because it reminded him of so many fatals he had been to in the past. Didn't stop him eating it though.

'What have we got then?' he asked of Nick, as they walked towards the vehicles. Jordan saw that the DAF seventeen tonne, rigid, curtain-sided truck appeared to have ploughed into the car and had pushed it hard against the barrier. It also appeared that it was a high-speed collision for the truck to do so much damage, that the smaller car had burst into flames on contact.

Looking round the vehicles, he asked, 'where's the truck driver?'

'Buggered off, by all accounts,' Nick always did have a limited vocabulary and sometimes could be quite irreverent. Probably one of the reasons he had abstained from becoming a Family Liaison Officer.

'OK. Are we looking for him?'

'Yeah, the local boys are going round to the owner.'

'And do we know who the owner of the lorry is?'

'Yeah, you know that hi-jacking yesterday?' Jordan nodded. 'Well, it's that truck.'

'Shit…OK, well in that case we need to be looking for one Bingham Tyler, if it is that truck. Can't have got far, if he's legged it. Get onto the local Division and get searching the area. And let's get the chopper up, as well, to help with the search.'

'Right-o,' Nick said, and turned to walk back towards his patrol car, but Jordan stopped him.

'What about the car driver? Do we know who? Is it a he or a she? I can't actually tell.'

'Yes, we know who the driver is –and you're not going to like it.'

'Well, let's have it then.'

Nick screwed his face up a bit and took a breath before saying, 'PNC owner comes back as Dr Kirsty Kingsfield.'

Jordan hesitated slightly at that information. 'Kingsfield, the forensic pathologist?'

'Yup.'

'You're joking, aren't you?'

'Nope.'

'As if my night couldn't get any worse!' Jordan turned to look at the Golf with what remained of the driver, a cloud of sadness descended on him, out of concern for her family and that of her husband.

***

Jordan left the scene of the collision some three hours later, as the pathologist was arriving, only speaking to him briefly as he got into his patrol car. It was 10am. He was tired. He wanted to get home to bed and put the last 24 hours behind him, but a call from the Traffic Superintendent didn't help matters one little bit. He knew that it was all going to hit the fan once the news got out. How could a local criminal manage to kill one of our own? Jordan always considered that anyone whose life was involved in the emergency services were part of 'the family.' This was going to look bad for everyone. He assumed that the call was because they hadn't found Tyler and the truck earlier.

Back at Traffic HQ, Jordan stood outside Superintendent Rebecca Burnett's office on the second floor, passing the time of day with some small talk with

Burnett's PA. Jordan had worked with Burnett, when they were both constables on the traffic department. She'd always told him that she wanted to be the first female Traffic Superintendent and rising through the ranks as a Sergeant and as an Inspector, she had achieved her goal, but at great cost to her marriage and her wayward son. Ambition is no lover of family life, Jordan thought, as he waited for her outside her office.

At one time, he had had a hope that they could have been more than just colleagues. When you work together for eight to ten hours a day, it is often said that a traffic crew knows each other better than their own partners. It would seem, Jordan mused, that there might be something in that considering his current personal circumstance. Rebecca stepped out of her office, dressed in uniform, with white shirt, superintendents red and silver crowned epaulettes, uniform trousers and black shoes. She invited him into her office with a slight wave of her hand.

'Jake, come in, come in,' she said, indicating for him to take a seat in the comfortable chairs she had set up in the corner of her overly large blue-carpeted office. Jordan thought that this was a good sign. 'Not in for a bollocking, then.'

'So, Beccy, what's so urgent you need to see me, unless it's just my magnetic personality?' Jordan said, as he wearily dropped down in the chair opposite her.

'On this occasion, it's about work,' Rebecca replied with a weak smile. She sat back in her chair –the smile left her and she looked solemn. Jordan picked up from her that all was not right.

'This murder is a delicate situation for the force. We need to be careful who we're going to assign to certain tasks. Now, I know you were the man at the scene and I know that you should be the senior investigating officer, but under these circumstances, that will be me.'

'I don't have issues with that. It's only right and if you hadn't offered I'd have come and told you to,' he smiled.

'But,' she continued, 'I do need you involved and I need you to act as Family Liaison Officer to his wife. I think you are just the man for the job.'

'His wife? But I thought that, well, PNC said the Golf was owned by her.'

'That was the case, but the pathologist at the scene…'

'Yes, I saw him arrive as I was leaving, only spoke to him in passing.'

'The pathologist at the scene confirmed that the body is that of a male, while you were en-route to me here.'

'But there are far better officers for the FLO job than me,' Jordan said quickly.

Burnett leaned forwards in her chair and flashed a broad grin at him, as she pushed a lock of her auburn hair behind her left ear, not responding to his comment. There was a knock on the door and her secretary brought in two cups of coffee. 'This must really be bad,' He thought. He didn't usually get this sort of treatment, even from Beccy.

'Black, two sugars, if I remember, and you look as if you need it?' she said.

'Yeah, thanks.'

Studying the coffee in her cup, Burnett took a sip and Jordan could see that she was thinking about what she was going to say next. He noticed her taking a deep breath.

'This is a really bad, Jake. The male in the Golf is believed to be Jim Kingsfield.'

'Oh, shit! How did we miss that?'

'You didn't. Nobody knew he'd worked through the night.'

'How did we find out?'

'His wife rang the DCS. Fortunately he was aware of the collision, but not who it was and so he couldn't give her any information.'

'Has she been told?'

'No, that's your job.'

Jordan didn't reply.

'Look, Jake, everyone knew Jim in one respect or another. He was one of the good guys and some little shit, excuse me, has taken him from us. The Chief wants us to put everything we have into catching this bastard. I think you are the only person I trust with looking after his wife.'

Jordan leaned forward in the chair, holding his cup between both hands. He looked straight at Burnett. He could see that she had been crying. There were still some remnants of red, puffy eyes that she'd tried to conceal.

'OK,' he said. 'Who else is in on the team?'

'Nobody–yet. The only people who know are those at the scene, me, the Chief and DCS MIT.'

Jordan knew that Kingsfield had been on the MIT for a couple of years, but in that time he had gained the respect of his colleagues and was an effective detective, so it was only right that the Detective Chief Superintendent, Major Incident Team, should conduct the criminal investigation, while Burnett conducted the collision investigation. Burnett got up and walked to the window, where she stood in silence for a few minutes. The mood in the office had changed considerably.

Interrupting the silence, Jordan said, 'we need to get Doctor Kingsfield told then. I wouldn't want her to find Jim lying on a slab, as she walked through the front door, not that she'd probably recognise him anyway. Why have we kept it from her this long?'

'No reason. We were just finding the right person to do the trauma message and that, as I have said, is you. And she won't find him in her mortuary–he's been taken to the John Radcliffe. So he's outside our area and her morgue. We have another forensic pathologist, who is going to do the Post-Mortem on the remains.'

Both stood looking out across the fields from her office window, with coffee cups in hand and keeping any further thoughts private. Then Jordan said, 'forgive me Beccy, but when we were crewed together you had a bloke. You wouldn't tell me who it was.'

Burnett kept her head forward and continued looking out of the window. 'It was him, wasn't it?' Jordan could see tears welling up in the corners of her eyes. She nodded and quickly turned away. He just wanted to take her in his arms and comfort her, but he knew that he could no longer do that, even though he had done the same thing countless times before, when times were bad for both of them. Jordan drained his coffee and placed the cup on the table.

'I'll get on with it then,' he said, walking towards the door.

'Thanks, Jake,' was all Burnett replied quietly.

Chapter 24

Jordan quietly left Burnett's office, carefully shutting the door and leaving her with her thoughts. He felt sad –his mood had changed considerably. It was flat when he left the scene. The knowledge that the person in the car was Jim Kingsfield made him even more dejected. But he was also unhappy for Dr Kingsfield and it was also a sad day for the Force. 'Why did we not see this coming?' he wondered. 'Somebody must have had some idea that Jim was on this idiot's hit list.' Subdued, Jordan left the carpeted executive suite of traffic headquarters, stepping through the glass doorway into the corridor that divides those who command from those who do not.

He was determined to pass the trauma message to Dr Kingsfield as quickly as possible and certainly before the press got hold of it, if they hadn't already. He looked at his watch. It had just turned 11:15am. Jim Kingsfield had been dead for nearly six hours and Jordan felt even more exhausted.

He followed the plain walled corridor adorned with pictures of old traffic scenes and traffic vehicles, then began to walk down the stairs, taking him to the rear of the Headquarters complex and back to his car. As he was about descend the stairs, his name was called.

'Jordan! Jake, wait up.'

Rebecca Burnett was walking swiftly down the corridor towards him. He saw that she had her hat and coat on. It was also nice to see that the traffic jacket she was wearing wasn't in the pristine condition of those generally worn by senior officers. He smiled at the thought of a police superintendent crawling under a goods vehicle to check the tachograph seals on the gear box, coning lanes off on the motorway and other jobs a traffic cop would do and he had seen her do these things on more than one occasion since her promotion.

'What are you doing, Beccy?' he asked, as she got closer to him.

'I can't let you do this one your own and, if I recall, is it not the responsibility of the Senior Investigator and the FLO to deliver such news?'

'It is —but do you think you should, knowing your history and all?'

'Kirsty knows who I am and what I was to Jim. Jim told her when we met a long time ago, that we 'stepped out' together. A quaint phrase, don't you think?' she smiled. 'She took the view that it was in the past and long before she met him. She didn't worry about it as far as I am aware.'

'OK.' he said, as he started to descend the stairs. 'Only if you're sure?'

'Yes, it'll be fine. Anyway, it's good to get out of the office, whatever the reason.'

Burnett had already determined where Kirsty was and that she had contacted the Detective Chief Superintendent again, enquiring about Kingsfield. The DCS did not give anything away.

It was a short trip from force headquarters to the hospital mortuary complex. They found Kirsty at work consulting some x-rays she'd attached to the light-box in her office. She had an open door policy. The door was half open when Jordan and Burnett arrived. Jordan tapped politely on the door.

Kirsty turned to see Jordan and Burnett. He saw the blood visibly drain from Kirsty's face. Her legs gave way a bit and Jordan stepped in to help her to the sofa in her office.

Jordan began talking to Kirsty as they say down. He became acutely aware that Kirsty had put two and two together.

'It's about Jim, isn't it?' she asked.

They both nodded slowly.

'I thought as much. Marland was too cagey when I spoke to him the second time. I knew something was wrong. Is he OK? Where is he?

'I don't know how I'm going to do this,' thought Jordan. 'This is the hardest thing I have ever had to do.' He could feel the welling of sorrow deep within him and it was difficult for him to maintain his composure. After all, he had worked with him and as he looked towards Beccy, he could see that she too was finding it extremely difficult. Jordan cleared his throat before speaking, but Kirsty had picked up on their mood. 'Tell me quickly Jake, is he alive or dead?' Beccy looked at Jordan, as he was about to speak.

'I'm sorry,' said Beccy, moving closer to her to comfort her. 'Jim died at the scene.'

'How?' asked Kirsty, who by now was crying.

As Kirsty wept, Jordan and Burnett gently and sensitively told her about the incident and collision involving her husband. Burnett offered her some tissues, which she took, wiping her eyes and face. As he watched and as they talked, Jordan was certain that he could physically see her heart break.

***

At lunchtime, DCS Marland marched into the Incident Room, where all his team had gathered. He had just come from a briefing with the Chief Constable and Superintendent Burnett. The news he was about to give was the most solemn duty he had ever had to perform. Never in his career had he needed to tell his officers that a multiple murderer had killed one of their own and he thought that at all costs, he must remained composed.

DS Dave Heart was sitting on the desk at the front of the Incident Room.

'I can't get any response from the DI,' said Heart to the Detective Support Officer.

'What about his HA?' enquired Jill.

'No reply, even rang the mortuary only to be told by Anton that Dr Kingsfield was unavailable at the moment.'

'Did he say anything else?'

'No, didn't give any other information at all – very strange. The DCS won't be pleased if he's not here.'

'When did you see him last?'

'Yesterday evening, said he was going to work late, wanted to get a better handle on this Smyth murder, but in all honesty I think we've got it well and truly wrapped up.'

He was going to try once more, concerned that he was not able to contact his boss and friend, as Marland asked for everyone's attention.

As the DCS stood at the front of the incident room, the raucous chatter became more subdued. The mere look on the DCS's face was enough to calm everyone down. They had all seen that face before and it was never followed by good news.

'Colleagues,' began Marland.

'Strange sort of start,' thought Heart.

'I've called this meeting to pass you some very grave news. I have just come from a meeting with the Chief Constable and the Head of Traffic, Superintendent Burnett. It saddens me to inform you that Detective Inspector Jim Kingsfield died this morning in a road accident, while on his way home at about 05:30.'

There were a few gasps and murmers around the room. Marland raised his hand to silence the room, as they listened to the DCS, the information he passed on to them sent the room cold and even quieter. Unusually, in the incident room you could hear a pin drop.

'Unfortunately,' Marland continued, 'the perpetrator of this collision is known to us and we are treating this incident as a cold-blooded murder.'

Silence still pervaded the room –even the computers seemed to go quieter out of respect for what was being said.

'Traffic and SOCO at the scene have determined that this was a deliberate act. Preliminary investigation also shows that there are a number of witnesses to what occurred, but none of them offered any help.' Murmurs followed, as Burnett and Jordan arrived and moved silently to stand against the back wall of the room. Marland acknowledged them with a nod and continued.

'The Chief, quite rightly, is taking a personal interest in this investigation and he has said that our department will work together with the traffic department.'

Some detective constables visibly cringed at that thought.

'To that end, I have asked Superintendent Burnett to come and give you an update on where we are with the Traffic side of the investigation.'

He waved Burnett and Jordan forward.

'Thank you, Colin,' Burnett said, as she walked briskly towards the front of the room.

'Morning, everyone. Most of you know me and some of you know Sgt Jordan at the back there.'

Jordan acknowledged everyone with a raise of his hand, as they turned to look at him, before turning their attention back to Burnett.

'In our meeting with the Chief, it was decided that the details of the collision will be investigated by my expert forensic collision investigators, some of whom are still at the scene. The road is closed and will be for some time. Scenes of Crime Units are also in attendance, along with a forensic pathologist from another area. The road will also remain closed until such time as the structural engineers have determined the safety of the over-bridge and barriers. Sgt Jordan will be the Family Liaison Officer for this tragic event. In fact, we have just come from Dr Kingsfield's office. As you would expect, she is devastated by this news and is being comforted by her family. Both Sergeant Jordan and I are concerned about her welfare, not just because of her husband's death, but also because of the criminal who committed this. I understand,' she continued, 'from what I have already been told that we are looking for one man in this case. One Bingham Tyler and...'

'That bastard! Sorry ma'am. I knew he'd have something to do with this. Said as much at our last meeting!' interjected Heart.

'You know this man?' Burnett said.

'Yes ma'am, long story.'

'OK, tell me about it, later.'

He nodded in agreement.

Burnett continued. 'I also understand that he had hijacked the vehicle he used to commit this dreadful act on DI Kingsfield from a haulage company in town, some of you and Sgt Jordan went to yesterday.' A few nods from around the room. 'As I understand it, you will be conducting an investigation into this company and their dealings with Tyler.'

'I've already started to collate information on Tyler and his associates, ma'am, after the photograph of him was identified,' said the Detective Support Officer.

'OK, good, we need to pool all our info on this man– see if we can smoke him out.' Burnett finished her briefing and moved aside for Marland.

'Chief wants a swift result–so do I. As I'm sure we all do, but I don't want any mavericks going after Tyler.

We've lost one of our own. We don't want to lose another one.' added Marland.

'What do we know about him already?' Burnett asked the room.

Several DCs and Dave Heart explained the history about Tyler to Burnett. Other officers who had information from a history of Tyler's previous convictions through to the information gained from the social services, also came forward with their own known information.

'I take it we are looking at the fostering angle?' asked Marland.

'Got Stevens and Okenewu down in London doing enquiries as we speak, Sir,' replied Heart.

'Has anyone told them what has happened up here?' enquired Marland.

'Don't think so, Sir,' said Heart.

'OK, Heart, get on to that will you? Just give them the basics, so they don't do anything rash when they get back. Right,' Marland continued, 'Any questions at this point?'

Heads shook. Some mouthed the words no, but most were too stunned to think about questions after the news they had just been given.

'OK, thanks, everyone. Let's knuckle down and find this little shit, before he does any more damage,' added Marland, as he re-buttoned his jacket ready to return to his office. He crossed the room to Dave Heart and gave him some instructions as to what to do with Kingsfield's effects. Jordan and Burnett had been quietly talking to some other detectives, as Marland walked over to them.

'You OK with all this, Rebecca?' asked Marland. Only the few got to call her Beccy.

'Yes, fine, Colin. We'll do our bit, don't you worry.'

'I'm counting on you and your department to work closely. You never know, it may be the start of a beautiful friendship.'

'What? Traffic and CID? You are joking, aren't you Colin?'

The laughter that followed the remark lightened the mood in the office a little. It had been a bad day, really bad, and it had only just started.

Chapter 25

Jordan's extra night shift had passed well into the day following Kingsfield's murder, the intimation of death to Dr Kirsty Kingsfield and the briefing with Marland. By late afternoon, Jordan had managed to get back home for some well-earned rest, before his wife arrived home from work.

Funny that she never mentioned anything about the incident with her boss –when he found her in his arms – comforting him. He couldn't believe that she had breezed into the house as if nothing had happened - nothing different. Probably to her nothing was different. 'How long had this affair been going on?' he wondered. 'Never said anything, never said a word' Jordan thought. Even though he was too tired to bring the subject up himself, it still weighed heavily on his mind. And even if he had brought it up he would have got very angry, very quickly and may have made matters worse.

He still could not believe it. He thought his marriage would survive anything after the discovery of not being able to have children and helping Rosie through that trauma. Quite obviously, this was not going to be the case and he didn't really know what to do. He quickly made himself a sandwich. He didn't really feel like it, but he hadn't had anything since meeting his crews on the motorway service area at 2.30am for breakfast. He looked at his watch –over twelve hours since his last proper meal! With these thoughts and those of the difficult case he was about to embark upon, he made his way up the stairs to their bedroom. He stripped off and had a long, hot shower, collapsing on the bed afterwards. He went out like a light.

The banging of the front door woke him in the twilight of the day. He looked at the bedside clock - 6.15pm - he'd been out for a good three hours.

Lying in the semi-darkness, he listened. He could hear Rosie downstairs, clattering noisily around the kitchen. Probably putting shopping away, he thought, and still acting normally. Well, I don't suppose she could do much else. He decided to stay where he was and closed his eyes.

Some thirty minutes later, the light in the bedroom came on and Rosie ushered her way into the bedroom with a large mug of tea for Jordan.

'Thought you might like a cup of tea,' said Rosie, as she placed the cup on the bedside table.

'Thanks,' was all that Jordan could manage in reply, while still half asleep.

Humming something quite nondescript to herself, Rosie left the bedroom and went back downstairs.

'Still acting like normal,' thought Jordan.

He lifted himself half up from the bed on one arm and reached for his tea. He could still hear Rosie downstairs, humming away to herself.

The humming stopped.

The TV went on.

The humming was replaced by a low murmur, which Jordan could hear from the kitchen below the bedroom.

He got up from the bed and threw on his dressing gown and went downstairs.

He walked into the kitchen and saw Rosie sitting at the kitchen table. The low murmur he heard was Rosie talking on her mobile phone.

Surprised by Jordan's appearance, Rosie quickly finished the call with a 'gotta go.' snapping her phone shut.

'Was that him?' Jordan asked irritated.

'Yes, it was.'

'Arranging your next assignation, no doubt?' Jordan responded with a snarl. Rosie just stared at him and said nothing.

'Well?'

'Well, what?'

'You have no intention of discussing this, have you?'

'I don't see that there is anything to discuss, do you?' Jordan looked at Rosie with incredulity.

'Jesus, you really know how to piss me off.'

'Well, you've pissed me off plenty of times.'

'Oh, so now we're into children's games are we?'

'No, it's just that there is NOTHING for us to discuss.'

'So, do you think our marriage is over then?'

'Yes.'

'And you don't want to work it out?'

'NO.'

'Why?'

'It just won't work out –you've only got to see some of our other friends who tried to patch it up to see what sort of a mess they're in.'

'Fine, if that's the way you feel, perhaps there is nothing to discuss then.'

Jordan stuffed his hands in the pockets of his dressing gown and turned to leave the kitchen.

'Jacob?' Rosie said, less defensively.

'I'm sorry, I really am.'

'Not as sorry as me, I can assure you that this is something that isn't going to go away you know. You've dropped yourself into a snake pit with that man. I just hope it works out for you.'

Silence.

'How long's it been going on?' Jordan sat down at the kitchen table opposite her.

Rosie stared at the table, squirming a little in her seat, but did not answer.

'Answer me!' Jordan raised his voice for the first time, rapping his knuckles on the kitchen table, making Rosie jump.

'I'll ask you again. How long has this been going on?'

Rosie quickly pushed the kitchen chair backward and stood up.

'No,' exclaimed Jordan, 'You're not going to walk away from this.' He got up out of his chair and blocked the kitchen doorway. 'SIT DOWN!'

'Hey, you're not interviewing one of your suspects now, you know.'

'I may as well be, for all the good it's doing.'

'Well, are you going to answer or not?'

Rosie, meekly sat down at the kitchen table, followed by Jordan. She put her head in her hands, and then removed a lock of her hair that had fallen across her face. Jordan had sat down opposite her again, staring hard at her, waiting for a response.

'About six months, I suppose,' Rosie finally replied.

'Six months! Jesus –do you love him?'

'I don't know.'

'You don't know? You don't know? Christ, he's been shagging your arse off for six months and you don't know!' Jordan was getting more and more angry at Rosie's responses, or lack of them.

'You don't have to be crude, Jacob,' Rosie came back at him immediately.

'OK, I'm sorry, but how else am I to look at it. Why, Rosie? Why?'

Not looking into Jordan's eyes, but staring off somewhere in the middle distance, Rosie considered her reply.

'I felt alone, unwanted – I felt –unloved.' She glared at Jordan in defiance. 'Other women my age look after their children –we don't. I spend my days sitting alone in an office at work and then I come home to an empty house, because you're at work, or working late. It depresses me Jacob, and –Adam –took that loneliness away.'

Rosie got up from the table and took a tissue from the box on the kitchen side, drying her eyes. She leant against the kitchen unit. Sobbing, she said, 'all, I ever wanted –was –a family –to love a husband –children –so I could love them back. Now I have –nothing.'

Jordan thought for a moment. 'If you think that you are going to turn this around and make it my fault, Rosie, you have another thing coming.'

'It is your fault, it's your bloody job, that's whose fault it is!'

'That's bollocks and you know it!'

'Don't you swear at me again,' Rosie raised her voice from the quiet tones that she had been using.

'If I want to swear, I think I have a fucking right to – don't you? Why the hell didn't you say something?'

'I didn't know where to start. I was overwhelmed by what was going on –the attention Adam gave me –and by the time I realised it was too late.'

'We've always managed to talk things through, Rosie, what's different?' Jordan said, softening somewhat.

'Because this is too big for me to cope with and I knew deep down that it would break our marriage, but it all got out of hand and I didn't know what to do.'

'Your dammed right that it's a marriage breaker. I thought you had more self-control, I thought we had something good between us –clearly I was wrong.' Any softness in Jordan's voice was now gone. Clearly riled by the conversation, he stood up from the kitchen table, pushing the chair noisily back.

'I'm sorry.'

'Sorry? Sorry doesn't cover it Rosie. How did you think I was going to react? When I saw you in his arms,

I just wanted to punch the bastard and give you a good slap, too. I thought our marriage was strong because of what we have been through, but now I see that it's all been a farce. I have to talk to mates at work about their marital problems and how it effects their work. I didn't think it would happen to us!'

Jordan pushed himself away from the kitchen table. He walked up to Rosie and stood directly in front of her. Pointing an index finger at her, he said, 'as I see it you have two options: one –stop seeing him and we'll try and work this out or two: leave!'

Rosie broke down. Jordan left her crying in the kitchen. He went back upstairs and threw on some clothes. Leaving the house in a fury, he slammed the front door as he did so. The silence that descended on the house was only accentuated by Rosie's quiet sobs.

Chapter 26

The day after the argument with Rosie, Jordan, with a thumping headache after the beer he'd consumed in his local pub out of anger and frustration, parked the unmarked police Mitsubishi Eno outside Kirsty Kingsfield's apartment. For a change, the morning was bright and sunny making the windows in Kirsty's apartment block sparkle, giving it a sense of ambient energy that Jordan certainly wasn't feeling.

The task for Jordan this morning was always more palatable when the sun was shining, despite his fatigue and the revelation of his own marital problems, he thought. He walked up to the front steps of her apartment. The long, two storey sandstone building used to be a major shoe factory in the town, employing a workforce of hundreds in its heyday. The large oak double doors in front of Jordan appeared to be the originals, but probably weren't.

He pressed the buzzer that just said, 'KINGSFIELD,' and waited for a response. Whilst waiting, he could not help but notice the CCTV camera on the opposite side of the street that had been pointing at their apartment. He had seen some of the footage that Tyler had kept on his computer. 'Deviant bastard,' he thought. But now the camera had its head bowed, as if sulking like a schoolboy caught doing something wrong.

The door clicked open, inviting Jordan in. He went up to the top floor apartment and rang the doorbell. The door was answered almost immediately.

Kirsty answered the door in a towelling robe and jogging bottoms. It looked as if she had been in them since she had received news of Kingsfield's death. He had tried to contact her a number of times, but she had not been answering the phone.

As a family liaison officer, he was was used to the relatives dealing with their bereavement in many different ways. Some cut themselves off from everyone, others gather their family around them and then find it difficult to let them go, knowing that they would be left on their own and some seek solace in religion. But humans are social animals we do not like to be left alone for too long a time. At some stage we all need to talk to someone, whether it's about our experience or just to keep company. He was not one to push her into talking. In time, she would come round.

She invited him in and, asking more sternly than she intended, said, 'what do you want, Jake?' Kirsty walked into the room and sat down on the long sofa.

'I need to know that you're OK and if there is anything I can do to help?' he answered, as he followed her. She invited him to sit in the chair to her right.

'I just want to know why?'

'Because it's my job.'

'No,' she replied, 'not why you're here–why has this happened?'

'I don't know,' he replied carefully.

He didn't really know how to answer the question that he has been asked at almost every FLO job he'd been to. Experience had taught him not to speculate or tell them that it was the 'will of God' or that they'd 'gone to a better place.'

'Have you found this Tyler prick yet?' she asked.

He was slightly surprised at the use of the expletive, but under the circumstances felt that it was appropriate.

'No, not yet, but I think we are close.'

'Well, tell me when you do, because I'm going to kill the bastard for taking my husband away from me.'

Tears welled up in her eyes and Jordan saw that she was desperately trying to hold them back. She pulled a tissue from the almost empty box that was on the table in front of her.

'I think that you may have to join the queue,' Jordan said. 'There is no easy way to say this, but I need you to come with me. There are some things that I need to show you. Things that you need to identify for us.'

'I cannot go into work, into my mortuary, knowing that he is there and not see him.' she said.

'He's not there, Kirsty. He is elsewhere. He has never been in your mortuary. We would not do that, knowing that is where you went to work every day.'

'Thank you for that,' she sniffed and blew her nose again.

Then she asked quietly, 'what do you need me to do then?'

'Well, there are some personal effects that we need you to identify.'

Kirsty looked down. Her shoulders dropped and she was even more deflated at that request. Jake thought how vulnerable she seemed and wondered whether he should have asked her. But she was the only one who could identify Kingsfield's effects.

After a long silence, she said quietly, 'alright, do you want me to do it right away?'

'Not if you don't want to, but it needs to be soon –for the Coroner. You understand?'

'Yes, I do, yes. But, can you give me an hour or so? I've not been looking after myself over the last couple of days. Even my mum commented on that before she and dad left last night,' she gave a nervous laugh.

'An hour is fine. Do you want me to come back then?'

'No, it's OK. You can wait.'

She went over to the kitchen area and showed Jordan where the coffee and tea was.

'Here,' she said, 'you can make a coffee or tea while you wait, if you like.'

'OK, if you don't mind me waiting.'

'No, not at all.'

Kirsty left the kitchen and headed off to her bedroom. Jordan heard the shower go on. He glanced around the apartment. With its modern furnishings, the big leather sofa dominating the living space and a large pine occasional table in front of it, it was very minimalistic. There were professional forensic and legal journals, interspersed with 'OK' magazine, a 'Radio Times' and the Force newspaper. On one side of the room was a bookshelf that reached to the ceiling. He wandered over to look at it and found an eclectic mix of both professional and personal favourites. A copy of 'The Encyclopaedia of Forensic and Legal medicine', sat next to a row of Peter James novels. He went into the Shaker-style kitchen area, with its large island unit, separating the living area from the kitchen, switched the kettle on and made himself a coffee.

After and hour or so, Kirsty appeared from the bedroom. She was dressed in a black suit, dark blue blouse and her hair had been tied up in a pony tail. 'Such a transformation,' Jordan thought. In fact, he was quite alarmed by his reaction to her, as he watched her walk from the bedroom toward him. It made him realise what Kingsfield saw in her and Jordan found himself extremely attracted to this forensic pathologist.

'OK, I think I'm ready for this,' she said.

Jordan nodded and they left the apartment. The drive to the John Radcliffe Hospital was subdued, only interspersed with some small talk. Jordan could see that Kirsty was deep in thought, watching the scenery pass by out of the passenger side window. There was no doubt in Jordan's mind that Kirsty was attempting to keep the tears at bay, as he glanced at her occasionally as he was driving.

Arriving at the hospital, they made their way to the mortuary, which was situated at the end of a long corridor with bright pale yellow painted walls.

'I wish the walls of my mortuary were as bright as this,' Kirsty spoke quietly, as they both walked along the corridor towards a set of double doors that led directly into the cutting room. The attendant met Jordan and Kirsty at the door. He escorted them to another part of the mortuary. He explained that what they had come to identify had been laid out behind the doors he indicated. The attendant withdrew to an appropriate distance from the pair, as Jordan stood quietly behind Kirsty. He saw that she was visibly composing herself for what she was about to do.

'Normally this is my domain, and although this is not my mortuary, I've always felt comfortable in any mortuary that I've visited in the past. But this is different,' she thought, bleakly. 'Today is different. Every day will be different from now on.' She bowed her head, trying to remain composed as Jordan leaned toward her.

'Are you ready?' he asked quietly.

Kirsty took a deep breath and nodded almost imperceptibly. Jordan stepped in front of her and gently pushed the door open. They entered a room that was no more than ten foot square. A stainless steel utility table had been placed in the centre of the room. There were curtains in each corner of the room but they had not been pulled around the plain walls. There was nothing to disguise what the room was used for.

Kirsty moved slowly towards the table, where she could see several items, charred, melted and almost unrecognisable, except for a couple of things: the gold watch she had bought him for their first anniversary and his wedding ring. She knew she shouldn't, but she picked both of them up.

The officer who had been standing in the shadows, guarding Kingsfield's belongings, had only acknowledged their entry, went to move forward to prevent Kirsty from picking them up. He was intercepted by Jordan, who looked at him and quickly shook his head, indicating not to interfere. The officer stepped back into the shadows.

Jordan said, 'Is there anything here that you recognise as belonging to your husband?'

Kirsty indicated the ring and the watch. She briefly explained how she recognised them, showing her wedding band against his. She slowly put the items back on the table. She let out a long and deep sigh and began to cry. Jordan, comforting her, led her out of the room and took her back to her apartment.

The journey back to the apartment was made in silence. Kirsty had kept quiet, with just the occasional sniff and a few tears. But when she got out of the car, she seemed to have composed herself. Jordan could see that the grief was only just hidden under the surface of that composure.

'Are you going to be OK?' he asked her as they walked into her apartment. 'Do you need me to call anyone to come and be with you?'

'No, I'll be alright, but, do you have to go straight away?' she asked.

'Not if you don't want me to. I can stay for a little while longer.'

'Only –only there is something I need to ask you.'

'OK, what would that be then?'

Kirsty offered him a seat on the sofa. She sat down next to him.

'Too close.' he thought or was it just his imagination?

'I want… no, need to be involved in the investigation,' she said.

'You know that can't happen, Kirsty.'

'Look, the investigation needs me from a forensic point of view. I don't want to be left out in the cold, wondering what's going on. And besides, I need to do something to take my mind off things. It won't, I know, but I think I'll be better off at work.'

'You could go and stay with your mum and dad for a few days, while we sort things out.'

'You've got to be kidding! I'd be smothered to death. I don't know which is worse, moping around here or being offered endless cups of tea and my parents not daring to say anything in case it's the wrong thing. No, Jake, I need to be involved.'

The little smile she gave brightened her face and was the first smile that Jordan had seen since the beginning of this terrible ordeal for her.

'I can't see that there will be anything that you can do as the pathologist. It's a difficult situation, I grant you, but I don't see them agreeing to you being involved. You are far too close to the investigation, they will say, you are… sorry…the victim here.'

'I understand, but you could ask, couldn't you?'

'I could ask, yes, but my role as your liaison is to keep you informed about how the investigation progresses.'

They sat in silence for a moment. Jordan could see that Kirsty was disappointed.

'Look,' he said, trying to placate her feelings. 'I'm not promising anything, but I'll ask. I'll talk to Beccy first. OK?'

'Thanks, Jake, I'm sure she will understand.'

In an effort to move the subject away from the investigation, Jordan asked, 'what about you? Who is Dr

Kirsty Kingsfield? I'll need the info for my liaison officers report, you understand.' He gave a broad smile.

'How much do you want to know? There's not a lot to tell.'

'Anything. Anything to take your mind off all this.'

Kirsty started to tell Jordan more about her. How she had always wanted to be a doctor, but later found forensics more fascinating so became a forensic pathologist after she qualified. It was a lot of hard work, she explained, as there are very few females in the job. She told him how she met Kingsfield at a crime conference and that they seemed to instinctively know they were good for each other.

They talked long into the evening. Jordan gave Kirsty a bit of history about himself, too. He told her that he had joined the police force after a string of menial jobs. Tried to get into the Army, but they changed his mind. Decided to try for the police and joined the force about fifteen years ago, took his sergeant's exam and here he was. Always wanted to drive fast cars though, which is why he liked the traffic department. Best job in the police, he concluded.

At the end of the evening, both seemed a little more relaxed. The talk between them had done them both good, Kirsty thought, as she relaxed a little after the trauma of the day. She sensed that she could feel safe in the hands of this traffic sergeant and instinctively knew that she could trust him.

Chapter 27

'*What are you doing, Bing?*'

'Completing my task, that's what I am doing.'

'*Why can you not give it up?*'

'Because I intend to make sure that nothing exists of my adversary and that means getting rid of the bitch, as well.'

'*You should not be doing this. You have done enough.*'

'No, I must.'

'*You must give this up.*'

'I cannot! It is in me now. It is like an addiction.'

'*You are addicted to what you want or just to the violence?*'

'Both.'

'*Then you need to be helped.*'

'I don't want to be helped.'

'*You must get help, Bing, you must. It will end badly. Do you want to die?*'

'I am not going to die! You sound as if you are someone different.'

'*That's because, we are. I am different to you. We are better than you, with feelings, feelings of remorse, feelings of sadness, not you with your anger, bitterness and hatred of all who do things against you. YOU MUST STOP THIS!*'

'Well, you know what they say?'

'*Who are they, Bing?*'

'How the fuck should I know? But if you've got an itch and I have, then you have to scratch it.'

'*But it's not an itch, is it, Bing? It is your vendetta. A drive to end someone's life. Your remorseless, cold and ruthless quest for misplaced justice, not just once, but by*' *all accounts at least three times. And you want to do another one. You are an evil man and I will do everything in my power to stop you.'*

'You cannot do anything!'

'You are talking with yourself. Look at the people walking past you, looking at you as you talk to us. They see no one. Just you. That is enough for some people to ring the police –some tramp sitting in a doorway talking to himself, sitting across the road from the home of a policeman, who you have just murdered, Bing. Murdered, murdered, murdered.'

'Shut up,' screamed Bingham. A couple walking past the doorway noticed Bingham sitting there and gave him a hard stare.

'What are you staring at? Fuck off!' he said to them, as they scurried away.

Having lost his electronic sight, Bingham had decided to camp out in a doorway across the road from the Kingsfield's apartment. He had not been able to go back to his own apartment for fear of being caught, so he'd stolen a coat from a market stall earlier in the day. The stall-holder chased him, but he soon gave up on him.

Bingham had seen Jake Jordan arrive and enter the apartment.

'Her husband's not even cold yet and she's already seeing another copper bastard,' he mumbled to himself.

'He's only doing his job, Bing, to ease her through the pain you have caused her by murdering her husband.'

'It was his own fault! He shouldn't have put me away.'

'You did wrong, Bing. You committed a crime. Crime must be punished.'

'Just go away, will you? I've heard enough of your crap for one day.'

He sat down in the doorway, waiting for an opportunity to strike. His mind was in turmoil, with the need to complete what he had set out to do.

He still had Kingsfield's baton, tucked away in his pocket. This was the only weapon he had, but it would have to do. He was sure he would be able to find something else if he needed it.

He waited all night outside Kingsfield's apartment, waiting for Jordan to leave and someone else to go into the block. The following morning after sleeping fitfully in the doorway, he saw a man enter through the front doors. As he crossed the road the man seemed oblivious to Bingham's presence, chatting away on his mobile phone. Bingham tailgated him into the apartment foyer and made his way to Kingsfield's top floor apartment.

It was 8.30am, when he knocked loudly on the apartment door. He hoped that she would just open the door and he would be able to burst in. But luck was not on his side.

'Who is it?' Kirsty shouted from behind the closed and locked door. Bingham thought quickly.

'Delivery for Dr Kingsfield,' he said in his best post-man voice. He had put his finger over the spyglass in the door, so she would have to open the door to see who it was. He hoped that she would open the door, so that he could force his way in. She did, but the chain was on. He kicked out at the door as it was opened, to try to smash through the chain and take her unawares. Again, luck was not on his side. His kick did nothing to the door. Kirsty screamed and tried to shut the door, but his foot was in the way. He charged at the door again and again, until the chain came away.

Kirsty ran into the kitchen to grab her phone and dialled 999. She managed to get to the police call handler, before he was on her. Bingham came up behind her and brought the baton down heavily on her shoulder, causing her to lose her balance. She fell onto her knees and dropped the phone. He grabbed her hair and dragged her into the living area. She was screaming and trying to get him to relinquish his grip.

'The more you struggle, the worse it will get, bitch!' he shouted at her through gritted teeth.

He threw her onto the sofa and hit her around the face several times, as he screamed at her to shut up. Kirsty screamed all the more loudly, trying to attract the attention of other residents. Nobody came to help.

With one final punch in the face, Kirsty dropped, semi-conscious onto the sofa.

Calmer now, Bingham said, 'That's better, isn't it?'

'You tell me, Bing.'

'Piss off,' he mumbled.

Bingham ripped the ties from the nearest curtain and straddled her body. Tying her hands at the same time, Bingham could feel a fullness growing in his trousers, as he ground his pelvis into hers. He was laughing, as he moved down towards her feet to tie them as well, but an unexpected upper-cut from Kirsty's bound hands caught Bingham's chin, which smashed his teeth into his tongue causing it to bleed. He struck her again, as there was a knock on the door.

'Kirsty?' It was Jordan. After their talk the previous evening, he was concerned about her being on her own in the apartment, knowing that Kingsfield's killer was still on the loose. He had arranged to visit Beccy Burnett and had called around to collect Kirsty. Even if Beccy hadn't wanted to see her, he would still have visited her, thought Jordan.

Jordan noticed the broken chain on the door. 'Kirsty, you OK?'

Jordan removed his pepper spray from his jacket and flicked the top. He placed his finger over the trigger and held it, hidden in his hand.

Bingham quickly pulled Kirsty up and clamped his hand over her mouth. She kicked out trying to make as much noise as she could, as he dragged her over to the kitchen area. He picked up a kitchen knife from the knife block on the side. He'd managed to do this, as Jordan appeared in the main apartment. Bingham held the knife to Kirsty's throat. Jordan stopped in his tracks.

'Bingham, what the hell are you doing?'

'Finishing what I started,' he growled.

'What do you mean?'

Jordan could see that Kirsty was in no fit state. The bruises on her face were beginning to show and her right eye was already closed. He saw that Bingham had his right hand over her mouth, his left hand holding a knife against her throat.

'I,' he said shouting, 'am going to leave here and you are not going to stop me.'

'You are not leaving here. There are others on the way.' Jordan desperately hoped that there might be. 'Traffic cops don't usually get caught up in this sort of shit,' he thought. 'Let's remain calm, shall we?' Jordan said, more for himself than Bingham. He looked at Kirsty and noticed she was trying indicate with her good eye to tell him something was on the floor near to her. He looked to his left and saw her mobile phone lying on the floor, just out of sight of Bingham. He saw that it was on an open call and he could make out the three 999 digits. Someone else was on the way, he thought.

'And what are you going to do with her, if I let you leave?'

'Oh, you will let me leave, or I'll slit her throat here and now. But she'll get the same treatment as her husband bastard.'

'I can't let that happen.'

'Well, believe me when I tell you that it is happening,' said Bingham, as he forced the knife harder against Kirsty's throat, making it bleed.

Jordan tried to take a couple of steps closer.

'Back off,' said Bingham threateningly.

'Why can't we talk about this sensibly, Bingham?'

'Because sensible doesn't come into it any more. I'm too far gone for that!'

Bingham had calmed down a little and Jordan thought that he almost resembled a different person. His face became more calm and not angry looking. He seemed to visibly relax slightly.

'But if you stop now,' he said, 'we can work something out.'

'You do talk a load of bollocks.'

The aggressive Bingham returned. It was then that Bingham noticed the pepper spray in Jordan's hand. He forced the knife harder against Kirsty's throat. More blood.

'I think you better put that down,' Bingham said, indicating that he had seen the spray can in Jordan's hand.

'Not going to happen,' Jordan said.

Bingham started to drag himself and Kirsty towards the front door. He held her tighter and tighter. She started to struggle more - he could see the determination in her eyes that told him that she was going to fight to get released from his grip. As Bingham tried to move closer to the door of the apartment, Jordan saw that they were now in range of his pepper spray.

Bingham still had a firm grip across Kirsty's mouth, but suddenly she decided to make a break for it towards Jordan. Both of them seemed to know what the other was about to do. Kirsty bit hard into Bingham's hand. He loosened his hold. She slid out from under his grip while at the same time Jordan raised his spray and pointed it in the direction of Bingham. The action was done too quickly for Bingham to react. He only managed to move his head slightly. The full force of the spray missed his eyes by mere fractions. Still, some of it found the spot. He did the wrong thing and started rubbing his eyes. Jordan took advantage and ran at him, both crashing to the apartment floor. Although Bingham was no match for Jordan, the fight was brutal and determined. Bingham tried in desperation to find the knife he had dropped, when Jordan had peppered him. Jordan was determined that he would not get hold of it or Kingsfield's baton, which was lying where Bingham had left it on the sofa.

The fight seemed to go on forever. Kirsty remembered the phone was on the floor. She crawled along the floor, bleeding heavily from the cuts to her neck and managed to retrieve the phone. She saw that the line was still open. She shouted into the phone, 'hello, help us please!' Then she remembered the police code for an officer requiring assistance. 'Ten zero, ten zero,' she croaked. She hoped that they'd got a location from the GPS in her phone. The fight was still going on behind her. She thought she could hear the sirens coming just as she passed out.

Jordan thought that he had got the better of Bingham, as they rolled around on the floor kicking and punching each other. For a slight man, Jordan soon realised Bingham had enormous reserves of strength. They both managed to get to their knees and Jordan head-butted Bingham. He fell backwards, but quickly recovered and brought a double-handed punch to Jordan's jaw, knocking him semi-conscious. With one final blow, Bingham struck Jordan squarely in the back, winding him further.

Bingham half-ran, half-limped to the door and was gone.

Jordan crawled on his hands and knees towards Kirsty, who he saw had collapsed by the phone. As he was crawling, he felt a sharp pain and oozing warmth from his right thigh. He seemed to remember landing on a glass vase during the struggle. As he got to Kirsty, he looked down at his thigh to see it bleeding quite heavily. He didn't know whether it had been done by Bingham or by the vase as they rolled around on the floor. No real damage though, he thought.

About a minute after Bingham had run off, re-enforcements arrived. Traffic, CID and the local area cars all converged on the apartment.

Dave Heart and DC Fred were first in the apartment, followed by Chris Prentice, Burnett and Marland.

Jordan told everyone what had happened, after they had asked for an ambulance for Kirsty, who by this time was sitting up on the floor with her back against the kitchen units. She was holding the cuts on her neck and weeping. It was difficult to maintain her composure. This was the last thing she had expected, after the death of her husband.

Jordan returned to her after briefing everyone.

'I'm sorry, Jake.' she said through tears. 'I'm sorry I couldn't help you. Are you OK?'

'I'm fine,' he said. 'I am more concerned about you. An ambulance is coming to check us both out.'

She nodded, exhausted and, not for the first time, he thought how vulnerable she looked. A respected forensic pathologist reduced to this, all because of one man's vendetta. He was determined that Bingham Tyler would not get away with it.

While Jordan was talking to Kirsty, he could hear Colin Marland in the background calling for more assistance to look for Bingham. Marland then came over to both of them. 'How are you feeling, Dr Kingsfield?' he asked.

'I've been better, I have to admit.'

'Mm, well, we'll get him, don't you worry about that.'

As he turned to walk away he added, as an aside, 'You OK, Jordan?'

'Yes, Sir, thanks for asking.'

'He can't go far on foot. I think. I've mobilised everyone for the search,' said Marland, as he walked away.

Chapter 28

'I told you this was a bad idea.

'So! It's not over yet! Why are you here, too, anyway?'

'You need to understand what you are doing –you're a bad man, Bingham, and after all I did for you.'

'You did nothing for me –nothing –you put me away with people I hated.'

'We didn't put you away, Bing, we wanted to make sure you enjoyed your childhood by putting you with people, who would help you.'

'Well, they didn't, did they? They didn't –they didn't.'

Silence.

Bingham left the apartment and just ran and ran. He didn't know where he was going to run. Leaving the apartment he ran towards the Abington Park, then decided to turn right down Ardington Road, quiet with few cars about or people walking. He knew that everyone would be looking for him now. There was nowhere to hide. He knew that he would just have to accept his fate.

'So, now is the time to hand yourself in, Bing. It's for the best, Bingham.'

'No, I'll never do that. They'll have to catch me. I need to get to a hospital.'

'That is the best thing, I think –don't you, to get some real help?'

'No, I'm only going there because that is where they will be taking her.'

'You can't get away with this, Bingham –you –need – help.'

He stopped running, bent forward to catch his breath and realised that he was outside a deserted shoe factory. He looked around to see if anyone was watching, before he slipped through a gap in the fencing. The factory, long closed following the decline of the boot and shoe industry in the town, had been standing derelict since the 1980s. The long red-bricked building stood two storeys high, had Georgian style architecture and was originally built in the early 1920s. It was built within a residential area and the façade of the building was made to look like an office block - not the quintessential style that one normally associates with urban factories of the early 1900s.

'I'll lay low here for a while,' he said. 'Then I'll make my way to the hospital.'

***

Kirsty was taken into the Accident & Emergency Department with Jordan in the same ambulance –he with his leg injury and she with her facial injuries. She was still tearful.

'Why did he come after me, Jake? What have I ever done to him?'

'Until we find him, I don't think we'll know. My guess is that he wanted you for himself –or maybe it was just the fact that you were married to Jim.'

'Did you hear him? It was like he was possessed, mumbling to himself, as if arguing with someone.'

'No, I can't say that I noticed that as I was rolling around on the floor with him.'

They both smiled weakly.

'No, I suppose you were a bit pre-occupied.'

She leaned forward. 'I'm sorry that I wasn't much help.'

'Understandable, after what he did. Don't go blaming yourself for anything. This is all down to him, nobody else.'

At the hospital they were seen quickly. Marland and Burnett arrived, after they had been cleared for discharge.

'Well?' Kirsty said. 'Have you found him?' she said with fortitude.

'No, not yet, but we will, Dr. Kingsfield, we will. Now I need to know what happened. Are you up to talking to me about it?'

Kirsty went through the details with Marland, with Jake joining in where appropriate.

Burnett had turned to ask Jordan a question when the group was approached by an out-of-breath Fred.

'We think we've got him,' he said panting and holding his sides to catch his breath.

'Where?' asked Marland, quickly.

'We think he is holed up.' Pant. 'In the disused Mobbs-Miller shoe factory on Ardington Road.' Pant. 'Someone called it in. We've mobilised everyone, including the dogs.' He exhaled deeply.

'Well done! OK, Fred, let's go,' said Marland. 'Oh, and Fred?'

'Yes, Sir?'

'You need to get in the force gym.' He slapped him heavily on his shoulders as he walked past him.

'Don't I know it,' panted Fred to himself.

'Er… excuse me,' Kirsty called to Marland as he walked away.

'I think we need to come, too,' she said.

Marland turned back to her. 'No, I don't think so. Both of you stay here. Neither of you are in any fit state to do anything useful.'

'Perhaps not,' replied Kirsty, 'but for my husband's sake, I want to come with you, to see you catch the bastard.'

Marland looked at everyone. Burnett just shrugged.

'Can't hurt boss, the more the merrier,' said Fred, a little more composed.

'Against my better judgement.'

He indicated for them to follow with a nod of his head.

By the time they all arrived at the disused leather factory, roads had been closed and tactical units were arriving at the scene. The same POLSA Sergeant who had been at the Fulborough Wood burial site was briefing his search teams in the same expressive manner. A few minutes later they all spread out around the building.

'I'm going in,' Jordan said to Kirsty. Both of them were still sitting in the police car.

'What!'

'I can't just sit here and watch. It's my job.'

'Well, I'm coming with you.'

'No, Kirsty, you stay here. You've had enough action for one day.'

'And you haven't?'

Jordan shook his head. 'Glutton for punishment, I suppose.'

With that, he was out of the car and dashing across to the nearest door he could see. It was all Kirsty could do to keep up with him, even with his leg strapped up.

Marland caught sight of them both running.

'Jordan, stay where you are,' he called in his best Sergeant Major's voice.

Jordan pretended he hadn't heard and kept going. He looked back to see Kirsty following. 'I told you to stay in the car.'

'Sorry, can't hear you.' Jordan couldn't believe how composed Kirsty was after all that had happened. He thought that she had either got a sure fire way of preventing emotions bleeding into everyday life –not that what they were doing happened everyday –or she was running high on adrenaline. He decided it was adrenaline. They managed to get to a side entrance, at the opposite end of the building from where the search team had entered. Jordan pushed on the door. It was open.

'Are you going in?' enquired Kirsty, tentatively.

'Yeah.'

'Okay,' she said, somewhat worriedly.

'You still want to carry on?'

'You bet I do.' But actually, she wasn't that sure what she was doing here and whether she really wanted to go into the factory. 'Haven't I had enough surprises for one day?' she thought. 'Still, too late to back out now.'

The door opened onto a large empty warehouse, at least a hundred metres long. It was dusty and smelled of curing leather. The concrete floor was covered with the fine dust of years of neglect. Pieces of machinery were scattered about, along with some leather pelts and other warehouse detritus, left behind when the factory closed. To his left, Jordan saw a set of steps going down to a basement area. He gestured silently to Kirsty to go towards the steps. All they could hear was the sound of police dogs outside the building, which echoed around the vast expanse of the warehouse. Just as they were approaching the basement steps, Jordan's radio went off. They both jumped at the noise. He answered in a whisper.

'Jordan, where are you?' growled Marland.

'Just about to enter the basement. Opposite where the search teams are.'

'Can't you do anything you're told? Traffic – you're all the same.'

'Sorry, sir, too much at stake. You'll have to discipline me later.'

'I'll have your bloody stripes, that's for sure. Is Dr. Kingsfield with you?'

'Yes.'

'Well, look after her, then.'

'That's my job, Sir.'

The radio went dead. A few seconds later Jordan heard Marland telling everyone else that he and Kirsty were in the building. Jordan knew that Marland would be stratospheric with rage at what they had both done. Well, he thought, he'd suffer the consequences later, but now this was personal. Bingham had attacked a person he was charged to look after. He had attacked him. So, whatever the consequences of this action, so be it.

Brick walls on both sides enclosed the concrete stairs down to the basement. Peeling green gloss paint hung from the walls and was scattered like confetti down the steps. They were unable to see anything. The brightness of the empty warehouse temporarily blinding them until their eyes got used to the dark and to what lay beyond the bottom of the stairs. Jordan removed a pen-torch out of his shirt pocket. He just hoped that it still worked, after scrapping with Bingham earlier.

They reached the bottom of the stairs and Jordan looked round the corner into the basement. It was all quiet. They slowly moved into the basement. It turned out that it was not completely dark. Around the top of the basement were small rectangular windows that let some light in. Even so there were enough large dark areas for a person to hide.

The basement was a room, probably only a quarter of the size of the factory floor above. And by the smell of it was probably used to store leather. Jordan indicated for Kirsty to stay close as they moved down the basement to the left.

Suddenly, there was a movement in a dark corner that startled them both. A cat ran out of the shadows and up the stairs.

With hearts pounding and adrenaline pumping, they moved on. They saw in the centre of the basement a pile of wooden crates and boxes with hessian sacking over them. Jordan indicated that he was going to search the boxes and headed towards them, but the light of his little pen torch hardly made a difference.

Chapter 29

Bingham heard someone coming. In his hideout in the dusty basement, all he could see was the movement of a small light getting closer.

'Ah, time's up.'

Bingham tried to keep still.

'Shut up and be quiet? They'll hear,' he whispered loudly.

'Of course they won't, it's just you and me.'

'But you make me talk, force me to answer you.'

'Do I?'

The small light moved inexorably closer. He could just about make out who it was.

'It's that fucking copper,' Bingham mumbled. 'Can't get away from the bastard, he's followed me.'

'He didn't know you were here, Bing.'

'No, he knew! He knew!'

'Yes, if you say so. What are you going to do, then?'

'I need to get out of here, now!' With that, Bingham leapt out of his hiding place and headed straight for Jordan. He slammed past him and ran for the exit.

Jordan heard the noise and was ready as Bingham came catapulting towards him. Bingham shoulder charged into him, trying to throw Jordan out of the way, but Jordan caught his arm and violently swung him around, so that he went sprawling over the floor. Bingham crawled to his feet and ran. Jordan, handicapped by his bandaged leg, went after him, only just catching him up before he got to the stairs. He rugby-tackled Bingham to the floor. He tried to get up, but Jordan was too quick for him and managed to get him pinned down with his knees in the centre of Bingham's back.

Jordan knew that his previous scrap with Bingham had been vicious and Bingham continued to writhe and kick under the weight of Jordan. Jordan's attention was momentarily distracted by another radio call from Marland. Before he could respond, Bingham let loose a back kick towards Jordan which caught him off guard. Managing to struggle free, Bingham then scrambled forward and tried to feel for anything on the floor to use as a weapon. He found a piece of wood and rolling over, took a swipe at Jordan as he came toward him. Bingham's strike caught Jordan in the shins, bringing him down. Kirsty, frightened by what was happening, could see that Jordan had been brought down in the dim light of the basement. She scrambled around for the piece of wood that Bingham had just dropped. Finding it she struck him across the shoulders with all the energy she could muster. Bingham whipped around with fists clenched. He struck Kirsty and sent her flying, giving Jordan time to recover and get on him again.

By this time, Bingham realised he was losing the fight. He was exhausted, but Jordan came at him again. With one last punch to the face, he sent Bingham crashing into some metal drums, dazed.

Jordan went towards him again with the intention, this time, of making sure he didn't get up. Bingham saw that he was coming for him again and put his hands up in surrender.

'OK, OK,' he said, breathing heavily and shuffling backwards until the wall stopped him. 'Time out, for Christ's sake.'

'You going to stay down, then or do I have to make sure?' Jordan demanded.

'Yeah, yeah.'

Jordan quickly handcuffed Bingham and radioed to Marland that he had Bingham in custody. Kirsty, having recovered from the punch she had received from

Bingham walked over to him and hit him hard around the face, twice, before Jordan stepped in.

'Why?' she shouted at him. 'Why did you kill my husband? Tell me. Why?'

Bingham looked at Kirsty and laughed. 'Because I could.' He smiled.

'You little bastard,' Jordan said. 'Don't you have an ounce of compassion?'

'Mm, it's something I've been asked before and apparently I don't,' Bingham replied, with a false smile.

'Still haven't answered my question,' Kirsty said, even angrier.

Bingham replied calmly. 'Do you know, I really don't know whether I want to.'

Kirsty took a step forward and raised her hand with the intention of hitting Bingham again, but was stopped by Jordan. He shook his head at her. 'No,' he said quietly.

Jordan had been standing in front of Bingham, as he sat with his back against the wall. He took a step forward and, with his right boot, placed it on the inside of Bingham's left foot, pressing down on it. Bingham squealed.

'Perhaps it is time to answer a few questions?' Jordan said.

'You can't do this. Ahhhhhhh, this is police brutality!'

'Police brutality? I don't see any. Do you, doctor?'

'No,' she replied, as Jordan applied more pressure, only with both his booted feet on both of Bingham's legs.

'OK, OK, just let up. I'll tell you, I'll tell you!'

Bingham seemed to have calmed down. It was weird, Kirsty thought, how he could become a completely different person.

'Well done, Bing, time for us to take control.'

'No,' Bingham shouted.

'What?' Exclaimed Jordan.

'I'm not talking to you,' said Bingham.

'I only see us here,' Jordan replied. 'You said you would tell us. Have you changed your mind –or do I need to remind you again?'

'I will, I will.'

'Get on with it then, before the others arrive to take you away,' Kirsty said, still with anger in her voice.

Bingham, still a little breathless, contemplated the floor in front of him. His mind was in a turmoil –part of him wanted to give up. Part of him wanted to get up and run away, get away from these two and the police outside. He knew there was nowhere to run. But he would run, if he had the chance. They just need to give me a little slack, he thought.

'It was a long time ago, when all this started, when I was a kid. My dad had been locked-up for murder. Me and my step-brother –you met him when I had one of his trucks away –and my step-sister got fostered.'

'Is that Adam Gaffney, the haulier?'

'Yeah, that's right.'

All the time hoping that he could get an opportunity to escape. If I could just lull them into a false sense of security.

'No, Bing, carry on, you can't escape now. I will see to it!'

'Shut up, will you?' shouted Bingham.

'Who are you talking to?' asked Jordan

Bingham ignored Jordan and went on. 'The social worker, Eleanor Smyth, split us up, but she is here with me, in here.' He pointed to his head. 'She won't let go, she won't let me go, so I have her talking to me now, constantly. I never get any peace.'

Kirsty and Jordan looked at each other. Jordan raised an eyebrow, hearing that from Bingham.

'I didn't want to go into foster care,' he continued, still calculating his chances of escape, '–blamed her for splitting us all up…'

'You shouldn't have done that, Bingham.'

'We were told never to contact each other…'

'Well, that's partly true I suppose, but I did tell the other two.'

'It wasn't until I came out of the nick after your husband put me away –' he looked contemptuously at Kirsty and nodded in her direction, 'that I started to look for her. I blamed her for the way my life had turned out. My foster homes gave me nothing but grief, while the other two were put into good homes. I got a good home, eventually…'

'So we did do you right –eventually.'

'But, by that time, the damage had been done. I found I was good at technology, so I trained for that.'

'So, why did you go and kill her? Was your desire for revenge that strong, after all those years?' Jordan asked.

'Yes, it was a means to an end. I hated Kingsfield for putting me away. I wanted, I needed, to get his attention. I wanted revenge. I wanted justice for me, for how my life turned out.'

'There were other ways you could have got his attention,' Kirsty said. 'You left that woman to rot in her own home, I know. I saw her.'

'I know you did and I saw you, too, in your white paper overalls, joking with your husband at MY job.'

'Why did you attack me?'

'You were too happy together. No couples are that happy,' Bingham retorted through gritted teeth.

'So, you wanted to kill me just because I was happy?'

Bingham shrugged. As he was talking and unbeknown to all three of them, Marland and Heart were standing listening to the conversation at the bottom of the basement stairs. Bingham went on.

'I found out where she lived and kept a watch on her house. That's what I do –I keep watch –I have electronic sight and sound, and you lot,' his handcuffed hands indicating Jordan, 'blinded me and took all my kit. To me, it was like leaving me without sight. I watched her for days, arguing with myself, with my conscience –with her –about what I was going to do - about what I had done. I'm a psycho. I know that. The doctors virtually admitted it to me when I was a teenager.'

Bingham dropped his head down onto his chest and slumped further against the wall. Jordan and Kirsty observed a change taking place in Bingham. There was a perceptible change in his facial expressions and the further relaxation of his body. It was as if another person had invaded his very being.

'So, who are we talking to now?' asked Kirsty.

A calmer, gentler voice began to speak.

'He never knows when I take over. I am much less 'volatile' shall we say, than Bingham.'

'How long do you stay with him?' asked Jordan.

'As long as I can, but he is very strong, I can only try and persuade.'

'Does it work?' asked Kirsty.

'Sometimes –we have fights, but I'm not a fighting man.'

'Does he regret anything he has done?' asked Kirsty.

'I do, but I don't believe he does. He is without morals. No redeeming features, except me of course. And he has Eleanor inside his head to help him through his troubles.'

'So, what happened to Eleanor Smyth? How did you do it, then?' asked Jordan.

The gentler Bingham began to relate the story of his killing of Eleanor Smyth. How he tracked her down, how he planned and prepared to kill her. And the trauma that followed the act of killing her – the first time he had ever experienced such a consequence.

Chapter 30

'So, now you know,' said Bingham

'Not all of it,' said Kirsty, 'What about my husband? You killed him just because you had a vendetta?' Kirsty shouted at him, while tears of anger and grief filled her eyes. 'I shouldn't be here,' she thought, 'in front of this animal.' What ever possessed her to follow Jake? Was revenge her motivation as well, the same as Bingham's?'

'Well, you know what they say?'

'What do they say, Bingham?' asked Jordan.

Bingham's demeanour had changed and he had become more aggressive.

'Shit happens!' and with that he laughed.

'Get up,' Jordan demanded.

'Fucking make me,' replied Bingham. Jordan bent down to grab Bingham's arm. As he did so, Bingham butted Jordan with his head. The telling of his story had given him a chance to recuperate. He sprung to his feet and ran towards the exit stairs, only to be confronted by Marland and Heart. They both grabbed an arm, as he tried to get past and force himself to run up the stairs. Bingham had the advantage, though, as he was facing forward. He rushed up the stairs with Marland and Heart in tow. Eventually, unable to keep up by running backwards up the stairs, they had to let go.

Bingham was up the stairs and out through the door, running for the nearest vehicle. It happened to be Burnett's traffic Volvo. He jumped into the driver's seat. The keys were still in and the engine was idling. His handcuffs restricted his hands, but he managed to throw the automatic box into drive and screeched out of the factory yard.

Jordan was trying to shout down his radio as he ran towards his traffic car. Kirsty got in beside him.

'Buckle up,' he said. 'This is going to get nasty.' He looked at her with some concern, but knew that if he told her to stay here she wouldn't –not with Bingham so close and not having heard what he'd said.

'Yeah, I'll take the nasty at this stage,' she said. Both of them were caught up in the adrenaline-induced action to chase after Bingham.

As Jordan manoeuvred the car in the factory yard, the rear door opened and Beccy Burnett leapt into the back seat.

'Christ, Beccy, where did you come from?' Jordan exclaimed, as he drove out of the yard.

'It's my bloody car he's nicked.'

'Leave the keys in again, did you?'

'Not a word,' she said, as she took up the middle seat in the back.

She sat on the edge of the rear seat and leaned forward, holding on to the passenger and driver's seats with each arm.

Jordan picked up Bingham, as he thrashed the traffic Volvo down the Ardington Road and turned right on Billing Road, towards the town centre, only just missing a bus on the main road.

'He's gonna try and lose us in town,' he said.

Beccy was co-ordinating other units, as Jordan gunned the patrol car through the traffic. Bingham jumped a couple of red lights, causing a number of kids on a pedestrian crossing to starburst out of the way.

Taking a right turn into York Road, nearly losing control of the stolen patrol car, Bingham put the lights and siren on to try to get other cars out of the way. He came up fast behind a slower moving car at Campbell Square traffic lights and tried to overtake the vehicle on the inside. Misjudging the distance, he smashed into the rear nearside wing, spinning the vehicle out of the way and into some oncoming cars.

He carried onto down to Regents Square. Police cars blocked his way to the right and left. He knew that if he could turn left there he had a chance of escape, but Bingham saw that the police car blocked the road. He knew what they were doing. He'd seen these tactics before. Channelling the fugitive in the direction that they wanted him to go, so that they could deflate his tyres, using a hollow point tyre 'stinger' trap.

But not him! Oh, no, he was going to head straight for the police car. The officer, seeing him heading his way, managed to move the car almost out of the way, but not quite. The front of Bingham's car slammed into the Ford Focus estate, pushing it out of the way and into a parked car.

Bingham accelerated away, laughing out loud. 'Outwitted them,' he thought

'No, Bing, just lucky.'

'No, I think not. The superior mind that I have saw to that - tactics, tactics that's what it's all about.'

Jordan chased Bingham past the wreck of the Focus. Bingham kept going at high speed through the town and out towards the motorway.

'If he gets to the motorway, we'll lose him for sure,' Burnett shouted at Jordan.

Bingham saw that Jordan was getting closer. Although both vehicles were evenly matched, Jordan's superior driving skills came to the fore. He knew how to extract the maximum power in each gear with the minimum of effort. Bingham didn't.

Bingham eventually turned into a winding country lane, as he got to the outskirts of the town. He still kept his foot hard down on the accelerator.

'We don't seem to be gaining on him,' Kirsty said loudly.

'I know,' Jordan replied.

'As long as we stay with him, we'll be OK. I'm getting other units into position to intercept him,' reassured Burnett.

'I think he'll start to slow down because he doesn't know this road very well, if at all. If he takes the next left towards Fenton's Bridge, we'll have him.'

'Why?' Kirsty asked.

'Railway crossing, gates are more down than up,' Jordan shouted over the scream of the engine and the wailing of the sirens.

'Left, left, left,' Burnett called into her radio. 'Towards Fenton's Bridge.'

As the road opens out towards Fenton Bridge railway crossing, the preceding three quarters of a mile, known as Fenton's Folly, is a Roman-road –straight. Speeds in excess of 100 mph could easily be achieved, but the folly was that drivers tried to beat the railway crossing. Some made it. Most didn't.

Bingham saw the straight road ahead of him and accelerated. 'I can do this,' he thought. 'I can get away from them.'

'No, you can't, Bing' replied his inner voice. *'You must slow down, accept your fate.'*

'The only fate left for me is to escape,' he shouted. He laughed, as he accelerated the Volvo along Fenton's Folly.

'He's accelerating. Speed one, zero, zero,' Jordan shouted.

Burnett pointed ahead. 'Look the gates are closing!'

'Yeah, and there is no view of approaching trains from either direction, because we're on a valley floor. I hope he doesn't do anything stupid.'

'Gates closed,' Burnett called down the radio. 'Target speed still increasing.'

'What are you doing, Bing. You must slow…………………'

'You don't think that…' Kirsty screamed.

'He bloody well is –brake you idiot, brake!' shouted Jordan.

But it was too late.

At the very last second, the Volvo was seen by the three in the chasing Volvo to brake heavily. All four wheels were smoking, as it tried to apply friction on the road surface to try and bring it to a stop. It failed and smashed through the gates of the crossing. Tenths of a second later, the car exploded as the front of the London to Birmingham express came into contact with the car. It destroyed the car, smashing it into thousands of pieces.

The train itself came to a grinding halt half a mile down the track. The convoy of police cars arrived at the scene seconds later. Everyone was convinced that no-one in that car could have survived.

Chapter 31

A week after the death of Bingham Tyler, Jim Kingsfield was laid to rest with full police honours. As is usual in these tragic situations, members of the force and other police forces turned out in full. DC Fred stood next to Jordan at the entrance to Northampton's civic church, All Saints. The sun had decided to shine and the clear blue sky produced a crisp and bright autumn morning. Standing in the square in front of the church portico, looking towards George Row, Fred turned to Jordan.

'You know,' he said quietly, 'I'm not really a church goer, but I do like the architecture.'

Jordan simply nodded, his mind on other things.

'Did you know,' Fred continued, making a wide sweeping motion with his right arm, 'that this portico was modelled on the one at St Paul's in London?'

Jordan turned to him. 'I would never have believed that you were into architecture, Fred, and no, I didn't,' Jordan replied.

'Yes, I think I could have been an architect, you know,' Fred mused. They both scanned the church looking up at the clock tower above the entrance –it was three minutes to eleven. 'Three minutes to go', Jordan thought.

'Did you also know,' Fred went on, 'that the resources to rebuild the church after Northampton's great fire in 1675 were given by Charles the second? That's why his statue is over the portico parapet.' He pointed to it, 'erected in 1715 it was.'

Jordan, who had been more concerned with the task that lay before him, as opposed to the church architecture, turned to look at Fred. The uniform tunic he was wearing was far too small for him, the tunic buttons straining against his paunch.

'Fred, I'm fascinated that you know all this and on any other day I'd probably like to hear about it, but…'

'Mm…' Fred went silent for a moment. 'Not really interested then,' he mumbled.

'Fred, it's not that I'm not interested –just not at the moment, that's all.'

'Yeah, I know. I do ramble on a bit when I'm nervous.'

'Can't ever believe that you'd be nervous about anything, Fred,' Jordan remarked.

'Well, it's not very often you get to have to bear a colleague's coffin, is it?' Fred countered.

'No, it isn't,' Jordan agreed.

They stood together for the last couple of minutes in silence, waiting for the cortege to arrive. As the FLO to Kirsty, Jordan was to look after her, her parents and Jim's parents for the ceremony. Jim's fellow detectives were to bear the coffin into the church, all looking conspicuously uncomfortable in a uniform.

The cortege appeared at the top of George Row and slowly moved into the square in front of the church. The section of CID pallbearers formed up smartly behind the hearse. Clearly DCS Marland had spent some time with his CID officers making them actually look as if they knew what they were doing –and smartly too.

The coffin, draped in the Force Standard, bearing a police cap, a wreath and Kingsfield's medals, was reverently borne into the church. Jordan had watched the family get out of the funeral car and move behind the coffin. Jordan stepped in behind the family, who acknowledged him with a solemn nod of their heads.

After the service, the cortege, with police outriders, made its way to the Cemetary where Jim was finally laid to rest. Kirsty held onto Jordan to steady herself, as the

Minister completed the ceremony by the graveside. During the whole ceremony, both at the church and at the graveside, Kirsty had not raised her head. She was distressed and had wept constantly, both sets of parents and Jordan taking time to support her.

The Chief Constable and all the senior officers gave their condolences to Kirsty, as they and the others had left the cemetery. Jordan was standing beside her, when Marland approached them.

'At least we got him,' he said quietly.

'I know –he won't be able to destroy other people's lives now,' Kirsty replied, still wiping her eyes.

'I am sorry that it came to all this,' Marland said. Kirsty nodded, wiping her eyes again with the handkerchief that had been her constant companion during the ceremony.

'What are you going to do now, Doctor?' Marland asked.

'I don't know. I'll take some time off. Eventually I'll have to come back I suppose. Do what I'm best at.'

'We certainly don't want to lose you,' Marland said. 'You going to look after her, Jordan?'

'Yes, Sir.'

'Good man.' And with that he turned and left the two alone.

'What are you really going to do?' Jordan pressed Kirsty.

'To be honest, Jake, I don't know. I need time to recover from all this.'

'Well, you know where I am. I'm still your liaison officer, even if Marland tells me I'm not.'

Kirsty gently touched Jordan's arm. 'Thank you for your support. You have become a good friend. I hope it continues?'

'No reason why it shouldn't,' Jordan replied. Kirsty stepped closer to Jordan and linked her arm through his. She looked at him directly for the first time.

'Do you know what?' she said secretively.

'No, what?'

'When we were chasing him from the factory, I...'

'Yes?'

'Well, is it wrong for me to have been –'

'Excited?' Jordan said. Kirsty nodded again.

'Not frightened by it, then?' He smiled.

'No –well –a little, perhaps.'

'OK, well, let's not make a habit of it, eh?'

There was the first glimmer of a smile from Kirsty as Jordan said that. Perhaps, Jordan thought, that these were the first steps to her being able to recover from this ordeal. In the time he had come to know Kirsty, Jordan considered that a friendship with this woman would be worth cultivating –not in the sexual sense, he understood. He was still a married man.

'Look, I tell you what,' Jordan suggested.

'Mm?' Kirsty responded nonchalantly, as they walked back towards the waiting car.

'After you have got over all this, been away, took stock, whatever you want to do, either on your own, with your family. I'll always be about. If you need to talk to somebody, night or day, then call me. OK?'

'Jake, that's very kind and I might even take you up on it!' Kirsty said, 'I think I do need to get away –put my house in order. I have an old girlfriend –lives in Spain. Perhaps I'll go and stay with her for a while. The sun'll do me good.'

Jordan smiled. 'We'd better go. Your driver's looked at his watch twice in the last ten minutes.'

Kirsty looked back and took one last look at the grave and blew her husband a kiss. As they turned back towards the car, a woman in a dark pencil skirted suit confronted them.

'Dr Kingsfield?' She asked.

'Yes,' Kirsty answered.

'I wanted to offer my condolences. I knew your husband.'

'Thank you, that's very kind. How did you know him?' she asked inquisitively.

'I used to work with him. My name is Stephanie Parker.'

Jordan looked at Kirsty, shocked.

'If you're Stephanie Parker,' he said to her, then turning to Kirsty said, 'who is in your morgue?'

Epilogue

The day after Kingsfield's funeral, Stephanie Parker agreed to meet Jordan and Kirsty in secret. Stephanie did not want everyone to be aware of her return. There were things she still had to do before returning fully to society, she said. And in all honesty, Jordan thought, even her agreeing to meet with them appeared to be somewhat reluctant.

Nevertheless, on a crisp autumn morning, they met in a small café outside Northampton and close to Althorp House.

Jordan had collected Kirsty from her apartment in his own car. He had decided to take the day off some time ago, so it didn't arouse any suspicions with his colleagues or supervisors. In fact, he had arranged to take Rosie out for the day, but in the light of recent developments, she had another think coming, he though wryly.

They had arrived before Parker and parked themselves in the corner of the café, which was furnished with rustic, handmade heavy oak tables and chairs. The café was adorned with horse tackle and other horsey paraphernalia was attached to the thick oak beams. They ordered coffee and pastries and sat in quiet conversation until Stephanie arrived.

'Do you think she'll come?' asked Kirsty.

'I'm not sure. She didn't seem particularly enthusiastic about it yesterday when we suggested it, did she?' Kirsty just shook her head in response.

A few minutes later, their concern about Stephanie turning up evaporated as she entered the café. She gave them a little wave as she spotted them and strode confidently to the table. She wore a pair of figure-hugging blue jeans, a pink blouse, matching scarf and a large black Fedora hat that was tilted to one side. She looks stunning, Jordan thought, and could understand now what colleagues, who only knew her as a probationary officer, saw in her. She had it and, clearly, she still flaunted it.

She sat down opposite them and they ordered more coffee.

'You seem a bit happier today?' said Jordan smiling.

'Yes, well, you're never at your best at a funeral.' She looked at Kirsty, 'sorry, I didn't mean any disrespect.'

'None taken, I assure you,' she said and gave her the briefest of smiles.

They engaged in small talk for a few moments then Jordan asked,

'So, Stephanie, tell me why we are sitting hear now and not four years ago –or how ever long it was?'

Stephanie looked away, taking in her surrounding of the café before she spoke.

'I don't know whether you were aware of the situation before I,' she hesitated, 'before I 'went away'.'

'Not really, no. I only knew what we were briefed about when you disappeared. You had apparently failed to turn up at Crown Court to give evidence against Tyler,' responded Jordan quietly. He didn't want others in the café to overhear his conversation with Stephanie. Not that anyone would be interested, he thought.

'I didn't turn up at Court because I had good reason to,' she paused, opening the large Burberry handbag she had been carrying and produced an envelope. She handed it over to Jordan. 'It was because of this.'

Jordan removed from the envelope a sheet of A4 paper, with closely spaced type on both sides of the paper. It was in pristine condition, as if it had been read only once and put back in the envelope, never to see the light of day again – until now. Jordan quickly scanned the letter and offered it to Kirsty. She shook her head and pushed it away from Jordan. She could see that it was signed by Bingham.

'This isn't the Bingham we knew, is it? It doesn't look as if it was penned by a psychopath?'

'Certainly not.'

'Why did he send you this?'

'I don't know. I think he wanted forgiveness. I think he knew what type of person he was. He always complained about voices in his head, telling him to do the opposite of what he actually wanted to do.'

'What was your relationship with him like?'

Stephanie thought for a moment. 'Fractious!'

'Fractious? I wouldn't describe him beating you up and trying to rape you as fractious,' Jordan said a little irritated.

'Well, to start with everything was OK. He picked me up in a bar down Bridge Street, at a time I was, shall we say, a free spirit. I knew I was unwell. I was addicted to alcohol, sex, some drugs and anything else that would take my mind off the job.' She paused, pondering. 'Stupid,' she said eventually. 'I see that now, but it has taken me all this time to get myself back together. This letter from Bingham made me understand what I needed to do. I know he made threats against me, if I gave evidence. And I knew that he would make good on those threats when he got out, so I wasn't going to wait around to find out. I think, even back than, he knew he wanted it to end. He couldn't cope with his alter egos –they'd come and go by all accounts, made him more aggressive – more paranoid about 'his people,' – his marks that he watched, including me, apparently.'

Kirsty and Jordan sat back in their seats and let Stephanie continue. Clearly, she felt the need to talk after all this time.

She continued, 'I don't think he ever thought or imagined what the result of sending the letter to me would do. Made me run away.' She laughed nervously.

'But where did you go?' asked Kirsty.

'Ever heard of Sir Reginald Parker?'

'Yes,' responded Jordan, 'isn't he something in the FCO?'

'He was,' Stephanie replied. She dropped her head forward and sighed. 'He passed away a few weeks ago. He was my father and it's the only reason I have come back to the UK.'

'Where have you been, then?' Jordan asked.

'I suppose you could say I was sent to the colonies.'

'Australia?'

'No, New Zealand – Christchurch to be exact, until the earthquake.'

'Couldn't have got much further away from the UK if you tried,' Jordan said with a grin. She responded in kind.

'I don't know what I would have done without my parents –my father in particular. One of the kindest men you would ever wish to meet.' She removed a tissue from her bag and wiped her eyes. 'He went out on a limb for me –broke the law, got me a new passport, new identity and packed me off to the furthest point away from the UK in the world, and fully supported me, because he said that was the best place for me to disappear.'

'Well, it certainly worked, didn't it?' Kirsty interjected. She had been sitting quietly listening to Stephanie. She couldn't believe what she was hearing about the same man who killed her husband and tried to kill her. Stephanie didn't know about those things she understood, but even hinting at what was in that letter that Bingham wrote to her still beggared belief about her naivety. She was trying not to get annoyed –after all, it wasn't Stephanie's fault, was it?

'It was my parent's idea that I go away. Sort myself out.'

'And have you?' asked Kirsty.

'Yes, I have.'

'And what are you going to do now? Officially, you're still a police officer.'

'I don't know. Honestly, I don't.'

'Are you going back to New Zealand?' Kirsty asked.

'Yes, scheduled flight on Monday –but in all honesty it's only to tie up my affairs. Mum doesn't want to come out there and all my family is here, so I'll come back for good.'

'You know that you will have to face an enquiry when you get back?' Jordan added.

'I know that and I am prepared for it. If they chuck me out, then so be it. I haven't really been a police officer, never really got into the role, if you understand.' Jordan nodded. 'I'll find something to do no doubt.'

'OK, let's get back to Bingham. He says in this letter that he 'did' her. What does he mean by that, do you think?'

'I don't know. I never heard him speak of such a thing. I was shocked to find out that he was the nine year old boy we found at the Hazelrig Close murder all those years ago.' She gave a nervous laugh. 'You know it was my first night out and my first job? Just my luck it screwed me up for the rest of my life, ha!'

A waitress appeared and asked if they need more coffee. They all had a refill.

'What was Bingham like when you were with him? Surely you must have remembered his name from that first job?'

'Look, Jake, I didn't find out until the night he assaulted me – he told me – I freaked – he hit me again.' She took a big swig of coffee.

'Sorry' Jordan said, '–shouldn't have brought it up.'

'No, it's OK. I've been talking about it for years with my counsellor, but it still upsets me.'

'Clearly.'

'And I wasn't told his name on the day. I got packed off into the Inspector's car and then sat with them back at the station, so you can see how it was a shock when I found out. What really got me was that fact that in his warped mind he targeted me for his own ends and when he didn't get them – well – you know the rest.'

'So, where do we go from here?' asked Kirsty.

'I go back to New Zealand and you say nothing at the moment, till I get back. If that's OK with you both?' Jordan looked at Kirsty.

'Fine by me,' she said.

'Right - when you get back, you better get in touch with me first before you go blundering into HQ and frighten everyone to death?'

They all agreed to meet in back in the café on Stephanie's return. They all shook hands and Stephanie walked out of their lives once again.

Book Two – available during 2015

If you enjoyed this, and need to see how things develop, then book two in the series will be ready for you soon.

Join Jake and Kirsty as they battle to find a killer who uses chemistry to murder, while people drive their cars.

Will Stephanie Parker overcome what awaits her back in the UK and re-join the police force? And who is the body recovered from Fulborough Wood? As the death of her husband comes back to haunt her, can Kirsty cope with the amorous intentions of the new Detective Inspector on the block, Fletcher Randall, and will Jake's inaction lose the woman he has become close to.

Acknowledgements

I would like to take the opportunity to thank the following people for their advice and help during the writing of this book. Professor Ian Wall – Forensic Physician and all round medicine man. Richard Jenkins – For the psychology stuff. Terry Charker – a crime reader's insights, and Julie Bowen- so I didn't make a fool of myself with the social services.

A big thank you to my Editor, Helen Jaeger, without whose inspirational support this book would still be in my head.

Last and by no means least to my partner Sarah, for the love, motivation, support, listening to all my ramblings and readings late into the night and being a sounding board for all my ideas.

Facts and Fiction

In writing this book, I have called upon my knowledge of Northampton. A town that I have worked in as a police officer for thirty years. For those reading this book who also have a knowledge of Northampton, I here separate fact from fiction.

All of the following places are figments of my imagination. Hazelrig Close on the De-Senlis estate. (Those who know Northampton will understand the relevance of those names.) Fulborough Wood and Estate, Fenton's Bridge and Fenton's Folly.

Willoughby, is on the Northamptonshire and Warwickshire county border. It is a pretty village, but the terrace of cottages on the outskirts of the village hidden in a copse are again figments of my imagination

The Mobbs-Miller factory on Ardington Road, does exist, but it is no longer deserted. It houses small business units and is not as big as I make out. Most of the street names and locations used exist, but I may have moved their location to fit in with the story. Kingsfield's apartment building was a boot and shoe manufacturer, but is in another part of the town and nowhere near Abington Park. They are apartments though.

Stephen Collier

Stephen Collier was born in England. He is a retired police officer, having served thirty years with the Northamptonshire Police. His service was predominantly with the traffic department, which has provided the background in the writing of his first novel.

Realising a long-held ambition to write, this is Stephen's debut novel, in a series of Jordan & Kingsfield dramas. Stephen lives with his partner Sarah, in Northamptonshire.

http://stephencollier-author.com

Lightning Source UK Ltd.
Milton Keynes UK
UKOW02n0650101014

239872UK00004B/8/P

Blind Murder

By Stephen G. Collier

Calculated revenge – cold, ruthless murder

Published by New Generation Publishing in 2014

Copyright © Stephen G. Collier 2014

First Edition

The author asserts the moral right under the Copyright,
Designs and Patents Act 1988 to be identified as the author
of this work.

All Rights reserved. No part of this publication may be
reproduced, stored in a retrieval system or transmitted, in any
form or by any means without the prior consent of the author,
nor be otherwise circulated in any form of binding or cover
other than that which it is published and without a similar
condition being imposed on the subsequent purchaser.

www.newgeneration-publishing.com

New Generation Publishing

For Ruth
For the inspiration she gave me, during her lifetime.

Prologue - July 1994

Stephanie Parker – a young, pretty, blonde, seventeen year old police cadet– was out on her first operational patrol with WPC Robyn Miller and PC Jim Kingsfield. They arrived outside the house they had been called to on the De-Senlis Estate, Northampton. Sitting in the rear of the blue Vauxhall Astra panda car, which Miller was driving, Stephanie immediately felt uncomfortable as they drew to a stop.

'This is a little different from what I've been used to,' thought Stephanie. Spending time inside the police station as a police cadet in the force was completely different from this experience. She wore the same uniform as her two colleagues sitting in the front of the car. The only difference was a plain blue band around her hat that was the only distinguishing feature from regular officers. Any member of the public would see her as just another police officer, and for a young seventeen-year-old that felt a heavy burden.

The two officers in the front of the car glanced at each other as they looked towards the red-bricked, half-concrete rendered house. The house, and the rest of the estate showed all the signs of a blighted and neglected community. The concrete path leading to this semi-detached council house in Hazelrig Close was shattered and overgrown. It resembled the crazy paving common to houses of the late 1970's, more than the single concrete pathway of its original design. The small front garden was split in half by this crazy pathway. Broken furniture, ripped-up carpet and other household rubbish had simply been abandoned, littering the whole garden.

It seemed to Stephanie that the arrival of a police car in the street had drawn no attention from other residents.